Hemingway's
Cats

Hemingway's Cats

Lindsey Hooper

KENSINGTON
PUBLISHING CORP.

www.kensingtonbooks.com

KENSINGTON BOOKS are published by
Kensington Publishing Corp.
119 West 40th Street
New York, NY 10018

All Kensington titles, imprints, and distributed lines are available at special quantity discounts for bulk purchases for sales promotion, premiums, fund-raising, educational, or institutional use.

This book is a work of fiction. Names, characters, businesses, organizations, places, events, and incidents either are the product of the author's imagination or are used fictitiously. Any resemblance to actual persons, living or dead, events, or locales is entirely coincidental.

To the extent that the image or images on the cover of this book depict a person or persons, such person or persons are merely models, and are not intended to portray any character or characters featured in the book.

Special book excerpts or customized printings can also be created to fit specific needs. For details, write or phone the office of the Kensington Sales Manager: Kensington Publishing Corp., 119 West 40th Street, New York, NY 10018. Attn. Sales Department. Phone: 1-800-221-2647.

The K logo is a trademark of Kensington Publishing Corp.

ISBN-13: 978-1-4967-2961-3 (ebook)
ISBN-10: 1-4967-2961-7 (ebook)

ISBN-13: 978-1-4967-2960-6
ISBN-10: 1-4967-2960-9
First Kensington Trade Paperback Printing: June 2021

10 9 8 7 6 5 4 3 2 1

Printed in the United States of America

For Gary Goldstein, my brilliant, hilarious, and incredibly patient editor, who did so much more for me than simply edit my book. I can't thank you enough, Gary.

And for the wonderful friends, family, and felines who inspired me along the way. You know who you are.

CONTENTS

A NOTE TO THE READER

In 2017, the world cheered as the famous six-toed cats of the Ernest Hemingway Home & Museum in Key West, Florida, bravely dug in their claws and triumphantly survived the catastrophic winds and rains of Hurricane Irma. This book is a work of fiction loosely inspired by these events. It is not a literal depiction of that specific hurricane or the museum or its employees. The characters (and cats) are not based on actual people (or cats) but are an invention of the author.

PART 1

WELCOME TO KEY WEST

I love to go to the zoo. But not on Sunday.
I don't like to see the people making fun of the animals,
when it should be the other way around.
—Ernest Hemingway

Chapter 1
A Cat Also Rises

Every morning, just before dawn, a funny thing happens on the southernmost island of the Florida Keys.

The sun refuses to get up.

Like a sleeping tourist who drank too many margaritas the night before, the sun buries its face under a blanket of clouds and tries to block out the sounds of the island's crack-of-dawn risers.

First up is the long-haired lighthouse keeper. He whistles a classic rock song while tossing handfuls of birdseed onto the road. *Come and get it!* Then there's the frenzied clucking of wild gypsy chickens, frantically eating their first-come, first-serve breakfast. *It's the Early Bird Special!* Finally, there's the fine-feathered, red-crowned king of them all. The Father of All Key West Roosters. *Who needs an alarm clock?* This old bird will tell you—ready or not—it's time to get up.

When this cock crows, everyone listens.

Even the sun.

Some folks call the rooster Old Faithful. Others are more creative, coming up with names like That Damned Bird or something more colorful. The rooster doesn't care. He lifts his head skyward, blinking once, then twice, to assess the morning light. *It's time.* Extending his crimson-puffed neck, he opens his beak and lets out a piercing, full-throated *ca-ca-ca-ca-caw!* The sound has a crazy syncopation that's somewhat off-kilter but somehow just right—sort of like the island of Key West itself.

It's a sound that cannot, will not, be ignored.

In the air-conditioned rooms of the Lighthouse Hotel, startled vacationers stir in their beds, lift up their heads, and murmur, "Cock-a-doodle-*what*? *Seriously?*" This is not the wake-up call they were expecting. In the low-fenced yards of candy-colored bungalows, tiny green lizards scramble for the nearest shrub, trying to hide from a possible predator. And off on the horizon, the sun shifts and rolls, ever so slightly, as if reaching for the snooze button to get more shut-eye but finally realizing it's time to get up.

Slowly, lazily—reluctantly—the sun rises over Key West.

It takes its sweet time at first. No need to rush things. Then suddenly, without further ado, it rises above the palm trees, spilling yellow-gold light over the entire island. Its warm rays shine across the shuttered shops and bars on Duval Street, the tour boats and sailboats bobbing against the docks, and the charmingly grand, two-storied Hemingway House with its iron-railed balconies and vintage green shutters. Everything under the sun gets the message:

Wake up, Key West. Time to rise and shine.

A cat also rises.

Sprawled out like a queen on the front porch of the Hemingway House—her favorite spot on the island—this magnificent golden-striped tabby twitches her ears and opens her sea-green eyes in the sun's first rays. She yawns. Extending her front legs and wiggling her toes—six of them on each paw—she stretches her entire body until it reaches full length. She is large but not too large, about six years old, and wise beyond her years.

Her official name is Ernestine Hemingway.

Everyone calls her Nessie.

Nessie is just one of the fifty-four cats who roam the historic home, museum, and palm-shaded gardens of the famous Ernest Hemingway House. Being a cat, Nessie has never read any of the Nobel Prize winner's acclaimed novels or stories. Also, being a cat, she has never actually counted the number of felines prowling the Hemingway estate—because cats can't count. Nessie does, however, know each and every one of the cats personally. She knows them like the back of her six-toed paw—or however many toes she has.

Remember, cats can't count.

The sun rises higher in the sky. From Nessie's point of view, it looks like a giant firefly climbing one of the palm trees to the tippy top. She squints her eyes as slashes of sunbeams glare through the leaves. Dragging herself up, she moves to a shadier spot on the porch. *Much better.* She stretches again, yawns again, and considers going back to sleep. But then a loud thump—followed by a frantic scrambling of paws—makes it clear that sleeping is not an option.

The kittens are awake.

And ready to rumble.

First up are the twins, Chew-Chew and Whiskey. They're a little older than the other kittens—and twice as rambunctious, like a pair of teenagers who just got their driver's licenses. They zoom across the Hemingway House porch like cat-shaped race cars, streaking past Nessie in a blur of gray and white fur.

Double trouble, as always.

Then comes Spinderella. She's a gangly prepubescent with gray and black stripes, gold-flecked eyes, and four comically large six-toed paws that are much too big for her body. She hasn't learned yet how to control her oversized feet, and sometimes it seems as if they're controlling her. She charges around the corner of the porch and tries to make a sharp turn—but her paws keep going straight. With a kittenish yowl, she slides and spins across the floorboards like a furry gray top, her tail whirling in the air until she slows to a stop.

Hence the name Spinderella.

Nessie watches the little cat as she tries to regain her footing. Dazed and confused, Spinderella shakes her little head, straightens out her paws, and scrambles off after the twins. As she scampers past Nessie, she trips over her own feet and almost slides off the edge of the porch. If Nessie could laugh out loud—like a human—she wouldn't be able to contain herself. Instead, she swishes her fluffy tail back and forth.

It's Nessie's version of "LOL."

Next up are the babies: Larry, Curly, and Moe. Three frisky bundles of whiskers and fur, the kittens hop, skip, and stumble across the porch in a free-falling jumble—like three balls of yarn tumbling out of a knitting basket. They're even younger than Spinderella and still learning the fundamentals of walking and running and navigating the world on six-toed paws.

Just watching their antics makes Nessie feel tired.

Is it too early for a cat nap?

The trio of kittens zigzag their way past her. Eventually they manage to reach the far end of the veranda. But then Moe collides into Larry, who smashes into Curly, who falls and rolls and ends up at the bottom of a squirming kitten pile.

Nessie swishes her tail. *LOL.*

Poor little Curly tries to push her brothers off, but she can't—so she starts mewling and crying for help.

Nessie to the rescue!

Jumping up from her shady spot, Nessie dashes across the porch and pushes the kittens off Curly with her nose. Free at last, the little tabby climbs to her feet and shakes herself off. Nessie gives her a nudge. Curly takes the hint and chases after her brothers as they make their way down the porch steps. Nessie meows after them. Then she returns to her spot in the shade—still sleepy but wide awake.

Who needs a cat nap anyway?

As the unofficial "House Mother" of the Hemingway cats, Nessie certainly has her paws full. Picking up clumsy kittens when they fall, breaking up unruly cat fights, chasing away the fence-climbing felines who terrorize the dogs across the street—Nessie is ready for anything. It's not like she *has* to take care of every cat in the house. It's just her nature. And being a cat, she has to follow her nature.

It's what cats do.

Nessie gazes at the kittens playing in the grass. They're fine. Satisfied, she tucks her legs beneath her gold-furred body and closes her eyes.

It's her last chance to enjoy the peace and quiet of the morning. Before the tourists show up.

And the chaos begins.

Meooooooooooow!

A loud screech echoes across the lawn, followed by a chorus of more screeches and meowing. The sounds escalate quickly, reaching a fierce and frenzied peak. Nessie lets out a sigh and opens her eyes.

What now?

"Children! Children!" a woman's deep, rich voice rings out.

Nessie gazes across the lawn to see a middle-aged brunette standing in the center of a cat-fueled free-for-all.

"Break it up! Break it up!"

The woman—Margarita Bouffet—is the general manager of the Hemingway House. She's very good at her job. But she's not very good at managing kittens.

"Break it up, I said!"

Nessie thinks of Margarita as "First Lady" because she's the first human to arrive every morning. On this particular morning, Margarita is wearing bright red cha-cha heels, Jackie O sunglasses, and a flowery yellow sundress that swirls around her legs as the kittens circle her ankles.

"Oh! That tickles!"

The twins, Chew-Chew and Whiskey, chase each other round and round Margarita's legs—while Larry, Curly, and Moe try to join in. The baby kittens trip and tumble and bump into the twins, who play peekaboo behind Margarita's dress before circling around again. Of course, Spinderella has to join the party, too. She puts her own unique spin on the circular cat chase—by getting in everyone's way.

"Stop it, kitties! You're getting fur all over my new shoes!"

Margarita bends over to separate the twins and push them away from the smaller cats. Chew-Chew takes off across the lawn, with

Whiskey right behind her. Spinderella scampers off after them. The three young cats disappear around the corner of the house, leaving the baby kittens alone, wide-eyed and confused.

Hey! Where did they go?

Margarita chuckles at their expressions. She gives Larry and Curly a few gentle rubs behind their ears. Then she reaches out for Moe, but it's too late. He's off and running after the older kittens. His sisters jump up and follow him. Margarita chuckles again, shaking her head softly as she brushes the cat fur off her shoes. She straightens up with a groan, then turns to face the house.

Nessie is staring at her. With those big green eyes.

"Why, look at you! Her Majesty Ernestine!"

Nessie doesn't react. Simply stares.

"You're just going to sit there on your throne and let me do all the work, huh, Nessie?"

Nessie yawns.

Margarita steps off the grass and onto the walkway. "Oh, I'm just teasing, sweetie. I know you've got your eye on the kids. What would I do without you? Nessie's my bestie!"

Nessie seems pleased.

Her tail—which resembles a fluffy feather duster—swishes from side to side, startling a tiny gecko behind a nearby flowerpot. Nessie yawns again. Then she lifts her hind haunches and stretches out her body full length. Butt in the air, chin down, front paws forward—it looks like she's doing a yoga routine.

But Margarita knows better. She knows exactly what Nessie is up to.

She's practically *begging* to be stroked.

Of course, being a cat, Nessie is much too proud to beg. She would never plead and paw for affection—like the shameless dogs across the street. No. She simply presents her golden-furred back and luxurious tail to a susceptible human and pretends to be pleasantly surprised when the stroking begins.

Margarita isn't fooled.

"I know what you want, sweetie," she coos, climbing the stairs of the porch. Her cha-cha heels click and clack on the steps like little firecrackers.

Clack! Clack! Clack!!!

Nessie jumps.

Margarita stops and laughs. "Don't you like my new shoes, Nessie?"

Nessie eyes the red pumps suspiciously.

"I need to break them in before I go dancing," Margarita explains.

Putting one red shoe forward, then the other, Margarita launches into a *one-two cha-cha-cha*. She hums a Cuban dance song under her breath, swaying her curvy hips to the beat. After a few twirls and taps, she smiles and winks at Nessie—who stares at the clacking heels nervously—then finishes the dance with a lively *one-two-stomp*.

Nessie pretends to be unimpressed. She yawns and arches her back.

Margarita laughs. "Okay, I can take a hint." Bending down, she runs her fingers through Nessie's golden fur.

Nessie purrs contentedly but keeps an eye on Margarita's shoes—just in case they start clacking again.

"That's a good girl," Margarita coos. She crouches down and continues stroking, from ears to tail, until Nessie melts into a helpless puddle of fur.

"I have a surprise for you, Nessie. We're getting a new tour guide today! Isn't that exciting?"

Nessie is too blissed out to react. She closes her eyes while Margarita rubs her ears.

"Her name is Laura, and she's a big Hemingway fan. She even wrote her college thesis on one of his books. What was the title again? Oh, yeah. '*The Sun Also Rises* and the Fall of the Male Ego.' Whatever that means."

Nessie yawns and stretches.

"Well, I'd better get her employment forms ready. She should be here pretty soon. She's flying in all the way from Syracuse, New York. Imagine that!"

Nessie opens one eye.

"It's very cold there, Nessie. Snows all the time. Not like here. I'm already sweating and the sun's barely up." Margarita fans her face with her hand. "I sure hope Laura can handle the humidity. It's terrible this year."

With a sigh, Margarita climbs to her feet and smooths out her sundress.

Nessie looks up, confused and annoyed that the stroking has stopped.

"Well, Nessie. If you see Laura, give her a big, warm Hemingway welcome and send her my way. I'll be in the gift shop."

Nessie waves her tail, as if she understands.

Margarita steps off the porch and heads toward the shop. After a few steps, she stops and looks back at Nessie. "It will be nice to have someone new here, don't you think? I have a feeling that something big is going to happen. Do you feel it, too?"

Nessie stares back, as if she's thinking about it.

"There's change in the air," Margarita continues. "It's like . . . something's coming. I feel it in my bones. Something . . . I don't know." She shrugs it off with a little laugh. "Whatever it is, I'm ready to rumba!"

With that, Margarita clicks her cha-cha heels and dances off to the gift shop.

Nessie watches her walk away. Then she repositions herself on her favorite perch and settles in, her legs tucked neatly beneath her golden-furred body. A warm breeze rustles the leaves of the palm trees overhead. It feels good on Nessie's face.

More of the cats are awake now. Some of them are slowly prowling the yard as if they're stalking something no one else can see. Others are frolicking and playing—taking advantage of the early-morning temperature before it's too hot to move. Chew-Chew and Whiskey are back. So are the kittens. Curly and Larry are rolling in the grass, swatting at flies. Moe is sitting perfectly still on the main path, staring intently at a tiny pebble. He thinks it's a bug. Or it *might* be a bug.

Just because it doesn't move doesn't mean it's *not* a bug.

Moe isn't taking any chances. He continues staring. Other cats walk around him, paying him no mind. But one of them—a slinky female named Eartha Katt—stops to see what Moe is staring at. Before long a few others join them, a small circle of very interested cats looking down at a pebble.

Nessie swishes her tail. *LOL.*

She starts to close her eyes when a sudden gust of wind blows across the island. It rips through the palm trees with surprising force, blasting the leaves and bending the trunks until they sway back and forth like hula dancers who've had too much caffeine. The sun disappears behind a large gray cloud, plunging the whole island into darkness. Nessie gazes across the yard. Most of the cats have stopped in their tracks, frozen in place. Some of them are running for cover. Nessie moves closer to the house—and braces herself.

The wind picks up momentum, tearing palm fronds from the trees. One of them crashes down on the roof of the gift shop with a loud bang.

From inside the shop, a voice rings out, "What the heck . . . ?"

The door swings open. Margarita steps out, takes one look at the wildly swaying trees, the angry billowing clouds, and the first fat drops of a heavy rain, and steps back inside.

There's change in the air.

Margarita sticks her head out again and looks toward the house. She can barely make out Nessie through the sudden downpour: a golden fluffy cat shape nestled against the front door.

The wind delivers another punishing gust. The palm trees bend in unison. The rain intensifies.

Something's coming.

Margarita looks down at her new red cha-cha shoes and wonders if she should risk ruining them to make a mad dash to the house.

Maybe she could do it barefoot? While she's thinking through her options, a funny thing happens.

The rain stops.

The wind dies down to a gentle breeze, and the sun reappears from behind the clouds. Almost immediately, the warm rays of light begin drying up the wet puddles on the ground. The palm trees stand up straight again, as if nothing ever happened. A minute later, the cats come out from their hiding places.

Well, that was weird, Margarita thinks. She'd seen plenty of summer storms before but never so quick, so short, and so intense.

"Are you okay, Nessie?" she shouts across the yard.

Nessie meows back.

The sun rises a little higher in the sky. The kittens are back in the yard again, lifting their paws high with every step as they cross the dampened ground. Larry and Moe lick raindrops off the grass. Curly joins them. Everything seems fine now, so Margarita goes back to work in the gift shop and Nessie returns to her favorite spot.

Time for that cat nap.

Nessie closes her eyes. A soft breeze wafts across her face and gently ruffles her fur. It feels good. Inside the shop, Margarita hums a folk song she remembers from her childhood in Cuba. On the street beyond the fence, the gypsy chickens cluck softly as they search for crumbs left behind by the lighthouse keeper. And two blocks away, a car makes its way down Whitehead Street—probably the next wave of tourists coming to check into the Lighthouse Hotel.

All is well on the island of Key West.

Nessie can relax now. But she can't shake the feeling that something is about to happen. Like Margarita, she feels it in her bones. Her whiskers, too. Either way, there's nothing she can do but wait for it to happen. Until then, she'll just lie here and enjoy the breeze and take a nap and—

Screeeeech!

A car with squeaky brakes pulls to a stop outside. A door opens and slams. Something—or someone—tumbles onto the road with a thud and a grunt.

Ooof!

The gypsy chickens go crazy, cackling and clucking like it's the end of the world.

Squawk! Squaaaawk!

A young woman screams.

"Help!"

And so it begins.

Chapter 2

"You're Not Allergic to Cats, Are You?"

Laura Lange knew Florida would be hot.

But not *this* hot.

She'd barely taken three steps outside the Key West International Airport and her clean white shirt was already soaked with sweat. Of course, flying in a tiny ten-seater plane did nothing to help her stay calm, cool, and collected. Neither did dragging a large rolling suitcase, carry-on, backpack, and shoulder bag out to the sidewalk to catch a cab.

"Need a ride, miss?"

Laura looked up to see a woman with dreadlocks leaning against a pink taxicab. She spoke with a lilting Jamaican accent, wore a Bob Marley concert shirt, and flashed a smile so big you could probably see it on Google Earth. Her taxi had a bright yellow sign on the roof—*Marley Car Service: The Best in Key West*—and the doors were decorated with musical notes and palm trees.

Laura smiled as she struggled with her luggage. "Yes! Thank you!"

"Let me help you with those," the woman said, popping open the trunk of her cab. She walked over to Laura and picked up the biggest, heaviest suitcase. "Whoa," she grunted. "You don't mess around. Planning to stay a while?"

Laura laughed. "Yeah. For a few months, at least."

The woman loaded the suitcase into the trunk with a grunt and reached for the carry-on, which was just as heavy.

Laura smiled apologetically. "Sorry. I have a lot of baggage."

"We all do, honey." The woman closed the trunk and glanced at Laura's sweat-soaked shirt. "Enjoying the humidity?"

"Uh, not really. I'm from upstate New York. It snows, like, nine months of the year there. I thought this would be a nice change of pace."

"Speaking of nice, I like your bra. Very pretty."

Laura glanced down at her chest and winced. *Oh, man, really?* Her white shirt was almost completely see-through from the sweat. Laura groaned.

"Welcome to the Conch Republic," the woman said with a big smile. She gestured toward a large sign above the airport entrance. It said: *Welcome to the Conch Republic.*

For a second, Laura wondered if she'd boarded the wrong flight.

The woman explained. "Back in the eighties, some of the locals tried to make Key West its own country. The Conch Republic. It didn't happen, but the name stuck."

"Oh, that's interesting. Are you a conch?" Laura asked. She had read that people born in Key West were referred to as "conchs" after the island's famous spiral seashells. Then she remembered the cab-driver's accent. "Or are you from Jamaica?"

"No. Chicago," she said, dropping the lilt in her voice. "My grandma came from Jamaica. That's how I learned the accent. I use it for the tourists. Helps me get better tips. But seeing that you're stay-ing a while . . ." She shrugged and held out her hand. "The name is Mama Marley, which isn't real either. I'll be your driver this morn-ing. Here's my card."

Laura smiled and took the bright pink business card. "I'm Laura. Laura Lange, which is my real name. I think. Unless my mom is lying."

"You never know. My mother told me I was allergic to the sun, to try to keep me from moving to Florida."

"My mom's not thrilled about me coming here either."

Laura made a mental note: *Call Mom. Let her know you didn't die in a ten-passenger plane crash.*

She climbed into the back seat of the cab with her shoulder bag and backpack. Mama Marley slid behind the wheel and revved up the engine. "Where to? Hotel? Boardinghouse? Airbnb?"

"No, the Hemingway House."

"You're staying at the Hemingway House?"

"No, I'll be working there. Starting today."

"You're not allergic to cats, are you?"

"No. But I've never worked at a place with animals before. Should be fun. I love cats."

Mama Marley made a *hmmmm* sound. "Okay then, but watch yourself, honey. Those Hemingway cats aren't normal cats. They're a little freaky, you know. Got all those toes. Way too many toes for a cat. And you know what that means. *More claws.*"

Laura laughed. "Yeah, I know. They're polydactyl. Descended from Hemingway's six-toed cat Snow White. They're supposed to bring good luck."

"You'll be lucky if you don't get scratched."

"You sound like my mom."

"They don't call me Mama for nothing." She stepped hard on the gas and steered the cab onto the southbound A1A. "Mama knows best."

Laura glanced out the window at the shimmering water of the Caribbean. Even in the early-morning light, it looked bluer and brighter than she remembered.

I made it. I'm here. I'm really here. Again.

Mama Marley kept talking. "When I was a little girl in Chicago, I got scratched by the neighbor's cat. Been scared of them ever since. You just can't trust them. Especially those Hemingway cats with all those freaky toes. It's just not right."

"But they're so cute!" Laura said, laughing. "My family visited here five years ago, and I'll never forget how cute the Hemingway cats were. This one kitten, she was so gorgeous, with golden fur and a big fluffy tail. For some reason, she took a liking to me. She followed me around through the whole tour and even sat on my lap afterward. She had six toes on each paw. I thought she was the prettiest thing I ever saw. From that day on, I've been kind of obsessed with Hemingway and his cats. I read all of his books. I even wrote my college thesis on Hemingway. And I owe it all to those cats. They're, like, ridiculously adorable."

Mama made another *hmmm* sound. "That's nice," she said, unconvinced.

Laura could tell she wasn't going to change Mama's mind on the cuteness of six-toed felines, so she stopped talking and gazed out the window. The view was stunning. Palm trees on one side, the deep blue sea on the other. The highway stretched out in front of her, a long blank slate of endless possibilities—or not.

She felt a sudden wave of self-doubt. Before she could stop it, her brain was off and running.

What am I doing here? Am I making the biggest mistake of my life? Am I wasting a college degree for a dead-end summer job? What if I had held out a little longer? What if a teaching position opens up and I'm not there to grab it? What if—and I can't believe I'm even thinking this—Mom was right all along?

Ugh. So many questions.

"Mind if I turn on the radio?"

"Not at all."

That was an easy one to answer.

Laura leaned back in her seat as Mama Marley fidgeted with the radio dials. After a few short bursts of crackling static, the gentle rhythms of soft Caribbean music filled the cab.

Reggae. Bob Marley. Of course.

Laura closed her eyes and surrendered to the gentle rhythms of the music. With every beat of the song, she felt her anxiety melting away and her excitement growing. Here she was, on this beautiful island—the world-famous home of Ernest Hemingway!—about to start a new chapter of her life. For better or worse.

Worse? Stop it!

The song ended, and a man's voice came over the radio.

"Goooood morning, Key West. This is Rooster McCloud, your friendly neighborhood deejay, lighthouse keeper, and chicken feeder."

Laura smiled. She liked the sound of his voice. It was deep and low with a gravelly tone that was strangely soothing.

"You've been listening to *Key West After Dark* on WKEY Radio, the southernmost point on your dial and in your heart. I've been up all night, but that's all right. We got to share some classic tunes, some local gossip, and some shocking secrets."

"Shocking secrets?" Laura asked.

"You bet," said Mama. "People call in with their problems, and some of them are real doozies."

"Sounds juicy. I'll have to tune in."

The man on the radio continued: "It looks like it's going to be a beautiful day here in Key West. Hope you all enjoy it. Me? I'm ready to sign off, hit the streets, and feed those hungry gypsy chickens."

Laura had a quick flashback to her family's vacation. She remembered the wild chickens wandering the streets of Key West like they owned the place. She thought it was bizarre and hilarious.

"Next up is Shelly with the weather," the deejay went on. "This is your friend Rooster McCloud, signing out. At the sound of the doodle-doo, it'll be exactly seven a.m."

"Doodle-doo?" Laura asked, only to get an immediate answer.

Ca-ca-ca-ca-caw!

The shrill crowing of a rooster erupted from the radio. Loud and clear—and earsplitting. Laura jumped in her seat, making Mama Marley laugh.

"Charming, huh?" she said. "That damned bird drives me nuts."

Laura shifted in her seat, catching a glimpse of herself in the cab's rearview mirror. At that moment, the sleepy morning sun came out from behind the clouds, spilling beams of light over the ocean, the highway—and Laura's face.

"Oh, no," she groaned. "I look like crap."

Her long auburn hair was starting to frizz from the humidity.

Well, not all of her hair. Some of it was matted to her face, with the ends sticking to her sweaty cheeks like some creature from an alien movie. She glanced down at her shirt to see if it was dry yet. Nope. Still see-through. *Ugh.* She thought about changing her shirt in the cab before getting to the Hemingway House—then remembered that her shirts were packed in the big suitcase in the trunk.

On the radio, a woman with a nasally news voice delivered the weather: "It's going to be a *perfect* day!"

Perfect? Laura thought. *I've been in steam rooms with less humidity.*

She leaned forward to check herself out in the rearview mirror. Using her fingers as combs, she managed to pull most of the hair off her face and smooth out at least some of the frizzies. Not perfect, but good enough. Her eyes were bright and green and her cheeks were flushed with a nice shade of pink—from the humidity—so she didn't need any makeup.

Lipstick, maybe?

It was Laura's first day, after all. She wanted to make a good impression. Reaching into her backpack, she pulled out the first plastic bag she could find. It wasn't her makeup. It was full of homemade Chex Party Mix.

Mom.

Laura's mother had insisted on packing a snack for the plane ride. Laura had forgotten all about it after being forced to change flights, spend a night in a cheap airport hotel in Fort Lauderdale, then transfer to a tiny ten-seat plane that rumbled and bounced like a bad carnival ride. It was terrifying, and Laura was way too nervous to eat anything—even Mom's Party Mix.

She dug deeper into the bag. Found the lipstick, removed the top, and started to apply.

Whoooosh!

A massive gust of wind slammed against the cab. It came from the direction of the water, rushing inland like a giant, invisible tidal wave. The force of it was strong enough to knock the car off course.

"Whoa!"

Mama Marley gripped the steering wheel as hard as she could.

"Hold on, honey!"

Another gust pummeled the side of the vehicle. Mama pulled leftward on the wheel to keep the car steady on the road. Laura had to brace herself on the seat in front of her.

Then the sky turned dark. A mass of billowy clouds rolled across the island, reminding Laura of an angry mob storming the castle in an old movie. She gazed out the window and watched the palm trees thrashing in the wind. Droplets of rain started pelting the windshield. In seconds, it was pouring and Mama had to turn on the wipers. Then the storm gained intensity, the rain pounding harder and wind howling louder. Laura was about to ask Mama to pull over and wait it out when . . .

It stopped.

As quickly as it started, the rain stopped falling, the wind stopped blowing, and the clouds stopped angrily mobbing. Thirty seconds later, the sun was shining again. Laura couldn't believe her eyes.

"Uh . . . that was weird."

Mama Marley shrugged. "Yes, well, sometimes we get these flash rainstorms. They last just a few minutes. Usually not this early, though."

Laura let out a sigh of relief and glanced down at her hands.

Her lipstick was broken.

The Party Mix was fine.

Grabbing a tissue from her bag, she wiped the Calypso Pink off her hand and tossed the broken lipstick into her backpack. She was about to pack up the Party Mix when a song came on the radio.

Jimmy Buffett's "Cheeseburger in Paradise."

Great. Now I'm hungry, she thought.

She eyed the Party Mix, realizing she hadn't eaten anything all morning. By the time Jimmy Buffett hit the second chorus of his heavenly cheeseburger anthem, she was ravenous. Unable to resist any longer, she tore open the bag of Party Mix and dug in. She pulled out a big handful of crispy baked cereal bits, pretzels, and nuts. Shoved them in her mouth and . . .

"Are you eating in my cab?"

Laura stopped chewing mid-crunch. She didn't know what to say and, even if she did, she couldn't. Her mouth was full.

"Mama Marley likes to run a clean cab. The consumption of food and/or beverages is strictly prohibited in accordance to Florida Regulation Twenty-Four A, Section B."

"I'm sorry," Laura mumbled through a mouthful of crumbs.

Mama Marley burst out laughing. "I'm just pulling your leg, honey. I don't care. You're probably hungry after your flight. What have you got there anyway?"

Laura chewed and swallowed. "It's my mom's Chex Party Mix."

"Mmm, mmm, sounds good."

"Want some?"

"No, thanks. I had a big breakfast. You go on, though."

Mama Marley pulled off the highway onto a quiet residential street lined with tall palm trees and pastel-colored bungalows. Laura gazed at the rows of neat picket fences and cute little houses, amazed at how charming they were. It was like driving through a life-sized Caribbean-style version of one of those toy villages beneath a Christmas tree. But instead of the rooftops being frosted with snow, they were dappled with sunlight streaming through palm trees. The roads were almost dry now, the sun baking away the last of the rain-drops, leaving a hint of steam rising from the pavement. Two small lizards dashed across the street in front of the cab. And somewhere in the distance, a rooster crowed to greet the sun's return.

"We're almost there," said Mama Marley. "We're crossing Duval now."

Laura turned her head to see dozens of colorful restaurants, bars, and gift shops stretching northward on Duval Street, Key West's busiest strip. At night, it was Party Central. But right now, it looked like a sleepy little village in a storybook. A few of the restaurants were already opened for breakfast, just waiting for the tourists to wake up. A pair of mustachioed men in Hawaiian shirts walked by with two waggle-tailed Chihuahuas on leashes. The men waved as the cab drove by.

Mama Marley waved back and turned onto Whitehead Street.

"Those are the owners of the Lighthouse Hotel," she told Laura. "I'm sure you'll get to meet them. And their little dogs, too!"

Laura laughed and leaned forward, taking it all in.

"Look! There's the famous Rooster McCloud." Mama Marley pointed at an older man on the side of the road. He had long salt-and-pepper hair under a red bandanna, wore a tie-dyed T-shirt and cargo shorts with flip-flops, and was tossing crumbs to a lively group of gypsy chickens.

"The radio guy?" Laura asked.

"And lighthouse keeper. A real character. Sweet guy, though."

Laura could see the gleaming white lighthouse up ahead, just beyond the entrance of the Lighthouse Hotel. Right across the street, nestled behind a redbrick wall and a jungle of foliage, was the Hemingway House. She could barely make out the Spanish colonial-style wraparound balcony and yellow-green shutters through the leaves of the trees. It was just enough of a glimpse to get her heart pounding.

This is it.

Mama Marley pulled the cab over, its brakes screeching as if they were in pain. "Here we are, honey!" She popped the trunk and hopped out of the cab.

Laura took a deep breath. Cramming the Party Mix into a side pocket of her shoulder bag, she grabbed one of the loops of her backpack and stumbled—awkwardly—out of the cab. Mama Marley glanced up from behind the trunk. She took one look at Laura's face and started laughing.

"Girl! You're a hot mess!" she hooted. "You've got lipstick all over you!"

Laura spun around—and tripped on the other loop of her backpack. With a loud grunt, she landed butt-first on the street.

Ooof!

Her elbow slammed against her shoulder bag, catapulting the bag of Party Mix onto her stomach. The plastic seal exploded, sending flying bits of Chex cereal, pretzels, and nuts into the air and onto the street—but mostly all over Laura.

In a flash, the gypsy chickens were on her, clucking and pecking and fighting over every spilled crumb.

Seriously, ladies?

Laura felt like she was in the middle of a turf war between rival street gangs. The birds swarmed over her, at least a dozen of them, flapping their wings in an all-out feeding frenzy. And for what?

Mom's Chex Party Mix.

Squawk! Squaaaawk!

Laura couldn't believe what was happening. She might have laughed at the absurdity of it all, except those damned birds were getting awfully close to her face. When one of them pecked at her chin, that was it. Enough already.

"Help!"

With a short, loud scream, she pushed the chin-pecking chicken off her chest. Glancing to the side, she saw Mama Marley standing frozen in shock. Behind her, down the street, was old Rooster McCloud flip-flopping toward them with his hands waving. And in front of the Lighthouse Hotel, the mustachioed dog walkers struggled with the leashes of their Chihuahuas, who unleashed a double-barreled blast of high-pitched yelps.

Is this how I die? she wondered. *In a Chex-related chicken attack? On the mean streets of Key West? In front of a stunned crowd of helpless onlookers?*

That's when Laura saw her.

A magnificent gold-striped tabby—with a huge fluffy tail.

Could it be?

It looked just like the kitten with the big fluffy tail who followed Laura around five years ago. But a lot bigger and a lot fluffier.

Is that you?

The cat had jumped onto the tall brick wall that surrounded the Hemingway House. Now she stood there, tail raised, claws out, and eyes flashing like a champion prizefighter sizing up an opponent—preparing to pounce.

And pounce she did.

With a ferocious battle screech, she leapt off the fence, charged across the road, and hurled herself into the feathered fray of Chex-crazed chickens. She hissed. She swatted. She swiped.

She showed those birds who's boss.

The gypsy chickens, of course, didn't stand a chance. They scattered and fled in all directions, running for their lives before the big bad cat made a Party Mix out of them. One of the chickens bumped into Mama Marley, who screamed and dashed. A few of the others made the mistake of running toward the Chihuahuas, who barked and sent them running the other way. Most of them headed for Rooster McCloud, who tossed some seeds on the ground to lure them away from that poor girl with lipstick on her face. It looked like she had enough problems to deal with for one day.

With a groan, Laura lifted her head and looked around.

The chickens were gone. Thank goodness.

No, she thought. *Thank Nessie.*

She watched the bushy-tailed cat chase away the last of the chickens. Once the birds were banished, the cat came back to Laura, sat down next to her, and stared.

It was almost like the cat was saying, *Okay, that's that. What's next?*

Laura looked the cat in the eye and whispered, "Nessie? Is that you?"

The cat blinked and licked one of her paws.

Laura heard footsteps approaching—probably people coming to help—drowned out by the loud clacking sound of cha-cha heels. The click-clacks grew louder, stopping just inches from her head.

"Oh, you poor thing! Are you all right?"

Laura looked up. A middle-aged woman with jet-black hair stood looming above her. She leaned over, her large hoop earrings dangling down over pink-blushed cheeks. Her eyes were filled with concern, but Laura couldn't help but stare at those crazy-big earrings.

"You must be Laura, right?" the woman said.

She recognized Margarita Bouffet immediately from their video chat interview three weeks ago. Laura thought she'd made a great first impression. It landed her the job, didn't it?

Now look at her—lying in the gutter, covered with chicken feathers and Chex Mix, face smeared with lipstick, shirt soaked through to the bra with sweat, hair frizzed and frazzled and matted to her skin—she was, as Mama Marley put it, "a hot mess." For a brief moment, she could almost hear her mother saying, *You never get a second chance to make a first impression.*

Yeah, Mom? What about really horrible second impressions? What then?

She sighed and smiled weakly at her new boss. "Yep, I'm Laura. You must be Ms. Bouffet."

"Call me Margarita. Everybody does. Here, let me help you."

Suddenly Laura became aware of the other people gathered around her.

"Careful!" said one of the mustachioed dog walkers. "She might have sprained something."

"Or broken something," said the other mustachioed man.

Laura shook her head. "No, I think I'm okay." She tried to get up on her own, but her leg was still tangled in the loop of her backpack.

"I got you," said a young man, stepping forward.

"Me, too," said another.

Laura felt herself being lifted up by two pairs of strong hands. One pair belonged to an incredibly cute guy with short dark hair, dreamy bedroom eyes, and a Hemingway House T-shirt that clung to his arms and chest in all the right ways. The other hands belonged to a taller, lankier guy who was equally as cute. He had shaggy blond hair, a short scruffy beard, and a devilish twinkle in his eye that made Laura weak in the knees.

Of course, hitting the concrete could explain her weak knees.

Get a grip, she told herself. *You're in no shape to flirt with cute guys right now.*

"Can you stand on your own?" asked T-Shirt Guy.

Laura gave it a try. "Yes, I'm fine," she said. "Just a little embarrassed."

Rooster McCloud stepped forward, shaking his head. "Don't be embarrassed. I've been feeding those chickens for years and, let me tell you, they can be awful aggressive. What was in that bag? It really drove them crazy."

Laura blushed. "My mom's Chex Party Mix."

Rooster nodded thoughtfully. "You'll have to give me her recipe. I'm Rooster McCloud. Local deejay and lighthouse keeper."

Laura smiled. "Yes, I know. I heard you on the radio earlier, thanks to Mama Marley here."

She looked around for the cabdriver but couldn't find her.

"I'm here, honey, inside my taxi!" Mama Marley shouted from the driver's seat.

She was using her fake Jamaican accent again.

Laura stifled a laugh.

"I'm sorry I couldn't help you, hon," Mama explained. "When I was a little girl, I got pecked by the neighbor's chicken. Been scared of them ever since. You just can't trust a chicken. Are they gone now? If the coast is clear, I'll help you with your luggage."

"I got it," said T-Shirt Guy, reaching into the trunk.

"No, I got it," said Scruff Guy, reaching in, too.

Mama Marley winked at Laura and waved her over to the car window. "Look at you, girl," she whispered. "You've got these boys fighting over you."

Laura laughed. "Not bad for a hot mess, huh?"

Mama Marley smiled. "Yeah, you still might want to find a mirror and . . . you know." She waved her hand in front of her face. With that, she revved up the engine, listened for the slam of the car trunk, then shifted into drive and took off.

Laura was tempted to yell, *Wait for me!* But when she saw the pink-colored taxi turn the corner, she knew it was too late. She had to turn around—hot messy face and all—and try to make the best of it. Somehow.

What would Hemingway do?

He wouldn't give a crap, she thought. *He'd roll up his sleeves, pour a stiff drink, and keep writing.*

It was a reassuring thought. Especially the stiff drink part.

"Everybody!" Margarita Bouffet said cheerfully to the others. "This is Laura Lange, our new tour guide! She came all the way from Syracuse! Laura, this is everybody."

Laura smiled sheepishly and gave a little wave, trying to ignore the lipstick on her hand.

"This is Rick and Ricardo," said Margarita, pointing to the mustachioed men. "They're the co-owners of the hotel across the street."

Rick—or maybe it was Ricardo—smiled at Laura, then squatted down next to the Chihuahuas. "And this is Desi and Lucy. They're very pleased to meet you."

Laura gazed down at the Chihuahuas and pretended not to notice that Lucy was sniffing Desi's butt. "Uh, the pleasure is mine," she said.

Ricardo—or maybe it was Rick—added, "They don't usually bark like that. They're very quiet dogs. Even the cats can't get a rise out of them."

"Not true," said the other owner. "They just know when they're outnumbered. How many cats do you have there, Margarita? Fifty-two? Fifty-three?"

Margarita turned to T-Shirt Guy. "I'm not sure. How many do we have now, Jake? What's the latest count?"

T-Shirt Guy shrugged. "I counted fifty-four last week, but the number changes every time I try."

Margarita shook her head, then turned back to Laura. "Laura, this is Jake. He's the cat keeper of the house. He makes sure they stay well fed and, hopefully, stay out of trouble. Right, Jake?"

"I try," Jake said to Laura with a warm smile. "It's not easy. They're troublemakers."

"Look who's talking," said Scruff Guy, stepping in front of Jake to greet Laura. "I'm Mack. Mack McCloud. Rooster is my great-uncle. I help him run the lighthouse museum down the street." He added with an endearingly goofy grin, "You'll be seeing a lot of me around here."

Jake shot Mack a dirty look.

Are they actually competing for me? Laura wondered. *They just met me! And I'm a hot mess! It's crazy.*

Instead of pondering the mysteries of men, she looked around to see if there was anyone else to meet.

Oh! There she is!

Just a few feet away, sitting calmly in the middle of the street, was the gorgeous golden cat with the big fluffy tail.

"And who is *this*?" Laura asked. "Besides my hero and savior and lifelong friend . . ."

Margarita chuckled. "Oh, this is Nessie. Her real name is Ernestine Hemingway, but we all call her Nessie. She's a beauty, isn't she?"

Laura gasped.

"So it *is* you! Nessie! So nice to see you again!"

She crouched down and ran her fingers through Nessie's thick fur, stroking from head to tail. Nessie arched her back in delight.

"Wait. You know Nessie?" asked Jake.

Laura nodded. "Yes, I met her when she was just a kitten. I was here with my family and . . . well, it's a long story."

"Well, I can't wait to hear it, dear," Margarita said. "Why don't you tell me all about it inside? Let's go into the gift shop. You need to fill out some paperwork and, maybe, um, clean up your . . ." She waved her hand in front of her face. "Boys, could you grab her luggage?"

Laura blushed. Standing up and smoothing out her skirt, she followed Margarita and the guys through the entry gate of the Hemingway House into the lush gardens of the front yard.

Nessie followed right behind her.

My hero!

Jake and Mack stacked the luggage outside of the gift shop and parted ways.

"See you later, Laura!"

"Yeah! Later!"

Margarita led Laura inside, closing the door behind them and turning on the air conditioner. "It'll take a minute for this to kick in," she explained. "The humidity is terrible this year. You'd think I'd be used to it by now." She pulled up a chair for Laura, then pulled out a hand mirror and box of tissues from under the counter. "Here you go."

Laura sat in the chair, looked in the mirror, and gasped.

It was worse than she thought.

Her hair was all over the place. Her face was spotted with Chex cereal bits. And her lipstick was smudged all the way to her ear.

"I look like the Joker."

"Nonsense, you look lovely, dear," said Margarita. "You're just having a bad day."

"Yeah, and it's the first day of my new job."

"Oh, you don't have to start today, dear. You've been through enough already. Go check out your new house share. Get settled in. Get some rest. You can start fresh tomorrow."

"Oh! Thank you!" Laura was more than relieved.

"But while you're here, you might as well fill out your employment forms. If I can find them. Where did I put those?"

Margarita rifled through some drawers, giving Laura a chance to study the merchandise in the gift shop. Lots of Hemingway books and biographies. Coffee mugs and knickknacks. Framed prints of the house and pictures of the cats and—

"Nessie!"

Nessie must have followed her inside. She rubbed against Laura's leg and hopped up onto her lap.

"Hello again!"

Margarita continued searching for the papers. She reached up to the highest shelf behind the cash register, pulled out a thick brown folder—and brought down a massive cloud of dust.

Laura sneezed. Twice.

Then sneezed again.

Margarita stopped and turned around. "I have to ask you something, Laura, and I want you to be honest."

Laura stopped petting Nessie. "Um, okay. Ask away."

Margarita looked her straight in the eye.

"You're not allergic to cats, are you?"

Chapter 3
Of Mice and Men (and Spiders and Snakes)

Of all the cats on the island, Pawpa Hemingway was the biggest, the oldest, and the wisest.

He was also the grumpiest.

Even as a kitten, Pawpa looked like a grumpy old man. With his ruffled gray fur, piercing blue eyes, and scruffy white beard, he was the spitting image of the house's most famous owner: old "Papa" Hemingway himself. And just like his namesake, Pawpa was a bit of a tomcat in his youth. He loved hunting (mice and lizards), fishing (goldfish in the neighbor's pond), and getting into fights (with any cat who rubbed him the wrong way). As he got older, Pawpa grew tired of the hunting, the fishing, and the fighting. But a lot of things still rubbed him the wrong way.

Like those squawking chickens this morning.

So much fuss and bother over a bunch of stupid birds. Pawpa knew—from experience—that chickens were not to be messed with. He had the scars to prove it. It only took one vicious street fight with the island's gypsy chickens for Pawpa to learn that some things—no matter how annoying—should be left alone.

Of course, that didn't stop Nessie.

When Nessie leapt over the gate to chase the chickens off that poor human girl, Pawpa had to admit he was impressed. But he had to wonder why. Why would Nessie risk getting pecked and clawed to save a complete stranger? Even more puzzling, why did she follow that stranger into the gift shop with Margarita, the house manager? As much as Pawpa enjoyed his role as the oldest, wisest, grumpiest cat in town—always aloof and above it all—he had to admit the mystery was killing him.

You know what they say about curiosity and cats.

Keeping one eye on the closed door of the gift shop, Pawpa sat patiently under a tree and pretended to be bored. He yawned a few times to make it more convincing. But inside, he was dying of curiosity. *What is going on in there? Who is that girl?*

The door swung open, startling Pawpa mid-yawn, and Margarita stepped out of the gift shop. Behind her was the girl, doing something Pawpa had never seen before.

She was holding Nessie in her arms!

Curiouser and curiouser.

Pawpa knew that Nessie didn't like to be held by humans. Like most of the four-legged inhabitants of the Hemingway House, she was a free-range cat with an independent nature and a limited tolerance for the cat-loving tourists who tried to pick them up.

Letting the tourists *stroke* them, however, was another story.

"Jake!" Margarita shouted across the yard. "Could you help Laura with her bags?"

The dark-haired cat keeper popped his head from around a large bush and let out a cheerful, "Can do!" It was as if he'd been waiting there the whole time, spying on the newcomer.

Just like Pawpa, he was curious, too.

"I'll see you tomorrow morning, dear," Margarita said to Laura with a wink. She turned and went back inside the gift shop.

Jake strode across the yard with a big smile and reached for Laura's rolling suitcase and carry-on. But his smile faded when he saw Nessie in her arms. "Um, I don't mean to be a jerk," he said apologetically, "but we ask our guests not to pick up the cats. It's house policy."

"Oh!" Laura blushed. "I'm sorry. She was sitting on my lap and wouldn't get off when I tried to stand up, so I, uh, brought her along with me."

Jake looked confused. "She sat on your lap?"

"Yes! After saving me from those chickens. Which was amazing. I think she likes me."

Jake looked down at Nessie, purring softly in Laura's arms, her long fluffy tail waving blissfully back and forth. "Yeah, I think she does, too. Huh."

"Why the 'huh'?"

Jake tilted his head and tried to explain. "It's just that Nessie is very particular about her humans. With her fellow cats, she's totally paws-on. We call her the House Mother because she takes care of all the kittens. But with people? She's very . . . choosy. Usually she's affectionate only with the people she knows. But you? You're a stranger."

Laura smiled mysteriously and stroked Nessie's fur. "Maybe I'm not."

Jake squinted his eyes. "You're not?"

"No, I'm not," said Laura. "Nessie and I go way back. We've been friends for years and years. Haven't we, Nessie?"

She lifted the cat to her face and rubbed their noses together. Which only confused Jake more.

"How is that possible? Margarita told me you're from upstate New York."

Laura shrugged and smiled. "Take a guess."

"You met her at an audition for a cat food commercial."

"No."

"You went to school together. You're sorority sisters."

"Nope."

"You pulled a thorn out of her paw when she was a kitten, and you bonded for life."

"No, but you're getting warmer."

"Okay, I give up."

"Already? You're no fun."

"Oh, I'm fun."

Laura raised an eyebrow. "Really? I wouldn't peg you as the fun type. You look so clean-cut and wholesome. I assumed you were the responsible type."

Jake blushed, which was very cute. "It's the new haircut. They cut it too short. I look like it's my first day at boot camp."

"I like it."

"Even though it's not fun?"

"Even though it's not fun. But your friend, what's his name? The scruffy cool one who helped you carry my bags? His hair is fun."

"Mack? You think he looks cool?"

"I do. Cool and fun."

Jake rolled his eyes, making Laura laugh.

"What's the deal with you two?" she asked.

"What do you mean? He's my best friend."

"I mean . . . I don't know. You both seem a little, um, competitive. Do you have some sort of rivalry going on?"

"It's a long story."

"I have time."

Jake sighed. "Okay. I'll tell you about Mack and me if you tell me how you and Nessie know each other. Deal?"

"Deal."

"You first."

"No, you."

"Ladies before gentlemen."

"Ladies before gentlemen? Did they teach you that at boot camp?"

"Very funny."

"Sorry about that. It's the hair."

"I know. It's too short, right?"

"It's not. I'm just messing with you."

"I'll get over it. Now will you please tell me about Nessie?"

"Sir, yes, sir."

★ ★ ★

Pawpa Hemingway was not happy.

As Laura told Jake the story of her childhood trip to Key West, meeting little Nessie at the house, and discovering her passion for books—especially those by Ernest Hemingway—the old gray cat sat quietly under his tree and watched them talk. He didn't understand a word they were saying, of course. But it was obvious to him that Jake—the Food Bringer—seemed just as smitten by this young female human as Nessie was.

But why?

Pawpa had no idea.

Maybe she smelled good?

He'd have to sniff her later and see. For now, he could only watch and wait for his chance to investigate more closely. It was like hunting a mouse that hid beneath the stairs. It required patience.

After a few minutes, the human male and female sat down in the shade on the front porch steps. Nessie settled into the female's lap, luxuriating in the gentle strokes of human hands. At one point, she even rolled over onto her back to let the girl rub her tummy!

Disgusting.

Pawpa would never let a human touch his stomach like that. If anyone tried it, they'd regret it. As far as Pawpa was concerned, that was off-limits. That was crossing the line. That was when the claws came out.

But Nessie? For some reason, Nessie trusted this human.

Not Pawpa.

He didn't trust this strange new person one bit. She could be dangerous. Like one of those little dogs that pretend to be your friend until suddenly—out of the blue—they bare their teeth and snap at you.

No, Pawpa did not trust this girl.

Whoever she was, whatever she was up to, this human was not like the other visitors who passed through the Hemingway House every day. She might have fooled Nessie, who had a soft heart and sweet nature. But she couldn't fool Pawpa Hemingway. Pawpa was the oldest. Pawpa was the wisest. And if anyone—human or otherwise—came to stir up trouble at the Hemingway House, they wouldn't get very far. . . .

Pawpa was watching.

"Don't look now," said Jake, "but I think we're being watched."

He nodded toward a broad-leafed tree across the garden. Laura turned to look but didn't see anything. She shielded her eyes from the sun and looked again. Finally, she spotted an old grumpy-looking cat sitting among the tree roots, its ruffled gray fur blending perfectly with the weathered trunk. With its camouflaged coloring and stealthy crouch, the cat reminded her of an undercover spy. Or a ninja.

An extremely *grumpy* ninja.

"Oh! Look at that face," Laura whispered to Jake.

The old cat stared back at her. Intensely.

"And those eyes!"

The cat's eyes narrowed and darkened and focused on her even harder.

"Yikes. Now I know how a mouse must feel when it's being stalked."

Jake chuckled. "That's Pawpa Hemingway. *P-a-w*-pa. Get it?"

"Of course! The white beard! The blue eyes! The gruff look! He's like Ernest Hemingway in cat form!"

"Exactly."

"So why does the feline reincarnation of Ernest Hemingway hate me so much?"

Jake laughed. "He doesn't hate you."

"He doesn't? He looks like he wants to kill me. And eat me for breakfast."

"You're new. He doesn't trust you. And he sees you being chummy with Nessie and the rest of us. He's just curious."

Laura wasn't sure she believed Jake. From the look on Pawpa's face, the old cat didn't just distrust her; he actively disliked her. But then again, they hadn't been formally introduced. She had to give it a try.

"Hello, Pawpa!" she called out across the yard. "My name is Laura. I'm going to be working here with you. I'm the new tour guide."

Pawpa's eyes widened slightly. But he didn't move. He just kept staring as if she'd challenged him to a staring contest to see who would blink first. It wouldn't be him.

"Won't you come and join us here on the porch?" she added sweetly.

Pawpa wasn't having it.

Laura took one hand off Nessie and patted a space on the porch next to her. "Come on, Pawpa. Come say hello."

Jake burst out laughing. "That's not going to work."

Laura ignored him. She called to Pawpa again and patted the porch step harder. Which startled Nessie, who jumped off Laura's lap and scampered across the yard. Which startled Pawpa, who leapt from his spying place and dashed around the side of the house.

"I told you it wouldn't work," said Jake. "Pawpa's not very sociable. With anyone."

Laura took that as a challenge. "I'll win him over."

"How?" asked Jake. "With your insights into the male animal that you found in the toxic masculine fiction of Ernest Hemingway?"

Laura sighed. "That was for my thesis paper. My professor was obsessed with gender studies. I knew she'd eat it up. Most of the other girls were writing about Jane Austen."

"So you think Hemingway was too . . . macho?"

"I think Hemingway artfully exposed the deep-seated vulnerabilities and insecurities hiding beneath men's socially constructed masculine armor."

"Whoa," said Jake. "They didn't teach us that in high school."

"Did you read Hemingway in high school?"

"Of course. I really liked *Of Mice and Men*."

"That was John Steinbeck."

"No, it wasn't. It was Hemingway."

"It was Steinbeck! I think I would know since I have a BFA in English and wrote my thesis on . . ."

Jake started laughing. "I'm just messing with you. I know it was Steinbeck."

Laura felt her face flush. "I guess I deserved that for teasing you about your military haircut."

"It really is too short, isn't it?"

Laura rolled her eyes and laughed. "Maybe Hemingway should have written about toxic male vanity, too. And speaking of guy stuff, are you going to tell me about your rivalry with Mack?"

Jake took a deep breath and started to speak but was interrupted by the sound of rapidly approaching paws. He and Laura turned to see two rambunctious cats dashing across the porch toward them. The dashing duo—a pair of tiger-striped tabbies—looked like photo negatives of each other. One was mostly black with brown stripes; the other, mostly brown with black stripes. Both had outlandishly large paws that looked more like baseball mitts or boxing gloves than cat paws. And both had the super-feline strength and energy to leap over Laura's lap in a single bound.

She let out a squeak. "What the . . . ?"

The two cats tumbled onto the lawn in front of her, a black and brown blur of fur and fury. Fighting like a pair of championship wrestlers, they rolled and tossed each other around on the grass until one of them managed to break free of the other. The mostly black cat reared up on its hind legs, standing upright and jabbing its huge brown paws back and forth in the air. The mostly brown cat did the same but waved its huge black paws from side to side.

"What is this . . . cat-on-cat violence?" Laura asked. "Should we break it up?"

Jake laughed. "No, they're just playing. That one's Boxer, and that one's Bullfighter."

"Very Hemingwayesque."

"Yeah. They're tough little guys. Fighting and brawling since the day they were born. You could probably guess they're brothers. And you know what brothers are like."

"Always trying to one-up each other? Like you and Mack?"

"Not exactly."

Laura was going to press him on the subject, but her attention was pulled away by the spectacle of the battling big-pawed cat brothers. With a few sharp jabs and a thrust, Boxer rushed at Bullfighter like a heavyweight champ. Bullfighter countered with a graceful spin and a swish of his tail. The move made Boxer lose his balance and fall to the grass on all fours. That didn't stop him, though, from throwing a left hook at Bullfighter's leg, sending him to the ground next to his brother. Both of them, however, bounced back instantly. In a flash, they were up on their hind legs again, facing off with big paws raised in the air.

"Why do their paws seem so much bigger than the other cats'?" Laura asked Jake.

"They have seven toes instead of the typical six-toed polydactyl," he explained. "Did you know that most of the cats here are descended from one polydactyl cat that was given as a gift to Hemingway by a sea captain?"

"Yes, I did know that," she said. "I memorized the entire Hemingway House handbook that Margarita sent me."

"Do you know the name of the original cat?"

"Snow White."

"Male or female?"

"Male."

"Where did Hemingway meet the sea captain?"

"At Sloppy Joe's Bar."

"Where is that?"

"Two-Oh-One Duval Street."

"Wow!" said Jake, clearly impressed. "I didn't expect you to know the street number. You are very well prepared."

Laura was about to respond when she heard a loud screech from Bullfighter. Or maybe it was Boxer. Either way, the two cat brothers—who were somehow still standing upright—had their big furry mitts locked around each other's bodies and were teetering back and forth in the grass.

"How cute, they're dancing," said Laura.

"Just wait," said Jake, leaning forward. "You're about to see Bullfighter's signature move."

Laura watched as the mostly brown cat twirled and spun and threw his mostly black brother to the ground.

"Body slam!" Jake cheered. "Boxer is great at bobbing and weaving and throwing punches, but Bullfighter's takedowns are poetry in motion."

Laura fanned herself with her hand like a Southern belle. "Gracious me, all this testosterone. I guess I really am at Hemingway's house."

Jake chuckled. "I assume you don't approve of the, uh, manly arts? Fighting, hunting, fishing?"

"Oh, I approve . . . sort of," she said. "My dad used to box, and my grandfather liked to hunt deer and fish for bass at Lake Onondaga. I'm not crazy about the hunting part, though. I like animals too much."

"Me, too," said Jake. "I used to want to be a veterinarian."

"Used to? What changed your mind?"

"Long story."

"I've got time."

"Well, I don't," said Jake, standing up and brushing some cat fur off his pants. "I've got to get back to work. Those litter boxes aren't going to clean themselves."

"I guess not." Laura stood up, pulled her phone out of her pocket, and checked the time. "So I guess I'll see you tomorrow."

"Bright and early. Do you need help with your luggage?"

"No, thanks, I'll manage. First I have to check in with my new roommates to see if they're home."

"Where are you staying?"

"With a couple women who run a snorkeling boat for tourists."

"The Crabb sisters?"

"You know them?"

"Everyone knows the Crabb sisters," Jake said with a sly smirk.

"I don't like that look on your face. What's wrong with the Crabb sisters?"

"Oh, nothing," he said, slowly backing away. "You said you like animals, right?"

"Love them."

"Great. You're going to love living with the Crabbs." With that, Jake turned and started walking away. "Later, Laura!" he said—a little too cheerfully—as he disappeared around the corner.

Laura was tempted to run after him for more details on the Crabb sisters but figured she'd find out soon enough. Instead, she checked her phone for messages. Three texts from Mom:

Did you make your flight?

Did you land safely?

How's the new job?

Laura sighed and typed a quick response:

Yes, yes, and I start tomorrow. Will call later.

Then she texted the Crabb sisters. Well, one of the Crabb sisters. Jolene, not Jilly.

I'm here in KW but got the day off. RU home now?

She hit send. Then she plopped herself down on the porch step and waited for a response. Which—she suddenly realized—might take a while if the Crabb sisters were working. They probably didn't check their text messages while snorkeling over the coral reef with tourists.

Laura stretched and yawned. Out of the corner of her eye, she saw a golden furry cat stretching and yawning, too.

"Nessie! You're back!"

She started to get up when her phone chimed. A text from Jolene Crabb:

We're home now but have a boat tour at 10. Can you get here fast?

Laura texted back:

Sure, no problem! See u soon!

Laura jumped up and started gathering her bags. "Sorry, Nessie, I have to run. See you tomorrow!" Hoisting her backpack on her shoulder, she grabbed her rolling luggage and headed for the front gate of the Hemingway House. As she stepped onto the sidewalk, she glanced back at the gorgeous Spanish colonial home with the yellow-green shutters—and the adorable cats who roamed back and forth across the garden. She waved at Nessie, who looked quite regal sitting calmly on the porch.

"Wait a minute. Where am I going?"

Pulling out her phone, Laura looked up the Crabbs' address. It was somewhere on Southard Street, but she wasn't sure how close it was—or if she could walk there in less than half an hour.

"Does the new tour guide need a tour guide?"

Laura looked up from her phone to see Rooster McCloud, the bandanna-wearing deejay and lighthouse keeper, standing on the sidewalk with a bag of chicken feed. She smiled.

"Ah, yes, I guess I do. Do you know where this is?" She showed him the address on her phone.

Rooster squinted his eyes, took one look at the address, and sighed. "Oh, I'm sorry. You can't get there from here."

"What?"

"It's just not possible."

"Not possible? Are you kidding?"

Rooster saw the alarmed look on Laura's face and immediately fessed up. "Of course I'm kidding! Of course you can get there from here! Sorry. Didn't mean to freak you out."

Laura breathed a sigh of relief. "That's okay. It's been a freaky day. So, this address . . . is it close by? Can I walk there in fifteen minutes or so?"

"With all that baggage you're carrying? Maybe. You'd be cutting it close, though."

Laura groaned. "Well, I'd better get moving then. Can you point me in the right direction?"

Rooster cleared his throat. "Well, you're on Whitehead now. If you go that way for about seven, no, maybe ten blocks or so, and then turn left and another left, no, right, wait . . . what's the street number again?"

Laura had the sinking feeling that she wasn't going to make it on time when she heard something in the distance. It sounded like reggae music, and it was growing louder every second. Suddenly, without warning, a car came roaring down the street and screeched to a stop behind her.

It was a bright pink taxicab with palm tree decals and musical notes on the side.

"Need a ride, miss?"

It wasn't by accident that Mama Marley showed up at the Hemingway House just when Laura needed a ride. It wasn't luck or fate either. Nor was it a weird hunch or mental telepathy or some kind of Caribbean magic that Mama learned from her Jamaican grandmother. No, it was really quite simple, and Mama didn't waste any time explaining it to Laura.

"You forgot to pay me."

"Oh! I'm sorry," said Laura, sliding into the back seat with her bags. "I guess I got a little flustered because of, you know . . ."

"Those damn birds."

"They were hungry."

"They're a menace." Mama shook her head and revved up the engine. "So where are we going? Far away from these chickens and cats, I hope."

Laura gave Mama the address on Southard Street. "This is where I'll be staying."

Mama squinted and made a face. "You're staying at the Crabb house? Really?"

"Yes. Why? Is something wrong?"

Mama didn't answer, just shook her head, cranked up the music, and started driving.

Laura sat back and tried to enjoy the ride. Which was impossible. The reggae music was too loud, the car brakes were too squeaky, and the anticipation of finally meeting the famous (or infamous?)

Crabb sisters was making her more than a little nervous. She turned on her phone to take another look at the roommate ad she answered:

> SUNNY PRIVATE ROOM FOR RENT IN CHARM-ING BUNGALOW. *Enjoy the flora & fauna of Key West in this perfectly located house share. Close to bars, restaurants, tourist sites, and marina. Female preferred for summer share or longer. Apply to Jilly & Jolene Crabb at . . .*

It sounded perfect.

A little too perfect, perhaps? Laura had to wonder. The sisters certainly sounded nice on the phone. Or at least the one sister she talked to—Jolene—sounded nice. She didn't speak to the other one. Jilly. For all Laura knew, Jilly was a raving psycho or an axe murder-ess or—

"I'm going to circle around the cemetery," said Mama Marley. "Southard is one-way."

Laura looked up from her phone. They were heading down a palm-shaded street lined with pastel-colored cottages and white picket fences. But the scenery changed abruptly when they reached the cemetery. The sky opened up above them, and the sun blazed down on a large, open expanse of white parched gravestones and blocky mausoleums surrounded by a wrought-iron fence.

As they drove by, Mama Marley took her right hand off the steering wheel and made the sign of the cross. "Always honor the dead. That's what my grandma taught me."

Laura read the words above the cemetery's entrance gate. " 'A Los Martires de Cuba.' "

"For the martyrs of Cuba," Mama explained. "They were free-dom fighters of the revolution. There's a lot of history in that old cemetery. But my favorite is the gravestone that reads: 'I Told You I Was Sick.' Ha!"

Laura laughed as they turned onto another postcard-pretty street. The homes here were just so beautiful and charming, like gingerbread houses decorated with pastel frosting and surrounded by lush little gardens full of tropical plants and flowers. Some of the homes were two full stories tall with wraparound balconies and verandas. A few were actually quite large and even had swimming pools, sparkling oases of shimmering blue against the bright green foliage and candy-colored siding.

"Wow, look at these homes," Laura whispered in awe. "I can't believe I'm going to be living in such a fancy neighborhood."

Mama shot her a look in the rearview mirror. "Don't get too excited," she said. "The Crabb house is the one coming up on the right."

Laura leaned forward to get a first glimpse of her new home.

"Oh. I see. It's very . . ."

"Shabby? Run-down?"

"I was going to say pink."

"Were you now?" Mama said with a laugh. "My senior prom corsage was pink, too. But now? It's like that house. Dried up, faded, and ready to crumble."

"Yeah, I guess it could use a fresh coat of paint."

"Couldn't we all," Mama mumbled. She stopped the car, popped the trunk, and got out to retrieve Laura's luggage.

Laura climbed out of the cab and onto the sidewalk, her eyes glued to the very small, very pale pink house in front of her. It was a typical Key West bungalow, short and narrow with an angled tin roof, covered porch, and white picket fence around a tiny front yard. The railings, shutters, and trim were painted white, which was very cute, but it was hard to see the details because of the wildly over-grown plants in the yard—which was probably for the best. Nestled among the dense foliage was a veritable flea market of odds and ends: a clamshell-shaped birdbath, a moss-covered mermaid statue, a spouting whale fountain, a fisherman's net full of shells and sea glass, a cracked mosaic sundial, a mirrored gazing ball, and a wildly eclectic assortment of bird feeders and wind chimes hanging from the trees. Leaning on the side of the house was a large inflatable dolphin next to a small wooden structure that looked like it could be either a chicken coop or a rabbit hutch.

You said you like animals, right?

Jake's words echoed in her head, only to be drowned out by something even more ominous: an extremely loud, birdlike squawk inside the house.

Awwwwrrrrrk!!!

Mama Marley let out a yelp and dropped Laura's luggage on the sidewalk. "Oh, I really don't like the sound of that," she said. "Quick, pay me so I can get the heck out of here."

Laura dug her credit card out of her purse and handed it to the cabdriver. Mama didn't waste any time. She processed the charge, handed Laura's card back, and hit the gas pedal so fast and hard Laura didn't have a chance to say thanks again. All she could do was wave good-bye as the taxicab turned the corner, taking its reggae music along with it. Reaching down for her luggage, she took a deep breath and prepared herself for . . . well, whatever was in that house.

"Welcome to Margaritaville, roomie!"

"Yes, welcome! Let us help you with those bags!"

Laura looked up to see two women in their mid-twenties— identical twins, apparently—crossing the front yard of the bungalow. They made quite a striking pair, with their long black hair, big brown eyes, and sultry yet classical features. They reminded Laura of foreign film stars from the 1960s. Their bodies looked ridiculously taut and tanned in their matching khaki shorts and yellow bikini tops. Obviously the Crabb sisters were very athletic—they sailed and scuba dived for a living, after all—and Laura might have felt intimidated if they didn't seem so incredibly nice, too.

"Come on inside. It's crazy stupid hot out here."

"Yeah, you must be melting. It doesn't get this hot in Syracuse, does it?"

"You look flushed. Are you okay? You might be experiencing heatstroke."

"You should probably take a shower to cool off."

The Crabb sisters kept talking—pretty much nonstop—as they grabbed Laura's bags and ushered her into the bungalow. As soon as they stepped inside, Laura felt a lovely cool breeze on her face from a pair of large ceiling fans with blades shaped like palm leaves. She tried glancing around the room, but her eyes hadn't adjusted to the dimmer light yet to see anything. She closed her eyes, waited a few seconds, then opened them again to take in her new home.

"Whoa!" she gasped.

It was a *lot* to take in.

And Laura thought the *yard* was packed full of flea market finds. The inside of the house could have been the actual flea market where those finds were found. The space was basically two medium-sized rooms divided by an arch with a narrow staircase on one side and a bamboo tiki bar on the other. Both rooms were colorful, cluttered, and crammed full of bizarre and interesting items. It would probably take Laura all summer to properly examine every oddball knick-knack and thingamabob. The living room was painted a pale lime green, which perfectly complemented the pale turquoise walls of the dining room. The ceiling was a muted pink, and the fans yellow. The furniture was a mix-and-match assortment of salvaged antiques, shabby chic stuffed armchairs, and what Laura could only assume were random treasures found in the trash. The combination of colors, styles, and dumpster dive doodads made for quite an eyeful.

But it wasn't the décor that made Laura gasp.

It was the wildlife.

Nestled among the shell-studded lampshades, dancing hula girl dolls, and vintage framed photographs of old bearded sea captains was an impressive variety of large glass aquariums, animal tanks, and birdcages. The largest of the cages filled the entire corner of the dining room. It had Victorian-style turrets and gables and made a magnificently grand home for a magnificently grand parrot.

Awwwwrrrrrk!!!

"Polly, hush!" said Jolene—or maybe it was Jilly. "Don't squawk at our new roommate. Her name is Laura. Can you say 'Laura'?"

The large, brightly colored parrot tilted her head to one side, then the other, then opened her beak and started to sing, "*Working nine to fiiiiiive . . .*"

Laura burst out laughing.

The Crabb sister rolled her eyes and sighed. "She loves Dolly Parton. Knows all her songs. That's why we named her Polly Parton."

"That's perfect," said Laura. "I love Dolly. *And* Polly." She glanced at the other cages and tanks in the room. "So who are these other . . . uh, roommates?"

The other sister took a deep breath. "Oh, yeah, well, this could take a while. Jilly, could you grab my bag in my room while I introduce Laura to the family?"

"Sure," said Jilly, heading to the stairs. "Make it fast, though. That nice family from Kansas is expecting us at ten. And did I mention that they've got two *gorgeous* college-aged sons who, I'm guessing, have never snorkeled before?" She wiggled her eyebrows suggestively and dashed up the stairs.

Jolene turned to Laura and lowered her voice. "You have to forgive Jilly. She's boy crazy. Which is why I advertised for a female roommate. Can you imagine if she dated and dumped some poor boy who lived with us? Things would get pretty weird around here."

"I can imagine," said Laura, shooting a glance at the aquariums and cages. "So, um . . . show me your pets."

"Animal companions," said Jolene, pulling Laura toward a brightly lit tank. "This is Antony and Cleopatra. They're tarantulas."

"I see. Very cute. And furry."

"And these are the lovebirds over here." She pointed to a cage with two separate perches, each with a small colorful bird sitting on it. "We thought they'd be super affectionate and loving, being lovebirds and all, but I don't think they like each other very much. We named them Romeo and Juliet. It's a tragedy."

"Yes, it is."

"And over here are our box turtles, Rocky and Rambo. One of them is female, but we're not sure which. They both look like tough guys to me."

Laura studied the turtles through the glass. They looked perfectly identical. Just like Jolene and Jilly. *I'll have to figure out a way to tell them apart*, she told herself.

"And in this corner," Jolene went on, "is the super handsome and super cool Iggy Popstar. He's an iguana."

"Yes, he is," said Laura, admiring the elegant way the green lizard held a pose on his rock. "Super handsome *and* super cool."

"We need to find Iggy a partner. I just can't imagine going through life all alone. Jilly and I always try to adopt our animals in pairs."

"A regular Noah's ark."

"You never know when the next big flood will hit."

Jolene glanced at her waterproof sports watch and started picking up the pace. She rushed through a seemingly endless collection of tropical fish, most of whom were named after famous pop music duos of the 1970s: Sonny and Cher, Peaches and Herb, Captain and Tennille, Elton John and Kiki Dee, Ike and Tina Turner, John and Yoko. A pair of angelfish, however, were named after Fred Astaire and Ginger Rogers.

"And who lives in here?" asked Laura, leaning over an empty glass tank lined with sand, some rocks, and a large dried branch.

Jolene turned and looked. Then she sighed heavily and shouted toward the stairs, "Jilly! Have you seen Sammy? He got out of his tank again!"

"No, I haven't seen him," said Jilly, descending the stairs with Jolene's bag. "We don't have time to look for him now. We have to go. Those corn-fed Kansas boys are waiting."

Jolene looked at Laura apologetically. "I'm sorry we're in such a rush. After work, we'll take you out for dinner and have some awesome key lime pie . . ."

"And margaritas!"

"Maybe. Laura's probably exhausted from her trip." She turned back to Laura. "You can unpack and take a shower while we're gone. Your room is through the kitchen there. It's a converted sun-room but really nice."

"Sounds great. Thanks." Laura gathered up her luggage and headed to her room.

The Crabb sisters waited until she was gone, then started whispering.

"She seems cool."

"Yeah, I like her."

"Do you think the animals freaked her out?"

"No, I don't think so."

A short, muffled scream came from the back room.

The sisters froze. "Laura? Are you all right?"

Laura shouted back, "I'm fine! But I have to ask. Is Sammy a snake?"

"Yes! He is!" shouted Jolene, grimacing.

"What color?" asked Jilly, suppressing a giggle.

"Orange and yellow!" Laura yelled back. "He matches the bedspread!"

"Oh," said Jilly. "That's not Sammy!"

"It's not?!!"

"No," said Jolene. "That's Delilah!"

Chapter 4
Key West After Dark

The typical Key West tourist may not know a lot about the life and literature of Ernest Hemingway—maybe they skipped reading *The Sun Also Rises* in high school—but they definitely know two essential facts about the quirky little island Hemingway called home:

The sun also sets there.

And it is glorious.

Every evening, as that blazing orb in the sky makes its slow, lazy descent into the shimmering waters of the Gulf of Mexico, hundreds of people head to Mallory Square and the nearby piers to watch one of Key West's magnificent, world-famous sunsets. It is a time-honored tradition here, one that feels more like a pop-up carnival than a natural daily occurrence. Local musicians and artists, street magicians and jugglers, jewelry makers and souvenir peddlers fill the square to entertain the crowds and—they hope—make a few bucks. Which can be quite a challenge. Most of their potential customers and tippers can barely take their eyes off the spectacular light show in the sky. Who can blame them? With each passing minute, the view only gets more dramatic, more dazzling, more Instagram-ready. As the sun sinks lower and the colors gleam brighter, the sightseers drift closer to the water's edge. Clutching their cameras, smartphones, and selfie sticks, they wait for the perfect moment to capture the perfect image for the perfect social media post. No Photoshop required.

Greetings from Key West! Wish you were here!

Not everyone is taking pictures, though.

Standing among the photo op seekers and selfie takers, a young college grad from Syracuse, New York, stares in awe at the brilliant display of blood-orange waters, raspberry clouds, and deep purple haze. It doesn't even occur to her to pull out her phone and take a picture. She's too overwhelmed, too . . . happy? excited? . . . just to be right here, right now, gazing at the sky over Key West. Less than twenty-four hours ago, she was looking up at the sky over Syracuse and worrying about her future. Now here she is. Living in the moment. Not thinking about anything. Just taking in that incredible, gorgeous sunset.

And waiting for her new roommates to decide on a place for dinner.

"Pepe's has the best key lime pie," says Jilly.

"You think? I prefer Kermit's," says Jolene.

"Whatever. What are you in the mood for, Laura?"

The grad student from Syracuse smiles gently, her eyes fixed on the horizon.

"Anything," she says. "Everything."

Meanwhile, at the Hemingway House . . .

Ernestine the cat—better known as Nessie—sat upright in her favorite spot on the front porch and watched the glowing red sun disappear behind the palm trees.

She knew what that meant.

It meant that the temperature would drop—and the cats would come out, restless and frisky after napping half the day in whatever shade they could find.

It meant that the gardening crew would start packing up their shovels and shears, bagging up their trimmings, and loading up their truck for the night.

It meant that the cleaning crew would arrive to sweep, dust, and mop away the daily grime of the tourists, the staff, and the cats who roamed the house. That meant it was time for Nessie to give up her favorite spot and go check on Margarita.

It was Happy Hour.

At the end of a long hot day, Margarita liked to reward herself with a well-deserved cocktail. Margarita on the rocks. With salt. And with Nessie. It gave the two old friends a chance to spend quality time together.

"Nessie! Hello there! Come join me for Happy Hour!"

Nessie meowed and crossed the garden toward the gift shop. Margarita opened the door to let the cat in. When Nessie was inside, Margarita glanced toward the house before closing and locking the door. Then she walked to the counter, reached down, and pulled out a clear glass tumbler, silver shaker, small saucer, large bottle of tequila, and triple sec. Nessie watched Margarita as she started mixing her drink, reaching into the mini-fridge for ice.

Nessie knew something was missing. And, just like the setting of the sun, she knew what that meant.

It meant that Margarita Bouffet would be searching for her lost shaker of salt.

"Now where is that saltshaker?" she mumbled under her breath. "Have you seen it, Nessie?"

Nessie blinked and waved her tail.

"Who keeps taking it?" Margarita sounded exasperated. "It's got to be either Chew-Chew or Whiskey, right?"

Nessie knew it wasn't Chew-Chew or Whiskey who stole Margarita's saltshaker. Yes, they were the most notorious cat thieves in the house. But Chew-Chew preferred to steal food—usually the staff's lunches—and Whiskey liked to steal sips from people's drinks, especially if they were alcoholic. Whiskey had a thing for whiskey. Whenever the Hemingway House hosted a wedding or other event, Chew-Chew and Whiskey were sure to be lurking in the background, pilfering snacks and slurping cocktails when no one was looking.

"Okay, where is it?" Margarita groaned. She crouched down and looked under the counter and store displays for the missing shaker of salt. "Why do cats love knocking things onto the floor? Will you answer me that, Nessie? Why?"

Nessie let out a sigh. She glanced up and saw another cat sitting quietly on one of the highest shelves in the gift shop. It was Kilimanjaro. Kilimanjaro was snowy white and slender with icy green eyes and an even icier disposition. She could usually be found sitting at the highest point of a room, silently looking down on everyone and everything. If anyone knew who the shaker thief was, it was Kilimanjaro.

Unless she was the culprit herself.

"Found it! What a relief." Margarita stood up and started shaking salt into the saucer. "You can't have a margarita without salt." She dipped the rim of her glass in the salt, added some ice, and poured herself a cocktail from the silver shaker. "Ah, that's better. Now tell me about your day, Nessie. What do you think of Laura, the new tour guide?"

Nessie's ears perked up when she heard Laura's name.

"I know you like her. I do, too," said Margarita with a smile. "I think she'll make an excellent tour guide. With a little practice, of course. Did you know she sent me an audition video? She pretended her home in Syracuse was the Hemingway House! It was very cute, very out-of-the-box. A little rough in spots, too, but it got her the job!"

Nessie gazed at her as if she were lost in thought.

"So, tell me, Nessie. Do you really remember Laura from her family's vacation? After all these years?"

Nessie looked at Margarita like she was about to answer when a sudden gust of wind made them both jump. A second storm-like gust made the roof above them rattle and moan as several large palm leaves slapped against the windows. Nessie hopped off her chair and ran around the counter next to Margarita, who crouched down beside her. Then, just as it seemed they were about to get hit with another flash rainstorm—just like the one this morning—the wind abruptly stopped. An eerie silence fell over the entire Hemingway estate.

Margarita picked up Nessie and slowly walked to the window. She peered outside.

Everything looked normal.

"Well, how about that, Nessie? Pretty strange, huh? It's like I was telling you this morning."

Margarita hugged the cat tighter and whispered in her ear.

"Something is coming."

Meanwhile, at the top of the Key West Lighthouse . . .

A tall, lanky, scruffy young man named Mark McCloud—better known as Mack—gripped the iron railing of the lighthouse catwalk and braced himself for another blast of wind. He waited. Looked up at the sky. Waited some more. Looked up again. And waited.

Nothing. No wind.

"Crazy weather," he mumbled to himself.

The first blast of wind almost knocked him off the catwalk, and he wasn't about to take any chances. Not when he was standing on a narrow catwalk at least fifty feet above the ground. The sudden gust reminded him of the freak mini-storm that hit the island this morning. Right before those gypsy chickens attacked that cute new girl at the Hemingway House.

"Crazy day all around," he muttered.

Mack leaned against the railing and took in the view: the darkening sky above with its orange and purple swirl of billowy clouds. The Lighthouse Hotel below with its sparkling blue swimming pool and gleaming white guest cabins. The Hemingway House across the street with its yellow-green shutters and dense tropical foliage. Even from this height, Mack could spot a few of the famous Hemingway cats wandering the grounds.

All quiet on the Key West front.

Mack sighed. Then he leaned over, picked up a rag and a spray bottle of industrial-strength glass cleaner, and went to work on the windows. His uncle—Key West's longtime lighthouse keeper and radio deejay Rooster McCloud—told him that just after sunset was the best time to clean the lantern panes. The lamp was lit so you could see the dirt on the inside, but there was still enough light in the sky so you could see the streaks on the outside.

Mack had to admit the crazy old bird was right.

"Never doubt the Rooster," he said, laughing to himself.

It was an inside joke Mack shared with his best friend, Jake. Whenever they questioned Mack's uncle on something—whether it was oddball trivia about chickens, the music of the seventies, or the long strange history of Key West—it always turned out Rooster was right. Mack and Jake learned their lesson in eighth grade. They were starting their own garage band and, being Key West locals, decided to do a punk rock version of the Jimmy Buffett song "Margaritaville." When they played it for Rooster, he kept narrowing his eyes and shaking his head. "Boys," he said when they finished. "Sounds good, but you messed up the lyrics. You switched the stanzas." The boys insisted they were doing it right. Rooster set them straight. "Look here, boys. I was a roadie for Jimmy Buffett's band for seven years. Must have heard them play 'Margaritaville' a thousand times. If anyone knows the lyrics, it's me." Then he leaned forward, adding, "Never doubt the Rooster."

It became a sort of mantra for Mack and Jake. If one of them turned out to be right about something—whether it was song lyrics or sports stats or scuba-diving equipment—he'd say the phrase to the other. And break up laughing.

"Never doubt the Rooster," Mack said again, wiping the streaks off a glass pane.

"But what if the Rooster is wrong?" a voice answered.

Mack stopped and looked up.

It was Jake, standing in the doorway to the stairs.

"Talking to yourself now?" he asked, stepping onto the catwalk. "You're getting more like your uncle every day. He told me you were up here."

Mack nodded. "Was he really talking to himself?"

"Yeah, he was rehearsing a bit for his radio show. I think. I hope."

Mack stood up and stretched. "I'm almost done here. What's up?"

Jake started to answer when he got distracted by the view. "Man, look at that sky! If you have to wash windows, this is the place to do it."

"Well, you get to play with cats all day. Want to help?"

Mack offered his rag to Jake.

"Sorry, I don't do windows. But I do play guitar and you play drums and Margarita needs a band for a wedding at the Hemingway House. The other band canceled at the last minute. The bride and groom are desperate."

"Desperate enough to hire The Off Keys?"

"Apparently so."

"When?"

"Two weeks from now. The twenty-eighth."

"I'm free. I mean, not free. It pays, right?"

"Of course. Double our usual rate."

"And the rest of the band . . . ?"

"Lilly and Kane are up for it. We'll need to schedule extra re-hearsal time and work on some new material. It's a wedding, after all, not a dive bar."

"What kind of music do they want?"

"The usual Key West wedding mix. Standards, dance hits, some Jimmy Buffett, a little reggae. The groom likes classic rock, but the bride wants it to have a Caribbean flavor. You know what that means."

"Bring the steel drums?"

"Bring the steel drums."

"Do we have to play Billy Joel? 'Just the Way You Are'?"

"I'm afraid so. But we also get to play 'The Girl from Ipanema,' which I know you love."

Mack laughed. "Okay. Sure. Count me in."

Jake grinned. "Great! I'll text Lilly and Kane and set everything up. Meanwhile, you dust off those steel pans and start working on 'The Girl from Ipanema.'"

Mack laughed again and leaned against the catwalk railing. "Speaking of girls," he said, "how's the girl from Syracuse?"

Jake gave his friend a little smile. "Why do you ask?"

"Why do you think? She's beautiful!"

Jake shrugged. "I suppose. In an upstate New York kind of way."

Mack scoffed. "Give me a break. You were practically panting over her."

"Look who's talking! You almost knocked me over helping with her luggage. And don't think she didn't notice. She thinks that you and I have some sort of stupid dude-bro rivalry thing going on."

"That's ridiculous," said Mack, stroking his beard. "Between you and me, there's no competition."

"Oh? Really?" Jake gave his friend the side-eye.

"Really. I win, hands down. No contest."

"Oh, I forgot. Ladies love the Mack."

"That's right. Once they date Mack . . ."

". . . they never call back."

They both broke out laughing. Another inside joke.

Jake gazed down at the Hemingway House, thinking about his chat with Laura. "You know what she said about you, Mack?"

"I can't imagine."

"She said you looked 'scruffy cool.'"

"Really? She did?"

"And fun. She said you looked 'scruffy cool' and 'fun.' But I wouldn't get too excited. I have a feeling she really likes me."

"It's the haircut. She must have a thing for military men."

"Shut up. She said she likes it."

"Wow. It must be true love."

"Don't be a jerk."

"No, I'm incredibly happy for you two lovebirds. I'll even play 'The Girl from Ipanema' at your wedding."

"Knock it off. I'm just saying I have a feeling . . ."

". . . that the girl from Syracuse is totally hot for you—"

"Her name is Laura."

". . . and your best friend Mack better back off because you saw her first."

"I never said that."

"You kind of implied it."

"Did not."

"No? You told me not to get too excited!"

"Well, are you? Are you excited?"

"I don't know!" said Mack, exasperated. "I only got a chance to say, 'Hi, nice to meet you.' But you—you're already having deep, meaningful conversations with her about haircuts and stuff. I guess that means she's all yours. She's off-limits."

"Of course not," said Jake. "She's a grown adult. She can make her own decisions. Also, it's her first day on the island. We need to just chill out, take it slow, and get to know each other. If she's interested in one of us, I'm sure she'll let us know."

"Well, that's a terrible plan," said Mack. "What if she ends up liking both of us but is waiting for one of us to make a move?"

"It's much more likely she won't like either one of us because of our stupid dude-bro rivalry thing."

"Who could blame her? We're terrible."

"Despicable."

"The worst."

The two chuckled. Then they leaned forward on the lighthouse railing, staring out at the island they called home. Above them, the sky had darkened to a deep violet hue. Below them, warm colored lights from the streetlamps and bungalows flickered and glowed like fireflies amid the palms. From where they were standing, the swimming pools on the ground looked like giant luminous emeralds from another world. Just a few blocks away, the Key West commercial district—with its brightly lit shops and bars and restaurants—looked like an alien spaceship had landed on Duval Street.

Jake squinted his eyes. He tried to see if he could spot a certain pink bungalow near the cemetery, but it was too dark already.

"Guess where Laura is staying," he said to Mack.

"Hotel? Motel? Holiday Inn?"

"No. She's staying with the Crabbs."

"Get. Out."

"Strange but true."

"What are the odds? Did you tell her?"

"About our history? No."

"Are you going to tell her?"

"I'm sure the Crabbs will. In fact, they're probably out there right now, sitting in a bar on Duval, sipping frozen margaritas, telling Laura the long sordid story of Jake Jacobs and the Crabb twins."

"Oh, man. You're done. Game over."

"It happened a long time ago. I was a dumb teenager."

"You're dead meat. The wedding is off."

Jake sighed. The two stood there silent for a while. Then Mack finally spoke.

"So I guess this increases my chances with Laura, right?"

"Jerk."

"Dumb teenager."

"Stupid dude-bro."

Just a few blocks away, in a bar on Duval Street...

Laura Lange—also known as the girl from Syracuse—sat on her stool, sipped her frozen margarita, and listened to the Crabb twins tell long, sordid stories of passion and heartbreak on the scandal-soaked island of Key West.

They told her about one guy Jilly dated who said he was a billionaire but turned out to be the assistant manager of a fast-food joint.

They told her about another guy Jolene dated who would steal a piece of her lingerie every time he came to the house. She discovered the truth one night when she caught him wearing one of her bras.

Then they told her about another guy that they were *both* dating. "At the same time!" said Jilly. "Without even realizing it!" added Jolene. The sisters said they should have suspected something was up because he kept getting them confused and calling them by the other's name. He actually got away with it for three or four weeks. Then one day, the two-timing liar made a fatal error. He accidentally asked both sisters on a dinner date at the same restaurant on the same night.

"What a creep," said Laura. "What happened?"

"What do you think happened?" said Jolene. "All hell broke loose. We threw a major fit."

"And some glasses and plates," said Jilly.

"We were like those tag team wrestlers on TV."

"Or the Real Housewives of New Jersey."

"We flipped the guy's table over."

"Yeah. The restaurant banned us for life."

"They should have banned *him*, not us."

"Well, we did break the dinnerware."

"We reimbursed them."

Laura enjoyed the twins' dating horror stories—she had a few of her own, too—but the local gossip was even juicier. Not that Laura believed any of it, of course. The Crabb sisters admitted that the stories were just rumors and probably not true. But that didn't stop anyone from repeating them. Either way, Laura got an earful that night. According to the biggest gossips on the island . . .

Rooster McCloud was a secret multi-millionaire who made his fortune by inventing the iPad and selling the idea to Steve Jobs.

Rick and Ricardo became the owners of the Lighthouse Hotel after winning it in a poker game with Las Vegas mobsters.

Mama Marley was a rich, successful reggae star in Jamaica until her fans discovered she was lip-syncing to someone else's voice.

Jimmy Buffett commissioned NASA to install a time machine at his Margaritaville Key West Resort and now he spends half his days living in the 1970s.

But the most shocking, and ridiculous, rumor was this one:

Margarita Bouffet was not the fun-loving, ballroom-dancing sweetheart she appeared to be. She was a gold-digging, all-too-merry widow who'd been married four times—maybe more. Three of her husbands died suddenly under mysterious circumstances. The only one still alive was her first husband in Cuba, whom she married when she was fifteen. She fled to America on an inflatable flamingo pool toy and sought out wealthy older men in the poshest resorts of Miami. One by one, she seduced them, married them, and, according to rumor, slowly poisoned them to death. The authorities never managed to catch Margarita because she kept changing her name and identity.

Laura couldn't believe it.

"That's insane," she said after Jilly finished the tale. "Margarita Bouffet? A bigamist and a murderer? I'm sorry, but she has to be one of the sweetest ladies I've ever met."

"Oh, I agree," said Jolene, standing up. "But people talk. And I need to use the restroom."

The second Jolene left, Jilly leaned forward and whispered in Laura's ear.

"While we're gossiping, I'll give you the dirt on Jolene. She's, like, totally boy crazy. Like right now, she doesn't need to use the restroom. That was just an excuse to talk to that hot guy over there."

Laura glanced across the bar and saw Jolene chatting with a very tall, very hot guy.

"That's why I insisted on a female roommate," Jilly went on. "Can you imagine if she dated our roomie and then dumped him? Things would get really weird in that house."

"Yeah," said Laura. "I imagine they would."

A few hours later, at the WKEY Radio station on Truman Avenue . . .

Russell T. McCloud—affectionately known as Rooster—sat alone in the deejay booth looking over his notes for this evening's *Key West After Dark*. He always tried to have extra material prepared, just in case nobody called in to the program and he was forced to ramble on about something to fill dead air. Usually it wasn't a problem. Rooster could talk for hours at a time about virtually anything. Heck, he could talk about nothing at all, for that matter.

Rooster McCloud liked to talk.

And tonight, he'd like nothing more than to talk about . . . (pause for dramatic effect) . . . *new beginnings.*

Inspired by an unfortunate incident involving gypsy chickens in the streets of Key West this morning, Rooster wanted to send a special message to the lovely young lady who happened to be the ill-fated target of a chicken-feeding frenzy. Not unlike the Tippi Hedren character in Alfred Hitchcock's horror classic *The Birds,* this unfairly attacked young woman was a newcomer in town. An outsider. A lone stranger at the mercy of the community or, in this case, the flock. She had come to this isolated place seeking adventure— and possibly romance—only to be assaulted and pecked and . . .

Wait, no, Rooster thought. *I don't want to scare the poor girl to death.*

He looked at his notes and crossed off the phrase "Hitchcock's Birds."

"Maybe an inspiring Hemingway quote instead," he said to himself. He remembered Margarita telling him that the new tour guide was a huge Hemingway fan—the girl even wrote her college thesis on him and, according to Margarita, it was "provocative."

He also remembered the way Margarita's eyes lit up when she talked about adding a fresh new voice to the house tours. Rooster found Margarita's enthusiasm downright infectious—and incredibly charming. But then again, he'd always found Margarita charming. He'd break into a boyish grin whenever she'd ask him, *What's new, pussycat?* It had become her trademark greeting as she passed him on the street on her way to work each morning.

Picking up his notebook, Rooster skimmed through the various Hemingway quotes he'd found on the Internet. . . .

"I drink to make other people more interesting."

Funny, but not really the message he wanted to convey.

"The best way to find out if you can trust somebody is to trust them."

Interesting, but not quite right.

"Always do sober what you said you'd do drunk. That will teach you to keep your mouth shut."

Man, that Hemingway thought an awful lot about drinking!

Rooster continued looking for the perfect quote, keeping one eye on the clock. He had four minutes left before going live. In the meantime, the Rolling Stones' "Beast of Burden" played over the airwaves—part of a prerecorded mixed tape of classic rock, reggae, and alternative hits put together by his nephew Mack and his buddy Jake. WKEY Radio didn't have any actual employees. Not paid ones, at least. It was more of a hobby than a business for Rooster, who set up the station in his own garage using money he made by selling the rights to a domain name he created on the Internet. The station was run by a ragtag assortment of local volunteers including his next-door neighbor Shelly, who was ninety-four years old and obsessed with the weather. More often than not, though, the station played prerecorded tapes all the way through to the end, leaving long moments of silence until someone showed up at the garage to take over the deejay booth.

Rooster ran a pretty loose ship.

He looked at the clock and waited for "Beast of Burden" to fade out. Then he counted down the seconds—*three, two, one*—and switched on the microphone.

"Good evening, ladies and schemers, lovers and dreamers, heart-breakers and homewreckers. This is *Key West After Dark* with your hard-to-shock host Rooster McCloud. I hope you're staying cool on this steamy night in paradise. And I hope you're staying out of trouble. But just in case you *aren't* staying out of trouble—if you've done something wicked, or shameful, or so embarrassing that you can't tell anyone—you can always call your old friend Rooster. Think of me as your lighthouse in the storm, a shining beacon of comfort and hope to guide you through the choppy waters of life . . . and love."

Rooster chuckled at his own corny metaphor. He hoped his listeners had a sense of humor.

"Before I take any calls tonight," he continued, "I'd like to say a little something about . . . *new beginnings*."

He launched into his prepared monologue about treating each day as a new opportunity, about taking risks and trying new things, exploring new places and meeting new people, *blah, blah, blah*. He was barely halfway through when he realized it sounded every bit as corny as his lighthouse metaphor. Maybe cornier. And what were the chances the young lady would be listening anyway? Tomorrow was her first day at work. She was probably sleeping.

A white light flashed on the call-in phone.

"Oh! Wait a second, listeners. It looks like we have a caller! How much do you want to bet they want me to cut the schmaltz and get to the good stuff?" Rooster pushed the flashing button. "Hello, caller! You're live on the air. This is *Key West After Dark*, the late-night talk show where everyday people share their deepest, darkest secrets. Don't be shy. Talk to the Rooster."

A man cleared his throat over the phone line. "Yes, hello, Rooster? I am a recently divorced gentleman of a certain age, and I have a problem concerning a disarmingly attractive widow with whom I've become acquainted."

Rooster recognized the voice immediately.

The lilting Southern drawl, the antiquated phrasing, the tortured syntax—it had to be Foster Lee Jackson, the absurdly pompous president of the Key West historical society.

"You *seeee*," the voice droned on, "I seem to have become quite smitten with the widow . . . against my better judgment, I'm afraid. Part of me would love nothing more than to throw caution to the wind and express my true feelings to her. And yet, another part of me fears that such a bold declaration would only lead to rejection and remorse. What's more, there could be immediate and unfortunate repercussions."

"Repercussions? What kind of repercussions?" Rooster asked, genuinely intrigued.

"Social and professional repercussions," the caller said gravely. "The lady and I are both actively involved in community affairs. Occasionally we have reason to interact directly on a professional level. What's more, we run in the same social circles. We see each other every week in a group of friends devoted to . . . um . . . a certain form of recreation. It's quite delightful, really. But I'm afraid if I make an advance and she swiftly rejects me, it could be . . ." He paused.

"Awkward," said Rooster.

"Yes, awkward."

"Hmmm. Have you tried asking her out for a drink after this . . . recreation?"

"That would be illogical. The cocktail bar is always fully stocked on Dance Night. And by evening's end, the widow is always a little tipsy and tuckered out."

Dance Night? Tipsy widow? Could it be?

Rooster didn't want to believe it—or even think about it—but all the clues added up.

Foster Lee Jackson had the hots for Margarita Bouffet!

Feeling a little nauseous, Rooster leaned closer to the microphone to dispense his advice. "That's quite a pickle you're in, my man. And normally, I would encourage every secret admirer to take a chance and take a shot at love. You only live once. But you? I think your situation is different."

"It is?"

"Yes. Your life is already too entangled with this woman's. You work together and play together. On a weekly basis! It's just too risky—"

"But weren't you saying earlier that we need to take risks? To explore new opportunities and meet new people?"

"Yes, but you've already met this woman and it's just not happening. Maybe you should try looking elsewhere."

"Elsewhere?"

"Yes, there are lots of dating sites online, and I'm sure they can help you find your perfect match."

"But what about—?"

"Thank you, caller! Good night and good luck!"

Click.

Rooster disconnected the call—and felt an instant pang of guilt. He had never done anything like that before. Never—in all of his years talking to hundreds of callers—had he ever given such terrible advice. And he did it on purpose!

Why? he asked himself. *Why did I do that?*

Rooster rubbed his eyes and stared blankly at the flashing lights on the call-in phone. He knew what he needed to do: punch one of the buttons, take another call, and move on with the program. But he just couldn't. Not right now.

Why not?

In his heart of hearts, he knew. In the course of that phone call with Foster Lee Jackson, he'd started to realize something that shook him to his very core. It was completely unexpected, weirdly exciting, and a little scary, too. But it was undeniably true.

Rooster McCloud—the hard-to-shock host of *Key West After Dark*—was hiding a shocking secret of his own:

I'm in love with Margarita Bouffet.

Two hours later, in the moonlit garden of a small pink bungalow . . .

A large six-toed cat with a magnificent bushy tail tiptoed her way through a shadowy obstacle course of mermaids and gnomes and clamshell birdbaths. The moon was bright enough to cast silvery beams through the overgrown greenery, but the cat didn't need any light. Using her sense of smell, she could easily find her way to the back of the house, even in the darkest of nights. Especially if one of the human females left a bowl of food for her on the back porch.

The cat hopped onto the porch and sniffed. The bowl was empty.

Maybe one of the neighborhood cats ate the food.

Or one of the humans forgot to fill the bowl.

Either way, the cat was hungry. She knew the females would feed her if she could get inside the house and wake them up. She also knew they slept in the upper rooms, and maybe—if the cat was lucky—they left one of the windows open. It was worth a try. The cat glanced up, crouched down, and sprang into action. Jumping and hopping from the porch floor to the wooden railing to a large tree branch, she made her way closer to the windowed sun-room attached to the back of the house. With amazing grace and confidence, she leapt from the tree branch to the sloping tin roof of the sun-room.

Thump!

It was not a graceful landing. But that didn't bother the cat. If she woke up the humans, all the better. That was her goal. The cat paused to get her footing, then started to climb the roof toward the small window above.

Screeee . . . screeee . . . screeee . . .

Like fingernails on a chalkboard, the cat's claws made a high-pitched scratching sound on the tin cladding of the roof. It hurt the cat's ears. She tried to walk softer. But the roof was too steep and she needed to use her claws, at least a little bit, to keep from sliding off.

Screeee . . .

One, two, three more steps and she reached the small darkened window at the highest point of the roof.

The window was closed.

The cat peered through the glass. Her large green eyes were immediately drawn to the glowing digital display of a small clock radio on the bedside table. The cat had no idea what the glowing box was or what it did, but the dim light helped her to see a sleeping human with long dark hair lying on the bed. The cat lifted a paw and scratched at the window. Nothing. She tried again. And again. Then she started scratching harder until she heard a sound down below.

It was the back door opening. And footsteps onto the porch.

Slowly, gingerly, the cat crept down the slope of the tin roof and poked her head over the edge to see who it was.

It was a female human with reddish-brown hair. Not one of the humans who lived here and gave her food. This was Someone New. And this Someone New was standing in the yard. Looking up at the roof. Staring straight at the cat.

The cat didn't move, just stared back. Then the human spoke.

"Nessie? Is that you?"

Two minutes earlier, in the converted sun-room of the Crabb twins' bungalow . . .

Laura Lange—also known as Someone New—awoke with a start. In spite of being dead tired after a bumpy ten-person plane flight, being mauled by a dozen Chex-crazed chickens, and drinking two frozen margaritas because her new roommates insisted, Laura was jolted from her hard-earned, much-needed sleep by a strange loud *thump* on the roof over her bed.

Now what? she thought.

She'd already been woken up twice that night: first by the very un-Shakespearean chattering of Romeo and Juliet, who were obviously having a lovers' quarrel, and then by Polly Parton, serenading the moon with a highly unusual rendition of "I Will Always Love You" that sounded absolutely nothing like the Dolly Parton or Whitney Houston versions.

And now there was something on the roof. Laura could hear it scratching on the tin.

Screeee . . .

She fumbled in the dark for the lamp next to her bed. The base of the lamp was a swashbuckling pirate holding a sword. Its pointy tip grazed Laura's hand as she flicked on the switch. "Ouch." It took a second for her eyes to adjust to the light—not to mention the tropical explosion of colors in the room. The Crabb sisters must have used all the leftover paint from the rest of the house when they converted the sun-room. A small writing desk was painted lime green; a large wardrobe, purple; a dresser of drawers, turquoise; the nightstand, canary yellow. The only furniture that wasn't painted was the antique brass bed and the bamboo roller shades that covered the windows on three sides of the room. Oh, and the tiny air conditioner in the window—they didn't paint that, which Laura found surprising.

Screeee . . .

Laura crawled out of bed to investigate. She crossed the room and rolled up one of the shades. The yard looked like a tropical paradise, an overgrown jungle glistening in the moonlight, beckoning her to explore its mysteries. She slipped on a pair of flip-flops, opened the back door, and stepped onto the porch.

Screeee . . .

Laura tiptoed down the steps and onto the grass. A car honked in the distance, and she was suddenly aware that she was standing outside wearing nothing but an oversized T-shirt and panties. But she didn't care. She had to know what was on that roof.

She gazed upward—and saw it. . . .

A hauntingly beautiful, magnificently furred cat standing regally at the edge of the rooftop, silhouetted against the moon like some feline fairy-tale queen of the night. The cat stared down at Laura with piercing green eyes that seemed to glow in the darkness.

Am I dreaming? Is this a vision?

Then she noticed something strangely familiar: The cat had a huge fluffy tail that waved slowly back and forth like a feather duster.

"Nessie? Is that you?"

Laura took a step closer. With the moonlight out of her eyes, she could see that the cat's fur wasn't gold with white streaks like Nessie's. It was jet black with white streaks. But the resemblance was uncanny. The cat on the roof could have been a photo negative of Nessie.

"Hello, gorgeous," she said to the cat. "Nice to meet you. I have a cat friend who looks just like you."

Oops. Laura's words seemed to break the spell. The cat rose up and dashed across the rooftop, jumping onto a nearby tree branch, then scrambling down and hopping to the ground. In two seconds flat she was gone, disappearing into the night like some otherworldly phantom. Laura was disappointed to see the cat go. But at least she learned what made the scratching sounds. She turned and went back inside, then climbed into bed and turned off the pirate lamp. This time, she was careful not to get stabbed by the pirate's sword.

She tried to fall back asleep. And tried. And tried. Finally, she decided to try something else: the radio on her nightstand. It was an old-timey wooden one, probably from the 1920s. She turned it on and—lo and behold—it worked! Even more surprising, it was tuned in to *Key West After Dark* starring Rooster McCloud!

Laura closed her eyes and listened to the lighthouse keeper's low, soothing voice. He was advising some poor woman who suspected her boyfriend was cheating on her. Rooster was very sympathetic and supportive. It was very sweet. By the end of the call, Laura could feel herself slowly drifting off. Rooster's voice had an oddly calming effect on her. . . .

"I'm going to end tonight's program with a quote from Ernest Hemingway," he said. "I'd like to dedicate it to all of you out there who are trying to start a new life but may be off to a rough start. Don't let it bother you. Just roll with it. Embrace it. Like Hemingway said: *'Live the full life of the mind, exhilarated by new ideas, intoxicated by the romance of the unusual.'*"

Those were the last words Laura heard before she fell asleep. And just like the mysterious cat in the moonlight, they worked their way into her dreams . . .

Especially the words "romance" and "unusual."

Chapter 5
Working Nine to Five
(with Six-Toed Cats)

In a 1958 interview in *The Paris Review*, Ernest Hemingway revealed something about himself that was even more surprising than his passion for felines.

He was a morning person.

Yes—in spite of Hemingway's well-earned reputation as a hard-drinking brawler who spent many a night ordering rounds at beloved dive bars like Sloppy Joe's Bar—the Nobel Prize–winning author somehow managed to wake up at dawn to work on his stories and novels. This surprised his readers, who assumed he'd be too hungover to write in the morning.

Today, the sun did something surprising, too.

Instead of lingering on the horizon, lazing in the haze, and trying to hide its head under a blanket of clouds, the sun rose quickly from its bed to face the new day without a hint of hesitation. Why? Because it had nowhere to hide!

There wasn't a cloud in the sky.

In the wee hours of the night, a gentle gulf breeze had coaxed all the clouds out to sea. By morning, the temperature was fifteen degrees cooler, the humidity was fifty percent lower, and everyone in Key West was a hundred times happier. This was the kind of weather every tourist hoped for when they visited the Florida Keys. Not too hot. Not too sticky. It was just right.

At the Lighthouse Hotel on Whitehead Street, early-rising guests headed straight to the palm-lined courtyard to enjoy a complimentary continental breakfast—with free mimosas!—before the best muffins and scones were gone. They grabbed their plates and cups and settled into the poolside lounge chairs, sipping and noshing and planning their day. *Should we take the glass-bottom boat tour? Go snorkeling over the coral reefs? How about a Key West pub crawl, see some local bands? Or maybe just stroll down to the Southernmost Point Buoy?*

For the tourists, it was another day in paradise.

But for the locals, it was another day of work.

Shopkeepers and housecleaners, cabdrivers and boat captains, tour guides and food servers—these hardworking islanders were up at the crack of dawn, thanks to the loudest alarm clock in Key West. The always-reliable rooster—also known as Old Faithful, That Damned Bird, and other fowl nicknames—announced today's sunrise with an especially earsplitting *ca-ca-ca-ca-caw!* His crowing scared a nearby flock of gypsy chickens and sent them skittering into the street, cackling for their breakfast. The squawking made Rooster McCloud reach for his bag of birdseed and head out the front door with a slam. And that woke up his ninety-four-year-old next-door neighbor, Shelly, who rolled out of bed, reached for her bifocals, and logged on to her computer to check the local weather.

"I knew it!" she said with a smirk. "Those big-city boys got it wrong again." The small but spry senior shifted her gaze from the meteorological charts on the screen to the glorious blue sky outside her window. "Yep, I was right. It's a beautiful day!"

Forecasting the weather was Shelly's number-one passion in life.

Being right was number two.

Meanwhile, all across the island, people began to rise and shine. . . .

Margarita Bouffet, one of Key West's earliest and shiniest risers, started her morning routine with a vigorous round of stretches, a few high kicks, and a long, hot shower—all while singing along to ABBA's *Greatest Hits*. *"You are the dancing queeeeen!"* Jake Jacobs, the young caretaker of the Hemingway cats, got out of bed earlier than usual to work out at the Old Town Gym—then worried that his body was too pumped for his T-shirt. *Will the new girl think I'm showing off? Like some dumb gym rat?* At the lighthouse museum, Mack McCloud arrived early to wipe down the display cases filled with old lighthouse artifacts—a task he told his uncle he did last night when he was actually practicing on his steel drums for the upcoming wedding gig. *It's just not a wedding without "The Girl from Ipanema."* On the other side of the island, Mama Marley steered her cab into the parking lot of the Key West International Airport. She pulled up in front of a well-dressed couple of wealthy-looking tourists, cranked up the reggae, turned off the engine—and turned on the charm. *Welcome to the Conch Republic!*

Some people took a little longer to wake up.

Some birds, too.

Like the parrot who lived inside a fancy cage in a small pink bungalow. Unlike the old rooster who crowed at the break of dawn, this fine-feathered bird—also known as Polly Parton—waited until one of the Crabb sisters' alarms started beeping upstairs. Then, instead of a cock-a-doodle-doo, the parrot serenaded the house with a squawky yet rousing melody. This, in turn, woke up the new girl sleeping in the sun-room. With a start, the girl bolted up in bed, reached for the nightstand, and then froze, confused by her strange, colorful surroundings.

Where am I? she wondered, still half-asleep. *What am I doing?*

Polly Parton gave her the answer.

"Working nine to fiiiiiive . . ."

At the Hemingway House, the polydactyl cats were wide awake and friskier than ever.

Thanks to the lower heat and humidity, they didn't spend the morning searching for a nice shady spot to stay cool. Instead, they basked in the sun, frolicked in the grass, and strolled up and down the garden paths—taking full advantage of the grounds before the tourists showed up. Boxer and Bullfighter engaged in a little post-breakfast warfare. Chew-Chew stole an empty candy wrapper from Larry, Curly, and Moe, who found the crinkly treasure near the front gate. Then Whiskey stole it from Chew-Chew, who tried to steal it back. Spinderella dashed back and forth across the veranda, sliding, skidding, and spinning around, over and over again. Just for the fun of it. Even grumpy old Pawpa Hemingway seemed to be enjoying the cooler weather. He crept along the outer perimeter of the garden wall, stalking a tiny green lizard through the foliage as if he were a big-game hunter. It made him feel young again.

And then there was Nessie.

Nessie sat quietly in her favorite spot on the front porch, watching the other cats roam the grounds. The sun began to rise above the trees, but it didn't feel too hot. Which was nice. Nessie didn't like the hot, humid days. Like yesterday. She twitched her ears and stretched. Then she sat up a little taller, fixing her gaze on the entry gate across the yard.

Is she coming back? she wondered.

Nessie didn't know why, but she felt a strange bond with the human girl who held her and stroked her in such a loving way. It was like reuniting with an old friend. She hoped it wouldn't be years and years before the girl came back again. Like the last time.

"Nessie! My darling!"

The golden-furred cat jumped to her feet when she saw a figure opening the front gate.

Is it her?

No. It was Margarita Bouffet. The First Lady of the House. Of course.

"How are you on this lovely, lovely day, Nessie?"

Margarita headed down the main path toward the porch, her cha-cha heels clicking and clacking on the stones. She walked up to Nessie and leaned over to stroke the cat's ears.

Nessie loved that.

"I wish I could stay here and scratch your pretty little ears all day, Ness, but I have too much work to do," Margarita cooed, giving the cat a few final strokes.

Nessie meowed when she stopped.

"Sorry, sweetie." Margarita stood upright and pulled a tiny notebook out of the pocket of her pink and green pleated skirt. "Let's see now. The pool guy is coming to change the filters at eight. The air conditioner repairman is dropping by at ten to check out our air ducts. That nice young couple from Key Largo wants to have a video conference call to confirm their wedding plans. And—heaven help us—Foster Lee Jackson from the historical society is dropping by this afternoon to look at our plans for the new ticket booth. What do you think of that, Nessie?"

Nessie yawned.

"I know. That man makes me yawn, too." Margarita glanced at her to-do list again. "And on top of all that, we have six different tour groups coming today. The tour guides are going to be booked solid. And it's the new girl's first day. You remember Laura, don't you, Nessie?"

Nessie looked up when she heard the name.

Laura?

"She's not ready to lead a tour yet, of course. I'll have her walk along with the other guides first, let her listen and learn the ropes, get to know the lay of the land and all that. Then, when she's ready, I'll give her a trial run. How does that sound, Nessie?"

Nessie meowed.

"Oh, look!" Margarita said, pointing to the gate. "There's the pool guy! Right on time! I'll talk to you later, Nessie. Have a lovely, lovely day!"

With that, Margarita clicked her heels and danced her way down the porch steps, her gold hoop earrings swinging against her cheeks as she clicked and clacked across the stone path.

"Buenos días, señor!"

Nessie settled back into her favorite spot. She swished her huge fluffy tail back and forth slowly and lazily, for no other reason than to feel the air wafting through her fur. It felt good. As the sun rose higher, she watched the humans arrive one by one through the front gate for another day of work at the Hemingway House.

"Morning, Nessie."

Jake Jacobs showed up first, fresh and pumped from his early-morning workout, high-protein shake, and numerous T shirt changes. He said hi to Margarita and the pool guy and quickly got down to business: replenishing the cats' food and water before taking on the dreaded task of cleaning the litter boxes.

Then came Millie the ticket booth attendant. She had bleached-blond hair pulled back in a ponytail and wore the same basic outfit she'd been wearing to work for the last twenty-five years: a starched white shirt, navy-blue scarf, and crisply ironed khaki pants. She always arrived early because she didn't want to miss anything.

Then there was Lucky Leo Trout the tour director. He checked in with Margarita first thing every morning to go over the tour group schedules. Leo was a little bald, a little short, a little chubby, and, according to him, the luckiest man alive. He loved to tell tall tales of his amazing good luck, but Margarita always managed to steer the conversation back to their schedule. Today was no exception.

"That's amazing, Leo," she said. "Down to your last dollar and you hit the jackpot? You really are one lucky man! Which reminds me, I think we may have hit the jackpot with this new tour guide. You saw Laura's video. Don't you think she has potential? So charming, and smart! Can you schedule her to take the tours with alternating guides today? Great, thanks, Leo."

Margarita hurried away before Leo launched into another story.

Nessie watched all this from her perch on the porch, keeping one eye on the front gate as others began to arrive.

Where is she?

Most of the employees were here already. The gift shop clerk, the tour guides, the groundskeepers and custodians—each of them said good morning to Nessie as they made their way to the employee lounge at the rear of the house. She thought it was strange that they couldn't start their day without drinking that dark hot liquid they seemed to love so much. Nessie tried it once, after someone knocked over a cup. It tasted terrible.

Nessie looked up at the sky and sighed.

She was about to give up waiting for the girl—and try to enjoy this beautiful day with the rest of the cats—when she caught a glimpse of someone outside the front gate. She stood up to get a better look. But the sun was in her eyes and it was hard to see. Then she heard a voice and knew instantly who it was.

"Nessie! I'm back!"

Laura Lange didn't want to be late for her first day of work.

After drinking two frozen margaritas the night before—and being woken mid-sleep by a cat on a hot tin roof—she was afraid she'd hit the snooze button on her phone and sleep until noon. Waking up, as it turned out, was no problem at all.

Thanks to Polly Parton.

The only problem with being woken by the parrot's enthusiastic rendition of "Nine to Five" was that Laura couldn't get the song out of her head. The whole time she showered, she couldn't stop singing it—no matter how hard she tried. Even as she dried off and dressed, she kept humming the tune to herself. Then she made the stupid mistake of belting out the chorus loud enough for everyone in the house to hear—including Polly, who started singing along.

"Laura, no!" one of the twins yelled from upstairs. "Don't encourage her!"

Laura blushed.

I haven't even left the house yet and I've already embarrassed myself, she thought.

Luckily, the rest of her morning went much smoother.

Her hair looked great, thanks to the drop in humidity. Her outfit, a simple gray skirt with a yellow and white patterned blouse, looked "professional casual" but cute, thanks to her mom's insistence on buying new clothes for Laura's new job. And her breakfast with the twins turned out to be the perfect cure for a mild hangover, thanks to the blueberry muffins purchased by Jilly and fresh-brewed coffee made by Jolene. While they ate, she told the twins about her late-night visitor, the fluffy, scratchy, six-toed cat on the roof.

"Oh, that's Tallulah," said Jolene.

"I didn't know you have a cat."

"It's more like she has us," said Jilly. "She comes and goes as she pleases."

"Yeah, she just showed up one day and adopted us. We gave her food and got her a bed and a litter box. It's like we're her personal Airbnb."

"I noticed she's a polydactyl," said Laura. "Do you think she's one of the Hemingway cats?"

The twins shrugged. "Maybe," said Jolene. "I guess it's possible."

"On this island, anything is possible." Jilly laughed.

Laura checked the time, thanked them for breakfast, grabbed her bag, and headed out the door. She made sure to have a map of Key West on her phone so she wouldn't get lost on her walk to work. Luckily, it was a gorgeous day and not very hot, so at least she wouldn't be drenched with sweat by the time she got there. She glanced at her phone. According to the map app, her estimated time of arrival at the Hemingway House was 8:45 a.m.

Perfect.

Laura smiled and—against her better judgment—started humming "Nine to Five" as she made her way down a picturesque street lined with palm trees, picket fences, and pastel houses. With each step, she could feel herself getting more excited.

And more nervous, too.

Will they ask me to lead a tour on my first day? she wondered. *Am I ready to lead a tour?*

Her thoughts were interrupted by the *toot-toot* of a car horn behind her, followed by the approaching sound of reggae music. She turned her head to see Mama Marley's pink taxicab coming down the street. As she drove by, Mama rolled down the window, waved at Laura, and shouted a cheerful greeting in Jamaican Patois. "*Gud mawnin*, Miss Tour Guide!"

Laura laughed and waved back. "Morning, Mama Marley!"

At first, she wondered why Mama was laying on the accent so thick—Laura was a local now and knew it was just an act—but then she noticed a pair of rich-looking tourists in the back seat of the cab. They seemed to be loving the whole Mama Marley Experience, loud reggae and all.

She sure knows how to put on a show, Laura thought, chuckling to herself. *Could those rumors about Mama being a lip-syncing reggae star actually be true?*

She shook her head. No, it was too crazy to believe.

Laura turned a corner and spotted Rooster McCloud halfway down the block. The bandanna-wearing lighthouse keeper was tossing bird feed to the gypsy chickens in the street, bobbing his head up and down to whatever music was playing on his headphones. He looked extraordinarily happy, even blissful. Laura, on the other hand, felt anything but blissful seeing those chickens again. Fearful, yes. Blissful, no. Even though she didn't have her mom's Chex Party Mix on her, she didn't want a repeat of yesterday's bird attack. So she crossed to the other side of the street.

Just to be safe.

"Miss Lange!" Rooster shouted, and waved as he saw her approach. He tugged the headphones from his ears. "Beautiful day, isn't it?"

"Yes, it is," she answered, smiling warmly but keeping a safe distance.

He noticed her glancing nervously at the gypsy chickens. "Oh, don't worry about them. They won't hurt you. I'm Rooster McCloud, in case you forgot. Key West lighthouse keeper and local radio host."

"Oh, yes, I know," Laura said. "In fact, I heard a little bit of your show last night. *Key West After Dark.*"

"You did? Really? Well, knock me over with a feather!"

"Yes, I really loved that Hemingway quote. Especially the part about living life 'intoxicated by the romance of the unusual.' I don't know why, but it really struck a nerve with me. It was exactly what I needed to hear, right here and right now."

"You don't say," Rooster murmured wryly. "What are the odds of me picking a quote that speaks directly to you? It must be the universe trying to tell you something."

"Must be," said Laura. "The universe and Hemingway."

"Yes, of course. Hemingway."

Rooster and Laura said their good-byes and went on their separate ways. As Laura walked down the street under the palms, she thought about the Hemingway quote—and the sly expression on Rooster's face when she brought it up. His eyes twinkled. Literally. They looked so playful, yet so wise, that Laura had to wonder if the rumors were true and Rooster really did invent the iPad.

Well, knock me over with a feather!

Laura had to laugh. The rumors in this town were pretty crazy. And hilarious. But . . . what if there was some truth in them? Key West was definitely an unusual place—the southernmost point in the contiguous United States located at the very end of a chain of tiny tropical islands—and it was bound to attract some unusual people.

She thought about that as she turned the corner onto Whitehead Street and nearly collided with two middle-aged men who didn't see her coming. It was Rick and Ricardo, the mustachioed owners of the Lighthouse Hotel.

And their little dogs, too.

"Lucy! Desi! No!"

The two Chihuahuas rushed at Laura, tails wagging and leashes crossing, causing Rick and Ricardo to bump into each other like a pair of vaudeville comedians. The couple apologized profusely as they tried to untangle the leashes. Lucy and Desi took advantage of the moment by pawing at Laura's shins, begging her to pet them. Which she did, happily.

"Hi, Lucy! Hi, Desi! Out for your morning walk?" she said, stroking the dogs' perky little ears.

"I am so sorry," Rick apologized, for the third time. "They usually don't go after people like that. Most of the time, they're very well behaved."

"No, they aren't," Ricardo rebutted. "You just think they are because you love them so much." He leaned toward Laura and lowered his voice. "The truth is, Rick spoiled them so much that they think they can get away with anything."

"Stop whispering about my little angels," Rick protested.

"Angels? They're devil dogs and you know it. Just admit it. You've raised a pair of banditos. We should have named them Bonnie and Clyde."

Laura laughed and continued petting the Chihuahuas. "Look at these innocent little faces. They're sweetie pies; I can tell."

"They're gangsters," said Ricardo, only half-joking.

The word "gangsters" made Laura think of the rumor she heard from the twins—that Rick and Ricardo won the Lighthouse Hotel in a card game with Vegas mobsters. She glanced up at the smiling couple with their matching mustaches and tropical shirts and adorable dog babies—and tried to imagine them gambling with the mob.

Nope. No way. It was preposterous. *Who comes up with this stuff?*

Laura straightened up and said good-bye to Rick and Ricardo and Lucy and Desi. Then she took a deep breath and headed down Whitehead Street, catching glimpses of the Key West Lighthouse rising up at the end of the block above the trees. To her left, she could see the redbrick wall that bordered the lush overgrown gardens of the Hemingway House. It looked as if it were the only thing keeping the explosion of tropical greenery from spilling onto the road and taking over the island. Somewhere, hidden behind the palm fronds, mangrove trees, and multiple flowering plants, was the grand old house itself. Laura could barely see it until she reached the iron front gate.

My new workplace, she mused, gazing up at the vintage green shutters, shaded veranda, and wrought-iron railings. *It sure beats an office cubicle.*

She fought the urge to start singing "Nine to Five."

Laura stepped through the gate and headed toward the house. As she walked past the boat-shaped fountain on the main path, she noticed a dozen or so cats wandering the grounds. She recognized two of them. Boxer and Bullfighter—the battling brothers—were locked in mortal combat. They bobbed up and down like prizefighters, playfully swiping at each other with their oversized mitts. Laura chuckled at the sight of them.

But her face really lit up when she saw her old friend sitting on the porch.

"Nessie! I'm back!"

By nine o'clock, a line of tourists had formed on the sidewalk outside of the Hemingway House. Vacationing families, travel companions, happy couples ranging from blushing honeymooners to smiling seniors, even a rowdy group of children from the local kindergarten, were there, ready to buy their tickets, take the tour, and discover the many wonders of Ernest Hemingway's famous home— and equally famous cats.

Laura was ready, too, for her very first tour.

As a tourist.

"Today is your lucky day, folks," said Leo Trout, addressing a small group—including Laura—standing on the front porch. "I'm Lucky Leo Trout, and I'll be your tour guide this morning."

Laura glanced down at Nessie, who crossed the porch and stood next to her. The cat seemed more than a little annoyed that one of the tourists had taken her favorite spot.

Leo continued with his introduction: "They call me Lucky because I've survived everything from tornadoes, fires, and floods to car crashes, train wrecks, and one very messy divorce. Let's just say I'm truly lucky to be alive."

He paused for laughter. Laura politely obliged, along with some of the group who chuckled.

"I'm also truly honored," Leo went on, "to tell you fine folks about this magnificent house. It was built in 1851 by marine architect Asa Tift, who designed it in the Spanish colonial style using limestone that was excavated right here on this very site. Asa dug so deep that the hole was big enough for a basement with nine-foot ceilings. It's one of the few houses in Key West to have a basement at all, and it's a darn good one, too. The limestone keeps it dry as a bone when it rains. Thanks to that limestone, this old house can withstand just about anything. Rain, wind, heat, tropical storms, hurricanes. Even the biggest of them all, the deadly Florida Keys Hurricane of 1919."

Laura felt something tickle her ankles. She glanced down and saw Nessie, swishing her tail slowly back and forth.

She looked bored.

Poor kitty, Laura thought. *I'm sure you've seen Leo do this a million times.*

Laura, on the other hand, found Leo's tour fascinating. Sure, his jokes were corny, but he was actually very entertaining. And very informative. By the time he ushered the group through the front door and into the long foyer, he'd managed to flash-forward through the decades to 1931—the year that Hemingway and his second wife, Pauline Pfeiffer, purchased the house after visiting Key West numerous times and falling totally in love with the island.

"The house was a dump," Leo explained to the group. "A real fixer-upper. Which is why the newlyweds nabbed it for the low, low price of eight thousand dollars. Pauline's uncle Gus bought it for them as a wedding present."

Leo led the tourists into the first room off the foyer, a surprisingly cool, airy space filled with romantic paintings of ships and seascapes, vintage framed photographs of Hemingway with friends, family, and famous celebrities, and colorful art and artifacts from the couple's world travels.

"Pauline was quite a collector," Leo explained. "She definitely had a flair for interior decorating. Notice the unique chandeliers she picked out for each of the rooms."

Laura stayed at the back of the group, taking mental notes of Lucky Leo's vast knowledge and skillful performance as a guide.

She wasn't alone.

Nessie stayed right by her side through the whole tour.

While Leo escorted the group from room to room—pointing out photos of Hemingway's fishing boat and crew, Pauline's French-inspired bathroom tiles, and artwork by famous and not-so-famous artists—Nessie followed Laura every step of the way. She even risked getting trampled when the tour group climbed the narrow stairs to the second-floor bedrooms.

"Who's that?" asked a little boy in overalls, pointing to a lazy-looking calico cat sleeping on one of the beds.

Leo laughed. "Oh, that's Lady Bratt Ashley. We named her after Lady Brett Ashley in *The Sun Also Rises*."

"Why do you call her Bratt?" asked the boy.

"Well, look at her," said Leo. "She lays on that bed all day and won't let any of the other cats sleep on it. As far as she's concerned, the bed belongs to her, and she's not willing to share it. Basically, she's just a little brat."

"And who's that?" asked the boy, pointing at a snowy white cat perched high atop the tallest cabinet in the room.

"That's Kilimanjaro."

"Like 'The Snows of Kilimanjaro'?" said the boy's father. "I read that story in high school. It was really good."

"One of Hemingway's best," Leo agreed.

The boy looked confused. "What's Kil . . . a . . . man . . . ja . . ."

"Kilimanjaro is the highest mountain in Africa," Leo explained. "It even has snow on top. Hemingway's story is about a husband and wife on a safari near Kilimanjaro. We named this cat after it because she's snowy white and likes to climb up things and look down."

"So do I," said the little boy.

Leo gave Laura a bemused look, then turned to address the group. "Okay, everyone, we need to move things along now. Please head out to the veranda. Then we'll take the stairs down to the pool."

As the tourists shuffled out onto the second-floor balcony, Leo whispered to Laura, "Sometimes people ask questions that might throw off the timing of the tour. It's important to keep an eye on your watch. You might need to skip some information to keep everything on schedule. You own a wristwatch, don't you?"

Laura stammered, "I, um, I have a cell phone . . ."

"Get a wristwatch," Leo said. "It's easier to glance at when you're talking." He turned and headed out to the veranda.

Laura looked down at Nessie, who looked back at her with concerned eyes.

"I guess I need to buy a wristwatch, Nessie," she said. "I haven't had one since fourth grade. Very old school."

As the two of them walked out of the bedroom onto the wraparound balcony, Laura glanced back at the bedroom behind her. She noticed a small gray shape in the hall doorway—the eyes, ears, and whiskers of an old gray cat—peeping around the corner like a little gray spy.

It was Pawpa Hemingway.

He was watching her.

Foster Lee Jackson arrived at the Hemingway House five hours early, dressed to the nines and carrying one large bouquet of pink long-stemmed roses. Known for his distinctive fashion sense and precise grooming habits—among other things—Foster looked every inch the Southern gentleman in his pale seersucker suit with bow tie and suspenders topped with a Panama straw hat. Today, his immaculately trimmed salt-and-pepper mustache and goatee seemed to be even more immaculately trimmed than usual. At least that's how it appeared to Millie the ticket booth manager, who couldn't help but notice the spring in his step as he strutted up to her window.

"A fine and beautiful morning to you, Miss . . ."

"Millie," she said with a smile. "Millie Graham."

"Of course! Miss Millie Graham! How could I forget such a unique name for such a charming lady!"

Millie blushed and smoothed down her bleached-blond hair with one hand, even though it was pulled back in a bow and never moved. "Why, thank you! How can I help you today?"

"I have an appointment with Ms. Bouffet," he said. "Could you please inform her that Foster Lee Jackson, president of the Key West historical society, is here?"

"I know who you are, Foster," said Millie with a girlish grin. "Everyone knows who you are. You're pretty hard to miss, with the way you look and all."

Foster raised a meticulously manicured eyebrow. "I hope you meant that kindly, Miss Millie."

"Oh, of course I do. You're just so stylish, is what I meant. Stylish and . . . debonair."

Now it was Foster's turn to blush. "That's very gracious of you, Miss Millie. My dear mother, God rest her soul, believed that a gentleman should always take pride in his appearance. I try my best, though I seem to be the last of a dying breed. Why, I've seen men my age enter a fine dining establishment wearing flip-flops and cargo shorts. It's sad, really."

"Yes, it is," said Millie, who'd been on plenty of dates with those men.

Foster smiled politely, then glanced at the house. "So . . . is Ms. Bouffet available now?"

"Oh! Let's see." Millie looked down at her schedule book. "Margarita wrote you in for three o'clock this afternoon. Hmmm, well, I'll try buzzing her desk." She pushed an intercom button on the ticket booth's office phone and waited. "Hello, Margarita? . . . Foster Lee Jackson is here to see you. . . . Yes, I know. . . . He's scheduled for three—"

"I was in the neighborhood and thought I'd drop by," Foster added, leaning into the window.

"He was in the neighborhood and thought he'd drop by." Millie paused. "Yes . . . okay." She hung up the phone. "She's coming out now with the plans."

"Oh, good," said Foster. "I knew I was taking a chance by coming here early. But you know what they say: 'Fortune favors the bold.'"

"Who said that? Hemingway?"

"No, it's an old Latin proverb, actually. Some attribute it to Virgil in his epic poem, *Aeneid*, but most scholars believe it was Pliny the Elder who—oh, Ms. Margarita Bouffet!" Foster turned away from Millie and tipped his hat. "Don't you look radiant this morning!"

Millie leaned out the window to see Margarita walking up the path carrying a packet of diagrams. She did, indeed, look positively radiant in the morning light.

And mildly annoyed.

"Good morning, Foster," she said with a strained smile. "I thought our appointment was at three."

"Yes, please forgive me. I happened to be in the neighborhood purchasing flowers for the office," Foster explained. "And when I saw these lovely pink roses, they reminded me of you."

Margarita looked confused. "They did?"

Foster gulped. "Yes, they, um, reminded me of your beautiful gardens here at the house, and I thought maybe I'd drop by while I'm here . . . though I shouldn't have presumed that I could interrupt your busy day, and I do apologize . . . profusely."

"It's fine, Foster," said Margarita. "Here are the contractor's plans."

She handed the diagrams to Foster, who took them and studied them carefully. "Again, I apologize," he said, "but as president of the Key West historical society, it's my job to assure the historic integrity of the island's most treasured homes and venues."

"The contractor based his design on the original ticket booth," said Margarita. "It's exactly the same. But hopefully, the roof won't leak when it rains."

Foster glanced back and forth between the ticket booth and the diagrams. "It appears you are correct," he said. "But what about the materials the contractor will be using? So many of today's builders use vinyl and other synthetics. It's a travesty." Foster shuddered at the thought.

"Nope," said Margarita. "Just good old-fashioned wood."

"What about the roofing?"

Margarita hesitated. "Um, I'm not sure exactly. I'll have to ask the contractor."

Foster looked upset. "Yes, you must. This is very important. The Hemingway House is one of the most famous historical sites on the island. Thousands of tourists come through these gates every day."

"Yes, I know, Foster. I work here, remember?"

"Of course. Forgive me, Margarita. Again." Foster blushed and handed the diagrams back to her. "Well, consult with your contractor, ask him for a detailed list of materials, and I'm sure you and I can work this out . . . together. Which reminds me. I hope you'll save a few dances for me at tomorrow night's soiree."

Margarita blinked twice and smiled through gritted teeth. "It'd be my pleasure, Foster."

"Well, then . . . until we meet again, Ms. Bouffet." He pulled a single long-stemmed rose from his bouquet and handed it to Margarita.

"Oh. Thank you," she said, trying not to roll her eyes.

"How sweet!" Millie gushed. "I love roses. They're so romantic."

Foster saw the look on Millie's face—and gave her a rose, too. "And to you, Miss Millie Graham. I hope to make your acquaintance again soon." With a tip of his Panama hat, he turned and walked out the front gate.

Margarita looked at her rose and groaned.

Millie smelled her rose and sighed. "What a gentleman. He's just so, I don't know, refined . . . and classy."

Margarita was about to tell Millie that Foster Lee Jackson was a pompous buffoon and total pain in the butt cheeks who was going to make her jump—and dance—through hoops before he'd approve the plans for the new ticket booth.

But then she had a better idea.

"Millie," she said. "How would you like to come to our Dance Night tomorrow?"

Lucky Leo Trout checked his wristwatch and waited for the tourists to finish taking pictures. "They like to linger here," he whispered to Laura. "But don't let them linger too long. We have a schedule to keep." He tapped his wristwatch with his finger.

It was easy for Laura to see why the tourists liked to linger here. The wraparound veranda on the second floor of the Hemingway House offered lovely views of the gardens and pool. You could even see the Key West Lighthouse. Which meant plenty of photo ops.

"Can I take a picture of you and your cat?" asked a silver-haired woman in sunglasses. "You look so cute together. Your outfits match!"

Laura glanced down at Nessie. "Well, she's not actually my cat—"

"Could have fooled me," said the woman. "She's been with you for the whole tour!"

Laura laughed. "We're old friends."

After the woman snapped a photo of them, Lucky Leo called the group together and led everyone down a side stairway to the outdoor pool area. Laura noticed Nessie hesitating, so she waited with her until the others descended before heading down. By the time she reached the others at the north end of the pool, Leo was enthusiastically describing the pool's dimensions (twenty-four by sixty feet!), the labor involved in digging it (in solid coral!), and the architectural significance of it (the first in-ground pool within a hundred miles!).

Leo obviously loved this part of the tour.

"See that penny?" he asked the group, pointing to a weathered coin embedded in concrete at the foot of the pool. "There's a great story about that penny. The year was 1937, and Hemingway's wife Pauline decided they needed a pool. Ernest agreed, even though she wanted to put it right where he'd set up a boxing ring. Sure, he liked to spar with the local boxers, but a pool sounded nice, too. So he said yes, then flew off to cover the Spanish Civil War as a news correspondent. That left Pauline alone to deal with the pool. Which she quickly discovered was a money pit. Just guess how much it cost."

"A million dollars?" asked the little boy who'd asked about the white cat named Kilimanjaro.

"Uh, no. Not that much," said Leo. "It cost twenty thousand dollars, which, in 1937, would be almost half a million dollars today. That's a lot of money! When Ernest returned from the war and learned how much the pool was costing them, he threw a fit. 'Pauline,' he said, exasperated. 'You've spent all but my last penny, so you might as well have that!' He fished a penny from his pocket and flung it on the ground. Well, Pauline didn't bat an eye. She picked up that penny and had it embedded right here. Hemingway's last cent."

Everyone in the tour group chuckled—even Laura, though she knew the story by heart. She glanced down at her feet, expecting to see Nessie by her side, swishing her tail back and forth.

Nessie wasn't there.

Laura scanned the pool area. A few of the kittens were playing tag under a large flowering shrub. Whiskey was chasing Chew-Chew behind the pool house. And old Pawpa Hemingway was crouched beneath the veranda stairs—staring at Laura with his piercing blue eyes.

But Nessie? Nessie was nowhere to be seen.

Where'd you go, old friend?

As much as Nessie wanted to follow her old friend through the entire tour, she just couldn't join Laura and the others by the side of the pool.

Nessie hated that pool.

Like most cats, she didn't like getting wet. But that wasn't the reason she hated the pool. She hated the pool because—somewhere inside her little cat brain—she retained bits and pieces of a terrifying memory of falling into the pool. She didn't remember any details of the event. Cats are not elephants and don't have the greatest memories. But she could never forget her feelings of sheer panic and helplessness whenever she got close to the pool. For Nessie, it was more of a natural physical response than an actual memory.

Either way, she knew she had to skip this part of the tour. She also knew where the group was heading to next, since she'd been watching people take this tour every day of her life. Instead of taking any chances getting near that pool, she'd go and wait for Laura at the next part of the tour . . .

The room with animals on the walls.

"And this is the room where Ernest Hemingway wrote seventy percent of his novels and stories," said Lucky Leo.

He glanced at his wristwatch and waited for the last of the stragglers to climb the stairs of the converted coach house next to the pool. Laura was in the back of the group and could only see small glimpses of the room's red tiled floor, pale blue walls, shelves of books and mementos—and, of course, Hemingway's hunting trophies.

"What is that? A skinny cow?" asked the little boy, pointing at a large horned head mounted on the wall.

"That's an antelope from Africa," said Leo. "Hemingway was quite the big-game hunter. He went on many safaris and brought back all sorts of pelts, skins, and trophies."

The boy's mother winced. "That's horrible," she said.

"Yes, I know what you mean," said Leo, not skipping a beat. "But you have to remember. Back in Hemingway's day, safaris were considered the supreme challenge for hunters. They were extremely popular among world-class sportsmen, and the trophies were proudly displayed in the finest homes. Things are very different today, of course."

As Leo moved on to point out other highlights of the room, Laura stepped around a pair of tourists—and got her first good look at Hemingway's round wooden writing desk.

A cat was sitting on it.

Nessie!

Right next to Hemingway's old manual typewriter.

As soon as Laura saw the typewriter, her heart started beating faster. She remembered seeing it on her family's trip to Key West—and falling absolutely in love with it. She'd already fallen in love with Hemingway's beautiful colonial house and Hemingway's cute polydactyl cats. But when she heard about all the great stories Hemingway wrote in that cool attic studio—and then she laid eyes on that old-timey typewriter with push-button keys—the fourteen-year-old Laura decided to set three life goals for herself:

1. She wanted to read everything Hemingway ever wrote.
2. She wanted to become a writer, too.
3. She wanted to write on a typewriter just like
   Hemingway's.

As soon as her family left Key West and returned to Syracuse, Laura went to the school library and started checking out books by Hemingway. For Christmas that year, her parents gave her an old typewriter from the 1930s that they found in a vintage store. Achieving goal number one took six months of dedicated reading. Achieving goal number three only required a few weeks of nagging her parents. But goal number two? Becoming a writer?

That's a whole other story.

Laura let out a sigh. Standing here now in Hemingway's actual writing studio, looking at Hemingway's actual typewriter, she remembered how hard she worked to bang out her own stories on that rickety antique her parents bought her. She also remembered the polite smile on her high school English teacher's face when he told her that her stories were very good—but her writing style could use some work. He said it sounded like she was imitating Hemingway and she needed to find her own "voice."

Laura was crushed. She still wanted to be a writer, but when it came time to apply to colleges her parents convinced her that it was more "practical" to go to Syracuse University—her father was a biology professor there, so her tuition would be free—and to major in English education for a career in teaching. Laura wanted to go to a school with a great writing program, like Iowa, but ultimately decided her parents were right. She needed to be "practical."

Nessie gazed at her from the top of Hemingway's desk. The cat seemed to sense the emotions Laura was feeling. Jumping off the desk, Nessie scampered to Laura's side and rubbed against her leg.

Laura looked down and smiled. She bent over to scratch Nessie's ears a few times, then stood up and looked at Hemingway's desk again.

She couldn't help but think of one of Hemingway's most famous sayings:

"There is nothing to writing. All you do is sit down at a typewriter and bleed."

★   ★   ★

Four tour groups and four tour guides later, Laura was told she could take an hour-long lunch break by her time-obsessed supervisor, Lucky Leo.

"Most employees brown-bag it, but some people head to a nearby restaurant," he explained. "That's fine with me, as long as you make it back in time." He pointed her in the direction of the employee lounge, then checked his wristwatch and dashed away.

Laura looked down at Nessie. "You hear that, kitty? We're on the clock, so we'd better get cracking."

As they headed down the garden path, Laura started wondering if cats even have a sense of time.

Probably not, she thought. *Cats seem to live in the eternal now.*

Which sounded like a pretty good way to live, as far as Laura was concerned. She'd wasted way too many hours of her life worrying about the future.

Nessie, however, seemed perfectly content to just walk along next to Laura in the here and now. She had stayed by Laura's side all morning long, accompanying her on all four of the tours—except the pool part.

What's up with that? Laura wondered.

When they got a little farther on the path, Laura had to stop and look at one of her favorite attractions: a five-foot-tall, perfect replica of the Hemingway House. It had little green shutters and little wraparound balconies, just like the real thing, only cat sized. An orange and black tabby was snoozing on the little front porch.

"Look, Nessie! That cat is sleeping in your favorite spot!"

Nessie blinked and yawned.

"Well, I wish I had a playhouse like that," Laura said. "It's like a Barbie's DreamHouse for cats!"

"I hope Barbie keeps her DreamHouse cleaner than this," said a male voice.

Laura froze. "Who said that?"

"Me: Jake." Jake Jacobs popped his head out from behind the miniature house.

"Oh! Me: Laura."

Jake laughed and came out of hiding, holding a greasy rag covered in cat fur. "How's your first day going, Me: Laura?"

"Good. I'm on my lunch break now."

"Are you going to eat in the lounge? If you don't mind, I can join you. I just need to clean up first."

"Sounds good. See you there! Come on, Nessie."

When they reached the employee lounge, Laura realized she'd forgotten something: to pack a lunch. It wasn't a big deal. She was still full from eating the twins' blueberry muffins. She decided to just have a cup of coffee from the pot on the counter when she noticed a neatly dressed woman with bleached-blond hair waving at her from a table in the corner.

"Laura! Laura Lange! Come sit with me, honey!"

Laura smiled politely and, feeling a little confused, joined the woman at the table.

"Hi, Laura. I'm Millie. Millie Graham, manager of the ticket booth. I brought you a sandwich. I figured you'd probably forget to bring a lunch on your first day. I hope you like tomato, basil, and mozzarella."

"I do. Thank you. It's my favorite," Laura said, accepting Millie's carefully wrapped sandwich. "How did you know . . . ?"

". . . that you'd forget? I've worked here forever, and I've seen everything. If you ever want to know what's going on around here, just ask me. I know everything about everybody."

"Yes, but how did you know . . . ?"

"That you like tomato, basil, and mozzarella? Just a wild guess. I figured you're from New York, so you might like something sophisticated and vegetarian."

Laura laughed. "I don't know if I'd call Syracuse sophisticated."

"Well, it's more sophisticated than Florida, believe me. Just ask Jake here."

Laura turned to see Jake crossing the lounge holding a brown paper bag.

"What kind of sandwich did you pack today, Jake?" Millie asked as he pulled up a chair.

Jake looked a little mystified but answered her anyway. "Peanut butter and jelly."

"See?" said Millie. "Florida men are not very sophisticated. Though I must say, Jake is looking mighty fine in that tight T-shirt. Have you been working out, Jake?"

Jake blushed. "Uh, yeah, I worked out this morning."

"Well, my goodness, it's really paying off," said Millie. "Do you know Laura?"

"Yes, we met yesterday," said Jake, happy to change the conversation. "So how's it going, Laura? How many tours of duty have you gone on so far?"

"Tours of duty?" she said with a sly smile. "I knew you were a military man."

Jake turned to Millie to explain. "It's the haircut. It makes me look like G.I. Joe."

"I think it makes you look very handsome," said Millie. "I'm sorry, Laura. Please go on."

Laura took a deep breath. "Well, I followed along on four tours this morning. The first was with Lucky Leo, then Sasha, then Carol, and finally Bob. It was really interesting to watch and compare them. They're giving the tourists the same basic information, but they each have their own style."

Millie leaned forward and lowered her voice. "So who do you think is the best guide? And who's the worst? You can tell me. I won't tell a soul."

Laura hesitated and had started to hem and haw when she was saved by the approaching sound of loud clacking heels.

It was Margarita Bouffet—and her brand-new cha-cha shoes.

"Jake! Laura! I was looking for you two!" she said, sashaying across the lounge. "I need to ask a favor. The Hemingway House is hosting my club's Dance Night tomorrow at eight. It's our monthly open ballroom party, so there's going to be more guests than usual, and I'm short on help. Would you two like to help me set up, monitor the refreshments, and clean up afterward?"

Laura glanced at Jake. "I, uh . . ."

"I'll pay you, of course. And it's hardly any work at all. You'll have plenty of time to join in on the fun. You like ballroom dancing, don't you, Laura?"

"Um, yeah—"

"Excellent! Invite your roommates, too. I know the Crabb girls enjoy a good time."

Jake glanced at Laura and tried not to laugh. "Sure, Margarita, I'll do it," he said. "Mack is the deejay, isn't he?"

"Yes, he is," said Margarita. "It'll be quite the party. Everyone's coming."

"I'm coming," said Millie.

"Yes, you are, bless your heart. And—get this—Mack promised me he'd try to talk his uncle Rooster into coming."

"That'll be something to see," said Jake.

"Indeed it will," said Margarita. "You can come at seven-thirty to help set up. Just remember to dress appropriately. And don't forget your dancing shoes!"

Margarita clicked her heels and danced her way out of the lounge.

Laura looked at Jake and burst out laughing. She was about to confess that she knew nothing about ballroom dancing when her cell phone dinged. A text message. She pulled the phone from her skirt pocket, looked at the screen—and groaned.

The message said: *I miss you. Can we talk?*

It was from Devin.

Her boyfriend.

Chapter 6
The Night Before Dance Night

'Twas the night before Dance Night and all through Key West, not a creature was sleeping . . .

Because they couldn't decide on what to wear.

Margarita Bouffet paced back and forth in her bedroom, mixing and matching various accessories—necklaces, earrings, bracelets, rings—with her favorite ballroom gowns. She'd narrowed the choices down to three. The Sultry Spanish Señorita. The Sexy Grecian Goddess. Or the Spicy Red Showstopper straight out of *Dirty Dancing: Havana Nights*. Margarita thought she looked pretty hot in all three of them. Smoking hot, with the right hair and makeup. But then she started having second thoughts.

Do I really want to drive Foster Lee Jackson mad with desire?

Foster, on the other hand, knew exactly what he wanted to wear—a mint-green tuxedo jacket with fine black trim—but he couldn't decide if he should wear the matching pants and vest or swap them out for black pants with a black cummerbund. He tried on the cummerbund, pulling it as tight as he could around his midsection. Then he posed—Argentine tango–style—in front of his full-length mirror. The cummerbund definitely had a slimming effect. He swore it made him look ten pounds thinner.

Cummerbund it is!

Millie Graham had absolutely no idea what one should wear to a ballroom dance party. But gazing into her closet, she knew she wouldn't find it there. Most of her wardrobe consisted of beige pants, white shirts, and assorted blue scarves. Sure, she had other options—a few flowery sundresses (too casual), a powder-blue sheath dress with beaded neckline (too mother-of-the-bride), and a plain black frock with lace overlay details (too grieving widow). Millie knew what she had to do. She had to swallow her pride and ask her neighbor Connie for help. Connie had excellent taste and a seemingly endless supply of coordinated outfits for every occasion. Not only was she a never-wear-the-same-thing-twice fashion plate; she was also a professional hair stylist and makeup "artiste" who'd been dying to give Millie a makeover for years.

Well, Connie, Millie thought as she knocked on her neighbor's door. *Tonight is your lucky night.*

Jake Jacobs stood stiffly in the middle of the living room wearing his father's old tuxedo while his mother pinned the seams of the pants and the back of the jacket. "Is this necessary?" he asked. "Do you even know what you're doing?"

His mother rolled her eyes and told him to hush up and stand still. "Or else I'll poke you with a pin," she added. When she finished pinning the suit, she stood back to see how it fit. "Oh, Jake, you look so handsome. Even more handsome than your dad. I wish he could see you now." Her eyes started filling with tears, which took Jake by surprise.

"Mom, don't."

She breathed in and blinked back the tears. "I'm sorry," she said. "I know it's been seven years now, but I still think of him every day."

Jake stepped forward to hug her. "I know, Mom. Me, too."

She pushed him back. "Don't hug me. You'll loosen the pins. Now take off the suit—carefully!—and bring me my sewing machine. It's in the hall closet." Jake shuffled out of the room, thought about how much he missed his dad, and wondered if his friend Mack had to ride an emotional rollercoaster every time he put on a suit.

Did Mack even own a suit?

Mack McCloud did, indeed, own a suit. Better yet, he didn't have to agonize over what to wear tomorrow like the other Dance Night attendees. When Margarita Bouffet asked him to deejay some of her club events, he simply ran to the thrift store and purchased a purple velvet damask tuxedo jacket, which he paired with black pants, white shirt, and a long skinny black tie. It was a miracle that the jacket fit his tall, lanky body. Margarita loved it, too. She said the swirly design of the damask matched the swirling movements of the dancers—and the bold purple color perfectly suited his unique personality. Whatever that meant. Mack decided to take it as a compliment. As he looked over Margarita's recommended playlist for tomorrow's party, he started thinking about the new tour guide at the Hemingway House. The girl from Syracuse. According to Jake, Laura would be helping them out with the party.

Will she be dancing with Jake all night? Mack wondered. *And would Jake mind if I asked to cut in?*

Rooster McCloud made sure his bedroom door was locked before he pulled the gray garment bag from the back of his closet. He didn't want his nephew to see what he was up to. Softly and lovingly, he laid the garment bag down on his bed and slowly unzipped the zipper. "Why, hello there," he whispered. "Long time, no see." He reached into the bag and carefully removed the treasure within: The Greatest Suit of All Time. *Mack is going to freak out when he sees me in this*, he thought, chuckling to himself. The shocked look on Mack's face when Rooster quickly and cheerfully agreed to attend Margarita's event was funny enough. *This* was going to totally blow his mind. Hell, it was going to blow *everybody's* minds.

Rooster chuckled again and, with great care, took the pieces of the suit off their padded hangers and tried it on. *Still fits! Well, knock me over with a feather!* He adjusted the collar and tie, then checked himself out in the mirror on the back of his door. "My, my, look at you," he said to his reflection. "The old bird's still got it." He struck a pose. "Looking good." He spun around and peered over his shoulder. "Even the butt looks good." Then he turned back and took a few steps away from the mirror to get the full effect. "Huh," he grunted. "I don't know." Besides his bare feet, which looked ridiculous, there was something seriously out of place that ruined the whole picture: his long salt-and-pepper hair and scraggly beard. As an experiment, he pulled his hair back with one hand, covered his beard with the other, and studied himself in the mirror. Then he glanced at a pair of scissors on his desk. *Should I?* he asked himself. *Could I?*

And if I did . . . would Margarita like it?

Laura Lange stepped out of her bedroom in her flirtiest party dress and did a little runway twirl for the twins. "What do you think? Will this work?"

Jilly and Jolene didn't answer right away. Not a good sign.

At least Polly Parton whistled at her.

"It's cute," said Jilly, finally. "I mean, really, totally cute. I love it. . . ."

"But . . . ?"

"But it's not really right for ballroom dancing."

"It's really cute, though," Jolene chimed in. "It's just . . . you ought to see some of these ladies on Dance Night. They go all out. It's crazy."

"We're talking ball gowns," said Jilly.

Laura sighed. "Well, stupid me, I forgot to pack my ball gown. The next best thing I have is a basic Little Black Dress. Maybe I could gussy it up with some accessories . . . ?"

Jilly and Jolene didn't say anything. Which told her everything she needed to know.

"What am I going to do? Margarita told Jake and me to 'dress appropriately.' I don't even know what that means." Laura groaned. "What are you two wearing?"

"Oh, we have a few dresses that'll work. We've been going to the open nights for a couple years now," said Jilly.

"Yeah," said Jolene. "We'd lend you one of ours, but . . . I don't think they'd fit you."

Laura laughed. "Don't rub it in. It's hard enough living with roommates who look like swimsuit models."

"Oh, please. You're beautiful, Laura," said Jolene.

"Gorgeous," Jilly agreed. She turned to her sister. "Do you think she could wear one of Mom's dresses? They look about the same size."

Jolene studied Laura up and down. "Yeah, maybe."

Laura was confused. "Um, is your mother here in Key West?"

"No, she's with Dad," said Jilly. "In Guam."

"Guam?" said Jolene. "I thought they were in Japan."

"No, they left there last week. They're in Guam now." Jilly turned back to Laura. "Our parents retired last year to travel the world. They left us this house."

"And their sailboat."

"And the snorkeling business."

"Oh," said Laura, a little surprised. It certainly explained how two young girls could afford their own cabana and sailboat in Key West. She'd wondered about that since she arrived but thought it impolite to ask. "So your mom's dresses are here? In the house?"

"Yes! Upstairs! Come on!"

Ninety minutes later, Laura returned to her bedroom with a lovely blue dress, a stunning pair of sequined dance shoes, and a huge sense of relief. She crawled into bed feeling good. At last, she could stop worrying about what to wear—and start worrying about leading her first tour group tomorrow.

Don't sweat it, Laura, you can do this, she told herself.

In all eight of the tours she observed today, there wasn't one fact about the Hemingway House that she didn't already know. She'd been studying and practicing for weeks and was totally prepared for anything. She even borrowed a Mickey Mouse wristwatch from Jilly so she could keep track of the time.

Lucky Leo would be pleased.

With that reassuring thought, Laura turned off the pirate lamp—successfully avoiding the pointy-tipped sword—and closed her eyes. She knew she wouldn't need to listen to Rooster McCloud's radio show to help her fall asleep. She was much too tired. And the house was unusually, blissfully quiet. Polly Parton wasn't singing, and Romeo and Juliet weren't fighting. In a matter of minutes, Laura felt herself drifting away to her own private island in a boundless sea of dreams.

'Twas the night before Dance Night and all through Key West, not a creature was stirring . . .

Except a black fluffy-tailed, six-toed cat on a hot tin roof. Laura's tin roof.

Tallulah was back.

The next morning, another fluffy-tailed, six-toed cat named Nessie took Laura's place as a tour group observer—while Laura led the group as their guide.

"The house had been long abandoned and in terrible disrepair by the time Hemingway and his second wife, Pauline, first visited the island in 1928," Laura explained to the tourists. "Two years later, they learned that the house could be theirs—if they paid the back taxes on it."

Nessie had no idea what Laura was talking about. But she liked the sound of her voice. It was a little scratchy but deeply soothing.

Almost like a purr.

As the tour group walked from the front porch into the entry hall, Nessie noticed that Lucky Leo was following along, too. From the living room to the dining room to the kitchen, he watched Laura like a cat watches a mouse.

Which made Laura nervous.

Which made Nessie nervous.

At one point, Lucky Leo interrupted Laura to point out something about the kitchen sink. "Laura is right about the house not having plumbing until 1940," he said to the group. "But before then, they used rainwater collected from two cisterns here on the estate. One is next to the carriage house, and the other is on the roof."

"Ah, thank you, Leo," Laura stammered.

Again, Nessie had no idea what they were talking about. But it didn't sound good. In fact, Laura seemed even more nervous after Leo spoke up—and the tension Nessie felt didn't go away until the tour group reached the second floor. Thankfully, once Laura started talking about the strangely shaped object on top of one of the cabinets, she seemed to grow more confident. Nessie noticed it right away.

"This delightful ceramic cat sculpture was designed by Pablo Picasso," she said, smiling to the group. "But it is not the original Picasso. What happened to it is a pretty wild story. Hemingway first met Picasso in 1922 through their mutual friend Gertrude Stein. When Hemingway saw Picasso's crazy geometric cat sculpture in his studio in Paris, he fell completely in love with it and just had to have it. He loved cats and wanted to give the sculpture to his wife as a gift. Picasso suggested a swap: his sculpture in exchange for a box of grenades Hemingway saved from the war. Hemingway agreed. For decades, Picasso's sculpture was on display here at the Hemingway House. But then . . ."

Laura paused, raising a finger for dramatic effect.

". . . in November 2000, someone in a tour group—just like ours—decided to steal it. The curators of the Hemingway House were very upset. They even offered a ten-thousand-dollar reward to get it back. But by the time the FBI apprehended the cat thief, Picasso's sculpture was damaged beyond repair."

"So that one's a fake?" asked one of the tourists.

"It's a magnificent reproduction by Bob Orlin, a very talented sculptor and painter and, oddly enough, an Ernest Hemingway look-alike," Laura answered.

Nessie didn't have a clue what Laura was saying, of course, but she could tell that Lucky Leo was pleased with whatever it was Laura said.

Leo also seemed pleased when Laura glanced down at the thing around her wrist.

"Okay, everyone, if you would just step this way out to the balcony, you'll be able to enjoy the views of the Hemingway gardens and Key West Lighthouse. Then we'll be going down the exterior stairs to the pool."

Laura watched the tourists file through the double-hung doors to the balcony with their cameras and phones raised and ready. She looked down at Nessie. "I guess you'll be skipping this part of the tour. I'll catch up with you later, okay, sweetie?"

This time, Nessie understood what her friend was saying.

She meowed and dashed out of the room—leaving Laura alone with Lucky Leo Trout.

Laura smiled at Leo, who smiled back at her. She wasn't sure if his smile was a happy you-go-girl smile or a condescending you-poor-thing smile. She was afraid to ask. But she had to know.

"How am I doing, boss?"

Leo smiled. "We'll talk later."

Later . . .

Millie Graham watched the last of the tourists stroll down the garden path to the front gate. Some lingered to say good-bye to a pair of cats who were lounging on bistro chairs like sophisticated diners at a Parisian café. Others stopped near the entrance to take one last selfie with Hemingway's house in the background. All of them received a warm smile and friendly wave from Millie, who bid each visitor farewell from the window of her ticket booth.

"I hope you enjoyed your visit!" she said, over and over. "Come back again soon!"

Even though she loved her job, she was glad the day was over. She couldn't stop thinking about the fancy dress that her neighbor Connie lent her—and the fancy hairdo she was going to give her as soon as she got home from work. Millie glanced at her watch.

Five minutes and counting . . .

Margarita Bouffet was watching the clock, too. She sat in her tiny cluttered office behind the Hemingway House gift shop and double-checked her appointments, making sure everything was ready for Dance Night. The party rental truck was scheduled to arrive in fifteen minutes to set up tables and chairs around the wooden dance floor in the side yard. Margarita prayed they'd show up on time—so she could rush home to do her hair and makeup and accessories. Then she had to rush back here to meet the caterers, who were scheduled for seven-thirty, along with Jake and Laura.

"Oh, Nessie, you know I love a party, but this is just exhausting," she said, before realizing that the cat wasn't there. She peeked under her desk. "Nessie?"

Realizing that the cat was probably with Laura, Margarita decided to go out and see if the rental truck had arrived yet. As she walked through the garden to the front gate, she noticed a cat and two people on one of the benches.

It was Nessie—sitting between Laura and Lucky Leo.

The new guide and her supervisor seemed to be having a serious but friendly discussion, with Leo doing most of the talking. Nessie kept looking from one to the other, as if she was trying to understand what was going on.

"Oh, Nessie, you poor sweet, innocent cat," Margarita muttered to herself. "Stuck in the middle of an employee performance review."

Jake Jacobs finished replenishing the cats' supplies and was about to wash up when he saw Laura saying good night to Lucky Leo. He waited for Leo's bald head to disappear around the corner of the house. Then he waved his arms to get Laura's attention.

She looked over and spotted him, then made a funny face and started staggering toward him like a soldier who'd been shot. Jake laughed.

"So? The reviews are in?" he asked. "Is the show a hit? Did you get a standing ovation?"

Laura sighed. "It went pretty well, all things considered," she said.

"What does that mean?"

"Well, Leo observed my first and last tours of the day. He said he noticed a big difference between the two, that I was really nervous at first but much more confident by the end."

"That's natural."

"He also said—and I quote—that I was 'exceptionally well prepared' to the point of being 'mechanical.' I need to be more 'relaxed and spontaneous.'"

"That monster. Who does he think he is?"

"I know, right? Anyway, he gave me some very good tips, some tricks of the trade, and some very specific notes. My biggest problem is my timing. I accidentally caused a traffic jam at one point. Two tour groups ended up crammed together on the upper balcony at the same time, which Leo called a 'serious safety hazard.'"

"To hell with that. Make them sign waivers. 'Enter at your own risk.'"

"I'll suggest it to Leo," Laura said, laughing.

Jake was about to make another joke when he noticed Margarita Bouffet at the front gate, waving wildly at a large truck in the street. Obviously something for the party.

He turned back to Laura. "So, I'll be seeing you here later tonight?"

"Yes, you will."

"Ready to bust a move on the dance floor?"

"Yes, I am."

"Dressed appropriately?"

"Dressed appropriately."

"Great! It's a date!"

"Is it, though?"

"No. It's just an expression."

"Is it, though?"

"Say good-bye, Laura."

"Good-bye, Laura."

Chapter 7
"What's New, Pussycat?"

As the sun lowered in the sky, the excitement began to rise.

Everyone on the island—or at least every member of the Key West Dance Club and their ballroom-curious guests—could feel the magic in the air.

Hemingway's cats felt it, too.

Something special was happening tonight, and the cats didn't want to miss it.

Especially the kittens.

Larry, Curly, and Moe had never seen an event like this at the Hemingway House. When the men showed up to arrange tables and chairs around the dance floor, the kittens literally fell all over each other to get a closer look. But once they saw all those table legs and chair legs and human feet moving around, they decided to back off and watch from a distance.

The adolescent cats—like Boxer and Bullfighter—were much bolder. When the sound equipment and party lights were installed, the raucous brothers started swatting at the cables and wires because they looked like snakes slithering across the ground. They weren't, of course, but that didn't stop the brothers from waging war against them.

The elder cats—like Nessie and Pawpa Hemingway—weren't

nearly as curious as the younger cats. They'd seen plenty of parties, weddings, and other events at the house, so this was nothing new. But that didn't stop Nessie and Pawpa from positioning themselves at key vantage points in the yard. They wanted to see everything—even though they pretended to be bored.

Kilimanjaro, as usual, acted like she was above it all. She found the perfect perch on the second-floor balcony where she could look down at everyone through the wrought-iron railing. She was joined there by Lady Bratt Ashley, who abandoned her coveted spot on Hemingway's bed to see what was going on. Below them on the dance floor, the black-and-gray-striped kitten Spinderella was having a ball, running, slipping, and sliding across the smooth wood surface.

For some of Hemingway's cats, the party had already started.

Especially Chew-Chew and Whiskey.

These highly skilled cat thieves began plotting their latest heist the moment they saw the bartender and caterers setting up the service tables. The twins knew, from past parties, that they needed to keep a low profile until the humans got up from their tables to dance, leaving their food and drinks unguarded. Because of the tuxedo pattern of their black and white fur, Chew-Chew and Whiskey found it easy to blend in at even the fanciest black-tie affairs—the ones with the fanciest hors d'oeuvres and cocktails. They just had to be patient.

And wait for the right moment to strike.

"Wow! Look at you boys! You're . . . dressed appropriately!"

Jake and Mack stopped fidgeting with the sound system and looked up to see Laura crossing the dance floor. She wore a shimmering electric-blue dress with a semi-sheer bodice and alternating panels of lace in a calf-length skirt that swirled as she walked. Her auburn hair was pinned up for the occasion, and her face positively glowed—thanks to the Crabb sisters' amazing makeup skills.

"Whoa," said Jake. "Who are you?"

"This can't be the new girl from Syracuse, can it?" said Mack.

"Last time I saw you, you were covered with chicken feathers. Don't tell me you had that dress packed in your carry-on."

"Why, this old thing?" said Laura, giving the dress a twirl. "It's Mrs. Crabb's. The twins went a little crazy dressing me up for this. I felt like their guinea pig."

"Well, the Crabb sisters are good with animals," said Mack.

"Yes, I noticed."

Jake glanced briefly at Mack, then pointed at Laura's shoes. "I know diamonds are a girl's best friend, but those shoes are insane," he said, steering the conversation away from the Crabb twins. "You didn't wear those walking here, did you?"

"No," said Laura, holding up a plastic bag. "I brought sneakers. They're not diamonds anyway, they're sequins and rhinestones. I'm still nervous about wearing them, though. Jilly and Jolene insisted."

"They're hard to resist, those girls," said Mack. "Right, Jake?"

Jake shot him a dirty look.

Laura noticed it but decided to change the subject. "Enough about me. What about you two? Jake, you look like a movie star from the forties. Or like James Bond ordering a martini."

"Shaken, not stirred," said Jake, suavely raising an eyebrow.

"And Mack? Holy mackerel! That is the coolest tuxedo jacket I've ever seen. You are a vision in purple. I love it! Did you steal it from the artist formerly known as Prince?"

"I did. Because tonight I'm gonna party like it's 1999." He raised his arms in the air and did a funny little dance.

Laura laughed. "Well, I think you both look incredible."

"I agree!" a voice rang across the yard.

It was Margarita Bouffet—gliding across the dance floor in her slinkiest, steamiest fire-engine-red salsa dress. The fabric hugged her womanly curves in all the right places, and the color matched her brand-new cha-cha shoes and high-gloss lipstick perfectly. But that wasn't all. With her jet-black hair swooped up to one side, an explosion of curls and ringlets cascading onto her shoulder, she no longer looked like the middle-aged manager of the Hemingway House.

She looked like a force of nature.

"Get out the fire hose," Mack muttered.

Jake and Laura were too stunned by Margarita's appearance to say anything at first. Which was fine, since Margarita did all of the talking.

"Just look at you three! I am seriously impressed! When I told you to dress appropriately, I didn't expect anything like this! Jake! My, but you clean up good. In that tux, you look like a young Cary Grant. So debonair. And Mack! You look handsomer than ever, I swear. What did you do? Trim some of that scruff? Whatever you did, I've never seen you look so dashing. Both of you boys are going to have all the ladies swooning!"

Then she turned to Laura, looked her up and down, and sighed.

"Laura, Laura, Laura. I had no idea that our new tour guide was such a beauty queen. That dress, those shoes, that hair . . . exquisite! You could be a Disney princess!"

Laura blushed. "I do feel kind of like Cinderella in this getup."

"Oh, you look magical! If I were your wicked stepmother I'd hide you away somewhere because I couldn't stand the competition. You're going to be the belle of the ball tonight!"

Laura laughed. "Oh, please! Look who's talking! Margarita, you look—pardon my French—hot as *hell*! I mean, *really* hot! Am I right, Jake? Mack?"

"You look amazing, Margarita," said Jake.

"Your best ballroom look yet," said Mack. "It should come with a warning: highly combustible."

Margarita giggled like a schoolgirl and did a quick salsa move. "Thank you, darlings," she said. "I try. Now . . . about the party. Mack, you have the playlist. Jake and Laura, I want you to keep your eyes on the service table. Just refill the food trays when they're low and clear off empty plates from the guest tables from time to time. Right now, you can place the centerpieces on the tables. They're in a box in the lounge. Beyond that, feel free to have a good time and dance the night away. As your boss, I insist."

She winked, smiled, and did some cha-cha steps across the dance floor—which startled Nessie, who was about to cross the floor to say hello to Laura. As soon the cat saw Margarita's cha-cha shoes, she changed her mind and returned to the edge of the yard.

"Oh, look, I scared Nessie," said Margarita. "Sorry, kitty! Which reminds me, Laura. Keep your eyes on the cats tonight. Especially Chew-Chew and Whiskey. They'll steal the food and sip the cock-tails if you let them."

With that, she spun around dramatically and dashed off toward the house, dress swirling, curls tossing, and cats scrambling to get out of her way.

Laura looked at Jake and Mack.

"This has to be the weirdest thing I've ever done," she said.

"Just wait," said Mack. "The night is young."

Thirty minutes later . . .

Things got weirder than Laura ever imagined.

At eight o'clock sharp, Mack cranked up the dance music—playing a little bit of everything from Latin salsas, sambas, and rumbas to Big Band standards, waltzes, and jive—while the guests started pouring in.

The members of the Key West Dance Club were just as eclectic as the music. A wildly diverse assortment of odd but lovable weirdos, the motley crew included sassy senior citizens in drop-dead gor-geous gowns and tuxedos, midlife-crisis baby boomers in flamboy-antly bizarre dance costumes—probably the result of watching too many episodes of *Dancing with the Stars*—and a boisterous bunch of merry millennials dressed in retro swing skirts and revealing Latin dancewear.

Laura couldn't tell if they were being "ironic" or not. But either way, she thought it was all pretty weird *and* wonderful.

"Buona sera, bella donna."

Out of nowhere, a slender young Lothario with slicked-back hair and a silky black shirt—unbuttoned to the waist—reached for

Laura's hand. Before she could respond, he grabbed her hand and kissed it, purring like a movie parody of a gigolo on the Italian Riviera.

She glanced over at Jake, who saw the whole exchange.

He made goofy goo-goo eyes at her and pantomimed ripping his shirt open to expose his chest. She tried not to laugh—because her would-be seducer was still standing right there, waiting for her reply. Luckily, she was saved by a familiar voice. A voice with a strong Jamaican accent—

"Miss Tour Guide! How you doing, girl?"

It was Mama Marley!

In a frilly pink ball gown!

Laura broke out in a grin. "Mama! What a great surprise! I hardly recognized you in that dress. It's gorgeous. You look absolutely stunning."

"I am *so* glad to hear you say that," Mama said, dropping the Jamaican accent. "This dress cost me two weeks of tips. From what I've heard about this party, I figure it's worth the investment. I've been dying to check it out."

"Are you interested in ballroom dancing?"

"I'm interested in finding a man," she said, scanning the crowd.

"Ah," said Laura. "That explains it. I thought you'd never step foot in this place because of all the 'freaky' multi-toed cats with their 'freaky' extra claws."

"Honey, the dating scene in this town is a hell of a lot freakier than any cat. And some of the ladies here got even sharper claws."

Laura chuckled and glanced over at Jake by the food table. He was chatting—and flirting, maybe?—with two young women with killer smiles, killer dresses, and killer bodies . . .

Jilly and Jolene Crabb.

"Oh, look!" said Mama Marley, tugging Laura's arm. "Your bare-chested boyfriend with the greasy hair is kissing another girl's hand!"

Laura turned to see the movie parody of a gigolo cornering some poor girl against a tree. "Oh, him," she groaned. "Thanks, Mama, for rescuing me in the nick of time."

"No problem. I didn't want to see you lose your innocence to a creep like him."

"Oh, please." Laura smirked. "I'm not that innocent."

"Not after that walking petri dish slobbered all over your hand. You should probably get tested tomorrow."

Mama continued scoping out the men at the party. Her eyes panned back and forth until finally fixing on someone on the far side of the dance floor. "Do you know that fine-looking gentleman over there talking to Margarita?"

Laura looked past the dancers to see Margarita at the deejay table, swaying to a salsa song and sipping a cocktail. She was saying something to Mack.

"You mean Mack McCloud? Rooster's nephew?"

Mama scoffed. "Hell, no. He's too young for me. I mean the man in the black suit and tie, to the left of Margarita."

Laura looked again. She glimpsed a man in a black suit, but her view was blocked by a pair of salsa dancers. When they finally shimmied out of the way, she got a better look.

"That's my supervisor! Lucky Leo Trout. You don't know Leo?"

Mama grabbed Laura's arm. "Good God, girl, you're right! I've never seen him dressed up like that before. Every time I've seen Leo, he's wearing one of his stupid golf shirts . . . which I hate."

"Golf or the shirts?"

"Both." Mama tilted her head and squinted her eyes. "Hmmm. I never noticed before, but he's actually quite handsome."

"Lucky Leo? Really?"

"Don't judge."

Mama Marley reached for a glass of champagne on the bar and smiled wickedly.

"If Lucky Leo plays his cards right," she said, "this just might be his lucky night."

★ ★ ★

When the brassy beats of the nineties hit song "Mambo No. 5" came to an end, Margarita Bouffet stepped onto the dance floor and started dinging her cocktail glass with a spoon.

"Attention! Attention, everyone!" she said to the crowd. "I'd like to officially welcome you to the open ballroom party of the Key West Dance Club. My name is Margaret Bouffet, but everyone calls me Margarita. For obvious reasons."

She raised her glass and took a sip. The crowd laughed.

"We're going to start the night off with a little dance review we put together. Our members will be performing samples of the various ballroom dances, starting with the classic fox-trot and Viennese waltz. Then we'll turn up the heat with a Latin samba, the rumba, and the cha-cha. After that, you're all invited to join us on the dance floor for a quick lesson in some of the basic moves. Even if you have two left feet, don't worry about it. The goal is to have fun."

As she spoke, half a dozen beautifully dressed couples took their places on the dance floor. Margarita set her drink down on the deejay table and nodded at Mack, who cued up the music.

"Without further ado, I present to you . . . the Key West Dance Club!"

The crowd held its breath as the dancers stood perfectly still, locked in their poses like department store mannequins. They looked as if they'd been frozen mid-dance. After a long silent pause, the music started—a bright, jaunty rendition of the old standard "Dream a Little Dream of Me"—and the dancers sprang to life. They bounced on their toes and trotted around the floor in unison, like Technicolor copies of Fred Astaire and Ginger Rogers. The crowd burst into applause.

"Are you ready for our number?" a voice whispered in Margarita's ear.

She swallowed her drink and turned to see Foster Lee Jackson—groomed to the gills, as usual, and admittedly resplendent in his mint-green tuxedo and black cummerbund.

"Foster! You made it!" she said with relief. "I was afraid I was going to have to do the cha-cha all by myself out there."

"Never fear, my dear," he crooned. "Foster is here."

Margarita smiled politely, then turned her gaze toward the crowd.

Where is Millie? she wondered. *If I'm going to survive this night, I'm going to need a good wing woman.*

She caught a glimpse of Mama Marley—everyone's favorite cab-driver, looking fabulous in a hot-pink dress that was the same color as her hot-pink cab—over by the food table. It looked like she was flirting with Lucky Leo Trout!

Lucky Leo? Really?

Margarita shook her head and chuckled to herself. As the music segued from the fox-trot to the waltz, the first group of dancers gave up the floor to other members of the club—a charming collection of seniors and boomers who swirled and twirled gracefully to the tune of Bryan Adams's "Have You Ever Really Loved a Woman?" The crowd clapped and swooned.

That's when Margarita spotted the thieves.

Chew-Chew and Whiskey.

Chew-Chew was standing on one of the guest chairs, nibbling hors d'oeuvres off an abandoned plate. Whiskey was up on the table, drinking from a highball glass of what appeared to be Seagram on the rocks.

"At least he can handle his liquor," Margarita muttered. "Hemingway would be proud."

She waved across the dance floor at Laura, who was watching the dancers alongside Jake, the Crabb sisters, and two tall blond young men—probably the Crabb sisters' dates. Margarita waved again until she caught Laura's attention. Then she nodded toward the cats.

Laura saw them, nodded back at Margarita, and shooed the cats off the table.

"You look ravishing tonight, I must say."

Margarita glanced at Foster Lee Jackson, who had somehow

moved closer to her without her even noticing. "Thank you, Foster," she said. "I was saving this dress for tonight."

Foster smiled dreamily. "It's perfect for you. I believe red is definitely your color. If you don't mind my saying, you're a knockout."

"Thank you, Foster."

He cleared his throat. "I just wish you had told me you were wearing red. I could have coordinated our outfits better, for the cha-cha number."

"You look great, Foster."

"I do? Well, that's mighty gracious of you."

Margarita sucked in her breath. *Where are you, Millie?*

The waltz music faded. The guests applauded and the dancers took their bows. Now it was time for the spicier part of the program. The Latin samba dancers, dressed in bright, florid colors, took their places on the dance floor. Mack cued up the music and cranked up the volume. The song was Gloria Estefan's "Rhythm Is Gonna Get You." The dancers were on fire. And the crowd went totally crazy.

Which scared the Hemingway kittens.

Laura nudged Jake and pointed across the yard at Larry, Curly, Moe, and Spinderella. The little cats were hightailing it out of the garden as fast as they could.

"I guess they're afraid the rhythm is gonna get them," said Jake.

"I think it already did," said Laura. "Poor little kittens."

"Gloria Estefan tried to warn them."

Laura laughed, then noticed Nessie watching her from across the yard. She waved at her old friend. Nessie swished her tail in response. Then Laura noticed Pawpa a few feet behind Nessie. He seemed to be watching them both.

"So this is the Hemingway place, huh?"

One of the Crabb sisters' dates—Brad or Chad or something like that—pointed to the house and looked at Laura.

"Yep, this is the place," she said.

"He's that writer guy, isn't he?" asked his brother. "Didn't he write *Of Mice and Men*?"

Laura shot a glance at Jake, who tried not to laugh.

"No, that's John Steinbeck. Ernest Hemingway wrote *The Sun Also Rises*, *For Whom the Bell Tolls*, *The Old Man and the Sea*—"

"Never heard of them."

"Hey, Chad, check out the cats! Here, kitty kitty. . . ."

The blond brothers took off after Nessie and Pawpa, who scampered away when they saw them coming. "Wait up, kitties!"

Jilly and Jolene looked at Laura and Jake and shrugged.

"Let me guess," said Laura. "Those are the cute college guys from Kansas?"

"Yeah," said Jolene. "They're not exactly brain surgeons, are they?"

"No," said Jilly. "But they're studying to be lawyers."

Laura shot a look at Jake, then turned her attention to the dance floor. A group of sexy rumba dancers were moving seductively to the song "Wicked Game" by Chris Isaak. The Crabb sisters started swaying along with the music—even more seductively than the dancers—which seemed to lure the Kansas college boys back from their cat-hunting safari. The boys snuck up behind the sisters and wrapped their arms around them. The girls didn't seem to mind.

I wonder if they can tell the twins apart, Laura thought. *Or if it even matters.*

As the sultry music ebbed and flowed, slowly building in feverish intensity, Laura gazed across the dance floor at the deejay table.

Mack was staring at her.

The look in his deep brown eyes startled her. She wasn't sure why. Maybe it was because he looked so lost—lost in his own thoughts—and those thoughts were focused on her. Laura returned Mack's gaze. It was a gaze full of sadness, curiosity, and . . . longing?

Laura didn't know how to react. So she broke into a smile.

And broke the spell.

"Look!" said Jake. "Margarita is up next!"

Laura shifted her focus back on the dancers. Margarita and Foster positioned themselves on the dance floor with four other couples.

Mack fumbled with the sound equipment and cued up the track—a Cuban-flavored version of "Lady Marmalade."

The music kicked off with a steamy *one-two cha-cha-cha*. The pulsating rhythm of the song—raucous and irresistible—seemed to surge through the dancers' bodies like a jolt of electricity. Their feet shimmied; their hips swayed. The crowd went wild.

Margarita went wilder.

"Look at her go!" Jake gasped. "She's fantastic!"

"Girl can dance," said Mama Marley, grabbing Lucky Leo by the arm.

Laura watched in amazement as Margarita Bouffet—her boss!—tore up the dance floor. Her partner, Foster Lee Jackson, was surprisingly good, too. Especially for a man who looked as buttoned-up and stuffy as he did. Laura broke out grinning and started clapping along to the music. The Crabb sisters cheered.

"Go, Margarita, go!"

After several scorching minutes of red-hot, go-for-broke dancing, the song reached its boiling point. With a final dramatic flourish, the dancers stopped dead in their tracks—each couple frozen in wildly suggestive poses. The crowd went nuts.

"Margarita! You are the queen!"

Mama Marley and the Crabb twins rushed onto the dance floor, dragging Laura along with them. They rushed up to Margarita and hugged her, jumping up and down and showering her with praise.

"That was so amazing! I can't believe how amazing that was!"

"Can you teach us? I want to do that, too!"

Margarita laughed. "Of course I can teach you. That's what this party is all about." She turned to the crowd. "Everybody, listen up! Now it's *your* turn to dance! Don't be shy; we'll show you the steps. Girls, grab a partner!"

She looked straight at Jake and Lucky Leo.

"Boys, let's cha-cha!"

Rooster McCloud stood outside the front gate of the Hemingway House, trying to work up the courage to go inside.

What's wrong with you, old bird? he asked himself. *You showered. You shaved. You're all dressed up with someplace to go. So what's the problem?*

He could see the party lights from the sidewalk. He could hear the music and laughter echoing through the garden. He could even feel the excitement in the air. *The rhythm of the night.* It was infectious. Even the palm trees were swaying to the beat.

Rooster adjusted his tie—for the hundredth time—and wondered if maybe it was the spiffy suit that made him feel like a teen-aged boy, self-conscious and full of doubt.

Never doubt the Rooster. Remember that?

He gazed thoughtfully at the Spanish colonial grandeur of the Hemingway House, with its wraparound balcony and wrought-iron railings and prowling polydactyl cats. The cats seemed friskier than usual. They wandered restlessly back and forth in the yard— obviously hyped up from the pounding music and dancing revelers who'd invaded their turf. Rooster didn't blame them for being a little miffed.

Sometimes a cat just wanted to be left alone.

He watched the felines for another minute, his eyes settling on a grumpy old gray cat sitting and sulking on the corner of the front porch.

It was Pawpa Hemingway.

He looked absolutely miserable.

Is that what I look like? Rooster wondered. *A grumpy old miserable cat who frumps and frowns on the sidelines while everyone else is having fun?*

He thought about Margarita. Her smile. Her eyes. Her genu- inely warm greetings every morning as she passed his lighthouse on her way to work: *What's new, pussycat?* They'd shared a lot of laughs together over the years—and more than a few of Margarita's namesake cocktails. She practically helped him raise Mack after the boy's crazy mother dropped him off with his uncle Rooster and then disappeared forever. Margarita was a true friend. But . . . was that all she was to him? Was it possible, after all these years, they could be more than just friends?

He took another look at grumpy old Pawpa sulking on the porch.

There's only one way to find out.

Taking a deep breath—and readjusting his tie—Rooster walked through the front gate of the Hemingway House. And joined the party.

"One-two cha-cha-cha, one-two cha-cha-cha . . . that's it! You've got it!"

Margarita clapped her hands and stood back to watch her "students" on the dance floor. The Crabb sisters swung their hips provocatively in perfect time with the music, the frills on their tight yellow dresses swishing wildly with every beat. This wasn't their first time at the ball. Their dates, however, seemed a little lost. But so what. The tall Kansas boys gave it the old college try, using any excuse to press up against the twins. To Margarita's delight, Laura and Jake were doing surprisingly well. Sure, Jake stepped on Laura's feet a few times. But that didn't seem to bother them. They just laughed it off and kept dancing—with Laura throwing in an occasional "one-two cha-cha-cha" to keep Jake on the beat. It was adorable.

But the ones who really surprised her? Mama Marley and Lucky Leo!

"Go, *mamacita*! Go!"

Margarita couldn't help but cheer them on.

For one thing, Lucky Leo was a veteran of these parties and already knew how to cha-cha. He was also lucky enough to have good rhythm, which was half the battle. In the past, Margarita had seen Leo master some pretty tricky dance moves. But tonight . . . wow. He really stepped up his game. And it was easy to see why. . . .

Mama Marley was on fire.

With her high-powered charisma and turbo-charged cha-cha moves, she commanded the dance floor as if she'd been performing like this her whole life. She grabbed Leo by the tie and pulled him to the middle of the dance floor. The others had to give them extra room—because Mama wasn't fooling around. She popped her hips and pouted her lips and pressed up against Leo teasingly, then spun away like a fireball. Leo loved every second of it.

And so did the crowd. They clapped and cheered through the entire dance.

"My, my, Ms. Marley is really quite good, isn't she?"

It was Foster Lee Jackson, breathing down Margarita's neck.

"It's hard to believe she's a cabdriver," he continued. "I'd swear she must have had professional dance training, though that seems unlikely. She's from Jamaica, no?"

"No. Chicago."

"Oh." Foster cleared his throat. "Well, anyway, the deejay told me that the next song is a tango. I would be delighted if you would honor me with a dance."

Margarita tried to look Foster in the eye—but she couldn't help notice the beautiful blonde standing behind him.

"Millie? Millie Graham? Is that you?"

"Yes! It's me! Can you believe it?"

"No! I can't! I can't believe it!"

Foster Lee Jackson spun around to see whom Margarita was talking to—and found himself face-to-face with the most ravishing creature he'd ever seen. Her shining blond hair was swept up in an elegant swirl at the top of her head. Seemingly random but perfectly placed curls tumbled down tastefully to frame the soft, delicate features of her face. She positively glowed. Her makeup was exquisite—not overdone like the "painted ladies" his mother warned him against. Her pale rose lipstick and blush brought out the blue in her eyes. And her dress—oh, my. It was perfection. A mint-green confection of taffeta and lace, both swirly and sexy, it revealed just the right amount of feminine curves—but left so much more to the imagination.

Foster was utterly enchanted. Her dress matched his tuxedo!

"You remember Millie, don't you, Foster?"

"Millie Graham," said the vision in green, extending her hand. "Ticket booth manager."

Foster reached for her hand—and kissed it.

Margarita was thrilled. "Doesn't Millie look fabulous? I didn't even recognize her!"

"I was wondering when you would," said Millie. "Both of you walked right past me three times tonight! Like I was a stranger!"

"Oh, dear, please forgive us, Miss Millie," said Foster. "Ms. Bouffet and I were distracted." He glanced at Margarita.

She wiggled her eyebrows at him and nodded toward the dance floor.

Foster got the message.

"Miss Millie, would you honor me with a dance?" he asked in his most charming voice. "In the immortal words of the Bard, 'I do desire we may be better strangers.'"

"Hemingway?"

"Shakespeare. Shall we?"

"Sure! I mean, we shall!"

Foster extended his hand, Millie took it in hers—and Margarita sighed with relief. She watched the hilariously mismatched pair walk to the dance floor in their matching mint-green eveningwear. If only their personalities matched as well as their outfits, Margarita would be off the hook. She wasn't sure how much more of Foster's fawning and leering she could take.

I hope this works, she thought, watching the couple assume a classic tango starting position. *I hate having to give a man the "I don't want to ruin our friendship" talk.*

The music started—a lusty instrumental version of "Hernando's Hideaway"—and the dancers came alive. The couples moved catlike across the floor, step by step, hand in hand, cheek to cheek. Foster held Millie tightly, smoothly guiding her through each seductive step. Margarita had to admit, Foster knew how to take the lead. And Millie, to her surprise, had some tricks of her own up her mint-green sleeves.

Margarita felt a sense of relief—and something else. She sensed someone standing behind her, watching her. Then she heard a low growly voice:

"What's new, pussycat?"

She turned around. And gasped.

Rooster McCloud—or some parallel universe version of Rooster McCloud—stood before her. Dressed in a perfectly fitted, stunningly gorgeous, silver sharkskin tuxedo with sleek black lapels, silver vest and pants, crisp white shirt, and black satin tie, he looked like he'd just stepped off a wedding cake—or out of a dream.

Even more shocking, his long hair and scraggly beard were gone.

"Rooster? Is that really you?"

Margarita stared in disbelief. His ruggedly handsome face—exposed for the first time in decades—was mostly clean-shaven except for a thick, trimmed mustache and rakish five o'clock shadow that only made him look handsomer. His salt-and-pepper hair was chopped to a medium length, the tousled locks of silver complementing the ocean-blue color of his eyes. When he saw the look on Margarita's face, he broke out in a dazzling smile.

"I can't believe it," she said. "You look like George Clooney!"

"Darn. I was going for Sam Elliott." Rooster struck a manly pose and stroked his mustache. "Do you care to dance?"

"Really?"

"Really. I dance a mean paso doble."

"You do?" Margarita was dumbstruck. She held up a finger, then dashed off to the deejay table. After saying a few words to Mack and the other dance club members, she turned around and motioned to Rooster. He smiled and joined them on the edge of the dance floor.

When the tango music ended, Margarita made an announcement to the crowd.

"Ladies and gentlemen, we have a special treat tonight. In honor of the great Ernest Hemingway, we will be dancing the paso doble. Hemingway, as you know, was a big fan of bullfighting. He wrote about it in *The Sun Also Rises* and *The Dangerous Summer*. Well, the paso doble is like bullfighting in dance form. One partner plays the role of the bullfighter. The other is the bull or the matador's cape. Sometimes it can be hard to tell which is which—or who wins the fight. But if all is fair in love and war, the same holds true . . . on the dance floor!"

With a snap of her fingers, the dancers took their places. Margarita turned to Rooster, her eyes sparkling. She lifted her arms as if holding an imaginary red cape, daring him to make the next move. The crowd gathered closer around the dance floor. A hush fell over the entire party. Then the music began—breaking the tension with the dramatic opening chords of the classic Cuban guitar song "Malagueña."

Rooster charged onto the dance floor like a wild animal.

And swept Margarita into his arms.

The crowd went crazy.

"Wait, is that Rooster McCloud?" Laura whispered to Jake.

"It can't be," he said, staring in amazement. "But it is! It's Rooster!"

Laura glanced at the other guests to see their reactions. Jolene and Jilly, Mama and Leo, Millie and Foster—everyone at the party had the same stunned look on their faces. When Rooster spun Margarita around, forcefully and masterfully, then dipped her backward down to the floor, all of their jaws dropped. Literally.

Laura looked over at the deejay table.

Mack was slack-jawed, too.

She turned her attention back to Rooster and Margarita. As the music grew more intense, so did their dancing. Rooster pulled her toward him. Margarita pushed him away. Back and forth, they waged a fiery battle of wills on the dance floor, two fierce opponents each locked in an escalating fight for control over the other. It was passionate. It was powerful. It was positively thrilling.

It was also sexy as hell.

Watching them dance, Laura felt a flutter of excitement rush through her. Then she felt something else: the tickle of fur against her leg. She looked down.

"Nessie! Are you seeing this?"

Reaching down, she picked up the golden-striped cat and held her in her arms. Nessie stared with wide-eyed wonder at Margarita and Rooster as they stomped and lunged and swirled across the dance floor. Nessie meowed once, then twice, then swished her tail. "Look at them go, Nessie," Laura whispered in her ear. "Did you know they could do that?"

Nessie knew Margarita could dance—and she knew to stay out of the way when Margarita put on her cha-cha shoes.

But she didn't know that the old human male could move like that.

Or look like that. He was shiny! And beardless!

If it hadn't been for her feline sense of smell, Nessie never would have recognized him.

Suddenly the music swelled to a feverish pitch.

Margarita spun around dramatically and grabbed the sides of her dress. Glaring at Rooster with dark smoldering eyes, she took a deep breath—and charged straight toward him. Swishing her dress wildly from side to side, she moved like a stalking predator closing in on its prey. Rooster tried to step aside. But she was too fast. She grabbed him by the arm and pulled him against her body. She ran her fingers up and down his neck, pulling him closer still. Their lips almost touched as they stared hungrily into each other's eyes. Then—as the music reached a sizzling climax—she pushed him to the floor and waved her imaginary cape, declaring victory. Rooster surrendered willingly to defeat, gazing up at his conqueror with eyes full of fire and longing. Then came the finishing stroke:

Margarita placed the heel of a cha-cha shoe on Rooster's chest—like a big-game hunter posing with her prize—and raised her arm in triumph.

The music ended. The crowd roared.

The party was a success.

As soon as the guests started leaving, Laura started cleaning up. Throughout the night, she'd been clearing away plates and glasses, so the final cleanup was pretty easy.

The hard part was keeping the cats away from the leftovers.

Especially Chew-Chew and Whiskey.

Laura could swear those two planned their heists with the kind of timing and precision you'd see in an Ocean's Eleven movie. As soon as Laura shooed Chew-Chew away from one table, Whiskey hopped onto another a few tables away. They made a great team.

While Laura stacked the plates in a bus tray, she kept one eye on the departing guests. Mama Marley left with Lucky Leo, Millie Graham left with Foster Lee Jackson, and the Crabb sisters left with their dates. Wishing them all good night on their way out was Margarita Bouffet—with Rooster by her side.

That's a lot of love connections for one night, Laura thought, picking up a glass. *What did they put in these drinks?*

She looked toward the deejay table. Jake and Mack were busy packing up the sound equipment. Jake saw her looking. He stopped what he was doing and crossed the dance floor. He had a funny look on his face.

"Laura, I feel bad about this, but I told Mack that I'd help him load up his van and take the sound equipment to our bandmate's garage. We're rehearsing there tomorrow."

Laura was confused. "Why do you feel bad about that?"

"Oh." Jake blushed a little. "I thought maybe I could walk you home tonight."

"That's okay. I'm a big girl. I can find my way home."

"I know, but, you know, you're new here and it's after dark—"

"It's no problem."

"Okay then." Jake turned and walked back to Mack.

Laura placed the last plate in the bus tray and flopped down in a chair. She looked over at the boys. Mack was looking back at her. She smiled. He smiled. Then Laura's cell phone dinged. She dug her phone out of her purse and looked.

Another text from Devin: *We really need to talk. PLEASE?*

Laura sighed and turned off her phone. She glanced back at Jake and Mack, then saw Nessie padding toward her. Without missing a beat, the cat jumped onto her lap and arched her back—an obvious ploy to get Laura to stroke her. Laura obliged.

"Tell me something, Nessie," she said, petting the cat softly from head to tail. "Just between us girls. Are cat boys as weird as human boys?"

If Nessie knew the answer, she wasn't talking.

Just purring.

Chapter 8
The Old Cat and the Sea

One week and three days later . . .

Pawpa Hemingway was still sulking.

The grumpy old cat had been watching the new girl—and Nessie along with her—every time the girl came to the house. Mostly in the mornings and afternoons. He thought maybe he could figure out why Nessie was drawn to this human.

But the more Pawpa watched them, the grumpier he got.

Today, like most days, he hid under a flowering shrub as Nessie greeted the new girl at the front gate. He observed their new morning ritual: Nessie sitting on the girl's lap on a garden bench while the girl sipped a cup of the bitter brown water. Then he followed them to the front of the house, where a small group of humans gathered around them. He watched the girl talk to the group for a while. Then—with Nessie by her side—the new girl led the humans inside the house, still talking as she guided them from room to room, pointing to pictures on the wall and other objects on display. This wasn't anything unusual. Pawpa had seen the other tour guides do this many times over the years.

What was unusual was Nessie's reaction to the pool.

When the new girl led the group of humans down the balcony stairs to the pool area, Nessie took off running. She did this every day. She'd run as fast as she could past the pool and dash up the stairs to the upper room of the pool house, where she'd wait for the new girl.

It didn't make any sense to Pawpa. It only added to the mystery.

And it was driving him crazy.

The old gray cat ducked behind a tree and watched the new girl as she led the other humans to the end of the pool. The girl smiled and laughed as she spoke. The humans smiled and laughed along with her. They seemed to like the new girl. *Everyone* seemed to like the new girl.

But not Pawpa.

Pawpa needed to know more about this human before he could trust her. She acted so nice when she was here—chatting with the other humans and petting the other cats—but where did she go after that? What did she do when she left the Hemingway House?

Pawpa was determined to find out. Even if it meant stalking her . . .

Beyond these garden walls.

Laura snuck up behind Jake in the cat supply storage room and—raising her hands like claws—gave her best imitation of a cat screech. Jake jumped and spun around.

"Oh, jeez, Laura! You almost gave me a heart attack!"

"Did you think I was a cat?"

"No. That did not sound like a cat. I thought maybe a seagull got in here somehow."

"Oh. I'll have to work on that."

"Well, you'll find plenty of teachers around here." He nodded toward a moody-looking cat peering at them from the doorway. "Right, Jackie Chan?"

The cat hissed at Jake and ran off.

Laura laughed. "Jackie Chan! What a great name for a cat!"

"Yeah," said Jake, pulling a large bag of cat food from the shelf. "Most of the cats around here are named after movie stars. Hemingway started that tradition."

"Yes, I've seen the headstones in the cat cemetery. Kim Novak, Liz Taylor, Willard Scott . . ."

She continued listing famous names as she followed Jake out of the storage room.

"But wait," she said. "What about Nessie and Pawpa, and Boxer and Bullfighter, and Kilimanjaro and Lady Bratt . . . ?"

Jake dropped the bag of food next to the cats' feeding trays and turned back to Laura. "The staff gets to vote on the names," he explained. "A few years ago, they decided it was okay to have some non-celebrity names as long as they were Hemingway related. I heard a rumor that it all started when someone suggested the name Kim Kardashian and the rest of the staff rebelled. I'm not sure that's true, though. You'll have to ask Millie."

"I will. Millie knows everything. She told me so herself."

Jake chuckled and nodded, then glanced at his watch. "So, um, I don't mean to be rude, but shouldn't you be working now?"

"My tour group canceled. They heard a big storm was coming, but . . ." Laura looked up at the sunny sky and shrugged. "So now I have a free hour. Leo suggested I use the time to pick the brains of my fellow employees, learn more about the house and the cats. Which is why I'm here."

"To pick my brain? I'm flattered. You think I have a brain?"

"The jury is still out. Anyway, a visitor asked me if all of the cats here were polydactyl. I wasn't sure, because some of the cats seem to have normal-looking paws."

"Yeah, about half the cats have the normal number of toes. But they all carry the polydactyl gene for extra toes because they're all descended from Hemingway's original cat Snow White," Jake explained. "By the way, did you know that some people say the original cat was named Snowball?"

"Maybe Hemingway changed it when he learned his cat was male. Or maybe he didn't want his cat to be named after a Disney princess."

"You never know. He was a real softie for cats."

"Like those two?"

Laura pointed at a pair of brown and white cats fighting over the food tray.

Jake laughed. "That's Bette Davis and Joan Clawford. They're always swiping at each other."

"So tell me more about the polydactyl gene. I'm interested. Really." Laura took a seat on a bench and leaned forward.

Jake joined her. "Well, it's a rare genetic mutation but completely harmless. In fact, it gives the cats certain advantages over other cats. The extra claws make them better mousers. Some people say they bring good luck. The sea captain who gave Hemingway his first cat had a bunch of them on board. He said their big paws gave them better footing for walking on ships."

"They had cats on their ships?"

"Yes, to kill the rats."

"Ew."

"Anyway, the polydactyl gene doesn't result in extra toes in all of the cats who have it, or on all of their feet either. Most of the polydactyls only have extra toes on their front paws. It's rare to see them on all four paws. Either way, any cat with the polydactyl gene will pass it on to their descendants."

"Where did all these descendants come from?"

"Well, as Hemingway put it, 'One cat just leads to another.'"

"I mean, the original litter. Who did Snow White breed with?"

"Hemingway's neighbor had a whole slew of cats. Snow White must have gotten frisky with at least a few of them. Over the years, the cats migrated from the neighbor's house to Hemingway's house and started interbreeding. That's how the polydactyl gene got passed down from generation to generation. They all have it now. Even the ones with normal-looking toes."

"Fascinating . . . oh, hi, Nessie!"

Nessie had been checking out the food trays but decided to wait until Bette Davis and Joan Clawford were finished with their cat fight. She hopped up on the bench and sat down between Laura and Jake. Laura gave her a couple strokes and was about to ask Jake another question about cat genetics when her phone rang.

"Oh! It's Jolene. Sorry, I have to take this."

Laura stood up and walked across the path, leaving Jake alone with Nessie on the bench. He looked at the cat and smiled. The cat looked back at him and blinked. Then they both turned their heads and looked at Laura chatting on the phone.

"No, that's fine. I'll ask him. . . . Great. See you later then." She clicked off her phone and returned to the bench.

Jake noticed a strange little smile on her face. "What's up? How's Jolene?"

"She and Jilly are taking me out snorkeling on their sailboat after work. I'm pretty psyched. I've never snorkeled before. Snorkeled? What a funny word. Anyway, they asked me to ask you if you'd like to come along."

Jake hesitated. "Well, um . . . I don't know. Sometimes I get a little seasick."

"Come on! It'll be fun. The coral reefs! The Crabb twins! In bikinis!"

"I don't have a bathing suit. I'd have to run home and change first."

"No, you don't. Just wear the shorts you're wearing now."

Jake sighed and shrugged. "Okay, sure. Why not."

"Great!" said Laura. "It's a date!"

Jake looked at her. "Is it, though?"

Later that day . . .

At the WKEY Radio station—also known as Rooster's garage—the final song of a classic rock block slowly faded out. And an old familiar voice weighed in.

"That was Key West's own Jimmy Buffett and his smash-hit song from 1978, 'Cheeseburger in Paradise.' This is your humble deejay Rooster McCloud, finishing up a two-hour nonstop block of wall-to-wall classic rock. I hope you're enjoying this beautiful day. It looks like that tropical storm we were warned about decided to head to Texas instead. Bad news for Texas, but great news for Key West. You can hear more about that after these messages from our sponsors. Coming up next is your trusted friend Shelly with the weather."

Rooster turned off his microphone and hit play on a prerecorded set of commercials. He got up from his chair and opened the door to the deejay booth. Shelly—the radio station's ninety-four-year-old "don't call me weather girl"—was sitting outside the booth on a folding lawn chair, hunched over her laptop, and looking very, very worried.

"Shelly, what's wrong?"

"I don't like the look of this," she said flatly. "I don't like it one bit."

"What?"

"Tropical Storm Sally. She isn't heading to Texas. The meteorologists got it wrong. She's heading for the Florida Panhandle. There's an air mass from the north that's changing her course. It's happening really fast, too. I've never seen anything like it."

"Is she going to hit us here?"

"No, but we're going to feel it," she said. "We're going to feel it real bad."

Rooster sighed and rubbed his eyes. "Well, you're on air in sixty seconds. You can warn people about it."

Shelly stood up and stepped into the deejay booth. "Yes, I can. And I will. But look at the time, Rooster." She pointed at the clock. "People are about to head out on sunset cruises now. If they sail out too far and get caught in a squall, well . . ."

She reached for the microphone, paused, and looked Rooster in the eye.

". . . they might not make it back."

It was still a couple of hours until sunset.

But that didn't stop the sun from putting on a show.

It hung over the gulf like a fiery red chandelier inside a vast aquamarine ballroom with pink and orange clouds painted on the ceiling—the perfect canvas for a dazzling display. The colors spilled across the sky in broad, billowy streaks, blending and deepening with every stroke of the sun's rays. In the distance a dark violet slash of angry-looking clouds sat glowering on the horizon line, adding drama and contrast to the brightly hued palette.

It was really something to see.

And everyone came to see it.

Tourists and locals alike flocked to the northwest coast of the island to catch a glimpse of this wildly impressionistic artwork in progress. Even some gypsy chickens flocked to the docks—though Laura suspected they were coming after *her*, not checking out the view.

"They're following me," she said to Jake as they passed a small group of chickens on their way to the pier.

"Who?" he asked. "The gypsy chickens?"

"Yes. I swear those are the same birds that attacked me."

"Maybe we should ask the Key West cops to round up the usual suspects. Then you can pick them out of a lineup."

"Seriously, Jake," she said, glancing over her shoulder. "I have a funny feeling we're being followed."

"By chickens?"

"No." She laughed. "I mean, I don't know. Never mind. I'm being paranoid."

"Just because you're paranoid doesn't mean they're not following you."

Jake stopped suddenly and gazed around at the other people on the pier. Then he looked straight at Laura.

"Just promise me this. If things turn ugly and the beaks come out, don't worry about me. Save yourself."

"Shut up."

"Just keep running and don't look back. I'll try to hold them off as long as I can."

"Stop."

"Wait for me at the rendezvous point. If I'm not there in five minutes, leave without me."

"Okay, I get it. I'm being ridiculous."

"Look!" said Jake, pointing to the end of the pier. "There's our getaway boat!"

Laura shielded her eyes from the sun and scanned the row of sailboats tied to the docks.

"Where?"

Then she spotted Jilly and Jolene, waving from the deck of *The Jolly Crabb.*

"Ahoy, mateys!"

The sight of her gorgeous roommates—in matching yellow bikinis—took Laura's breath away. The sunlight glistening on their tanned skin, the sea breeze wafting through their long, dark hair, the sails billowing behind them . . .

They looked like an ad campaign for the Key West tourism board.

"Ahoy, roomies!" Laura shouted back. "Permission to come aboard?"

"Of course," said Jilly. "Get your butt up here."

"And get out of those work clothes," said Jolene. "It's party time!"

Jilly held up a large silver thermos. "I made margaritas!"

Jolene saw the surprise on Laura's face. "Don't worry," she said. "I'm the designated driver. I'm not drinking."

Jake gave Laura a hand climbing aboard the boat, then joined her on deck. Jolene gave Laura a quick rundown. "So this is *The Jolly Crabb.* It's a Tartan Thirty-Seven, thirty-seven feet long, with a teak cockpit and two single berths below. It's got a diesel engine, electric and manual bilge pumps, and a battened mainsail with furling genoa and spinnaker."

Laura nodded and grinned. "I have absolutely no idea what you just said, but I love this boat! It's beautiful! I can't believe you can actually sail this thing."

"Believe it," a male voice chimed in.

Laura turned around to see Mack McCloud climbing up the steps from the cabin below. He was wearing tropical flowered board shorts—and nothing else.

Except a lot of colorful tattoos.

They wrapped around his lean-muscled arms and legs like sea

monsters from the deep. Some of them, in fact, *were* sea monsters from the deep. Large, menacing squids and whales, octopuses and jellyfish—and something that looked like the legendary kraken— swirled among gorgeously detailed images of shipwrecks, fishnets, and treasure chests.

"Mack?" Laura tried not to stare at his tattoos. Or his body. "I didn't know you were coming."

"Yeah, Mack," said Jake. "I thought you were manning the lighthouse for Rooster."

Mack shrugged. "He gave me the night off."

"And I invited him," said Jilly, holding up the thermos. "Who's ready for a margarita?"

As Jilly filled three plastic cups for her guests, Jolene leaned over the side of the boat to grab the mooring line. She started to untether it but then stopped.

"Hey, guys . . . ? I think somebody followed you here."

Laura shot Jake a look. They crossed the deck and stood next to Jolene. She pointed to something on the dock.

"Isn't that one of the Hemingway cats?" she asked.

Laura and Jake gasped simultaneously when they saw who it was. Pawpa Hemingway.

The old gray cat was crouched down on the gray wooden pier, about thirty feet away from them. Just staring.

"That's crazy," Jake murmured.

"That's Pawpa," Laura added. "I told you we were being fol- lowed."

Jake shook his head. "Unbelievable. In his younger days, Pawpa used to sneak off to go fishing in Rick and Ricardo's goldfish pond. It drove them nuts. But he hasn't done that in years. And as far as I know, he's never strayed this far from home."

"What are we going to do?"

Jake sighed. "I guess I'll have to take him back to the Heming- way House." He turned and looked at Jolene. "Do I have time to do that? Can you guys wait for me?"

Jolene glanced at the sun and sucked in her breath. "Ah, I'd rather not wait much longer. We really should leave now if we want to sail out to the reef and make it back before dark."

"And what about that tropical storm?" said Jilly. "We don't want to get caught out there if it heads our way."

"It won't," said Jolene. "I checked the weather earlier and they said it's heading west. Even so, we should leave now."

Laura looked at Jake. "Couldn't we bring him along?"

Jake sighed. "I don't know. It seems risky. If anyone at the house finds out . . ."

"I won't tell."

"Me neither," said Mack. "Come on, Jake. He'll be fine. Look at him. He came all the way out on this pier. He's obviously not afraid of the water. If you don't believe me, just ask Rick and Ricardo's goldfish."

Jake snorted, then let out another heavy sigh. "Okay," he said after a long pause. "But I can't believe we're doing this."

As Jake climbed onto the pier to lure Pawpa onto the boat, Jolene led Laura down to the cabin below so she could change into her swimsuit.

"This is so cozy down here," said Laura, eyeing up the paneled walls and clever little compartments. "I love all this wood."

"It's teak," said Jolene. "Look, I want to say that I'm sorry if having Mack here is awkward for you. Inviting him was Jilly's idea."

"Awkward? Why would it be awkward?"

Jolene gave her a funny look. "Because they both like you! Duh."

"They do? Both of them?"

"Of course they do! And who could blame them? You're smart, you're funny, you're pretty . . . and you're the new girl in town."

"Ha." Laura turned around and started undressing.

"I'm gonna let you in on a little secret about Key West," Jolene continued. "It sucks to be single here. This is a resort town with just a handful of locals who stay year round. Most of the people who come here are tourists. They visit for a few days, maybe a week or two; then they leave. Which is fine if you're like Jilly, who loves to sample everything on the menu without actually ordering anything."

Laura laughed and stepped into her one-piece swimsuit.

"If you're looking for a long-term relationship, well, good luck. Young, eligible, single people don't come to live here permanently very often. You're the rare exception. And a hot commodity, too, I might add. That swimsuit looks great on you!"

Laura blushed. "Thanks. I like it better than the frilly pink one my mom picked out."

"The blue is perfect. The boys will love it. I just hope they don't start fighting over you."

"Oh, come on."

"Well, they've been best friends forever. I think they're just waiting to see which one of them you like better before making a move. You know what that means, don't you? You're the one in control here. You can take your pick. Or not. It's up to you."

Laura scoffed. "I'm still just getting to know them. So far, I like them both."

Jolene smiled wickedly. "That's an option, too," she said.

The boat made a sudden lurch, throwing Laura off-balance. Jolene grabbed her by the arm to keep her from falling.

"We're pushing off," she said. "Come on, let's join the others. You can leave your stuff down here so it doesn't roll around on deck." She led Laura to the cabin steps but stopped before heading up. "Remember, Laura. You're in control."

Laura laughed. "I don't feel like I'm in control. I never feel like I'm in control."

"That's ridiculous. You took control of your life to move here, didn't you?"

Laura thought about it. "Yeah. I guess I did."

"Well, don't stop now. There are two hot boys up there and a thermos full of margaritas. What are you waiting for?"

"Don't you mean *we*? You and Jilly are still single."

"Us?" Jolene giggled. "Oh, we already dated Jake and Mack. Years ago. So much drama. Come on!" She dashed up the steps.

"Wait, what?"

Pawpa Hemingway was having the time of his life.

With his paws tucked beneath him like an ancient Egyptian sphinx, he gazed out at the sea from the bow of *The Jolly Crabb* as it sliced through the swells toward the sun. From his newly claimed throne, he could see, hear, and feel everything. The water rushing toward him. The wind stroking his face. The waves crashing below him and sails rippling above him.

Pawpa loved it all.

Of course, he wouldn't let the humans know that. He was here on a mission—to see what the new girl was up to—but that didn't mean he couldn't enjoy himself, too. From time to time, he'd look back at the humans on the deck of the boat. They talked and laughed and seemed very happy together. The male humans seemed especially happy to talk and laugh with the new girl—while the other two females spent a lot of time adjusting the sails and turning the big wheel at the back of the boat. Everyone seemed happy and relaxed and contented.

Even Pawpa Hemingway, the grumpiest cat in Key West.

He turned back to look at the sea. The sun was a little lower in the sky now. The clouds on the horizon were a little darker, too—and the boat seemed to be heading straight for them. That was okay with Pawpa. In fact, he found it thrilling.

What had started as a simple reconnaissance mission for the old gray cat was turning out to be something so much more.

A real adventure.

Laura couldn't stop staring at the tentacled sea monster that wrapped around Mack's upper right arm. Ever since they set sail, she'd been trying to stay focused on the gorgeous sea-green water around them. But between Mack's amazing tattoos and Jake's gleaming muscles, it was impossible not to gawk. Besides being incredibly nice and incredibly funny, these boys were incredibly easy on the eyes.

"Is that a kraken?" she asked, touching Mack's arm. "Like in those Greek god movies? 'Release the kraken!'"

He laughed. "Indeed it is. It's the first tattoo I ever got, and still my favorite."

"His uncle Rooster wasn't very happy about it," said Jake.

"I was only fifteen," Mack explained. "But that wasn't what bothered Rooster. He was afraid that I'd waste all my money getting more and more tattoos. He said one of his fellow roadies for Jimmy Buffett got hooked on getting them after his first one. He spent thousands of dollars covering his whole body. It was like an addiction."

"Turns out your uncle was right," said Jake, nodding at Mack's body.

The two of them looked at each other and grinned.

"Never doubt the Rooster!" they said in unison, laughing.

Laura could tell it was an inside joke and was about to ask them for the origin story when Mack jumped up off his beach towel, stretching his long, lanky limbs.

"Well, I'm going to have another margarita and chat with the Crabbs for a while," he said. "If you talk about me when I'm gone—and you will—be kind."

Mack grabbed his cup and crossed the deck to join the twins in the cockpit. As he walked away, Laura got a good look at his massive back tattoo—a finely detailed rendering of the Key West Lighthouse rising above palm trees with a nineteenth-century schooner sailing in the background. Laura had to admit, Mack's tattoos were impressive. She rolled onto her stomach and turned toward Jake. That's when she noticed that he looked a little pale—and queasy.

"Are you okay?" she asked. "Feeling seasick?"

Jake shrugged. "I'm fine. Just a bit nauseous. It'll pass . . . I hope."

Laura gave him a sympathetic look, then turned toward the bow of the boat.

"Check out Pawpa," she said. "He looks like an old sea captain."

Jake chuckled. "Oh, he's loving this. I had a feeling he would. He used to be quite the wildcat in his youth. A real scrapper. Always getting into things. Fights, fishponds, henhouses, you name it . . ."

"How did you lure him onto the boat?"

Jake reached into the leg pocket of his cargo shorts and pulled out a cat treat. "I always carry some extra treats with me. You never know when you'll need them."

"Ingenious." Laura nodded. "Gotta love cargo shorts. They're functional *and* stylish."

"Are you making fun of my shorts?"

"I would never make fun of a man's questionable fashion choices. I'm not that kind of girl. But if I was, I would have to ask you something."

"What?"

"Is that a cat treat in your pocket or are you just glad to see me?"

Jake groaned. "That's bad. You're a bad girl. Ask me something else."

Laura thought for a second. "Oh! I know! I have a cat question for you."

"Shoot."

"Okay, here goes. All of the polydactyl cats in Key West are descended from Hemingway's cat, right?" Jake nodded, and Laura continued: "So . . . that would mean that Tallulah, the cat on my hot tin roof, must have come from the Hemingway House. True?"

"Wait. You have a cat on a hot tin roof?"

"You don't know about Tallulah?"

"Who's Tallulah?"

Laura took a deep breath and told him the whole story: how she was woken up by a midnight visitor scratching on the roof who turned out to be the Crabb sisters' kind-of-sort-of semi-adopted cat—and who looked as if she could be Nessie's twin.

"Her name is Tallulah and she has the exact same fluffy tail and six-toed paws as Nessie," Laura explained. "But her fur is black instead of gold. What do you think, Jake? Could they be related?"

Jake thought about it and shrugged. "I *suppose* she could have come from the Hemingway House," he said. "Maybe a distant cousin from way back. It's hard to say."

Laura looked disappointed.

"But—speaking of *Cat on a Hot Tin Roof*—did you know that the play's author, Tennessee Williams, lived in Key West for thirty years?"

Laura perked up. "Really? I didn't know that! I love Tennessee Williams! How did I not know that he lived here? Where is his house?"

"I could show you. It's not set up like a museum, like the Hemingway House. But we can walk by and check it out."

"Okay. Maybe after work sometime this week?"

"Sure."

"Great!" said Laura, playfully adding, "It's a date!"

Jake was about to say, *Is it, though?* when the sailboat started bobbing violently up and down, crashing its way through a sudden rough patch of incoming waves.

It was enough to make Pawpa spring from his perch and scamper to a safer spot . . .

Right in between Laura and Jake.

"Well, well, well, look who it is," said Laura. "Hello, Pawpa!"

She was tempted to put her arm around him—maybe stroke him a little—but decided against it. Pawpa would hate that. So instead, she simply looked the old gray cat in his big blue eyes and smiled. He didn't seem to mind. His expression was blank. For all she could tell, he was smiling back at her.

"I think Pawpa's starting to like me. What do you think?"

She glanced at Jake—and stopped smiling.

"Jake, are you all right? Your face . . . it's green."

"I'm gonna be sick."

Covering his mouth with his hand, Jake jumped to his feet and dashed to the side of the boat. Laura cringed as she watched him lean over the rail, coughing and heaving. Shaking her head, she looked down at Pawpa. He seemed every bit as disgusted as she was.

Of course, that's how he always looked.

"Hold tight, everyone! Big swell coming up!"

It was Jolene, shouting from the cockpit. She gripped the wheel with both hands while Jilly grabbed one of the sail lines. Mack braced himself against a cabin rail and pointed straight ahead. "Thar she blows!" he yelled.

A huge rolling wave rose up like a creature from the sea, lifting the front end of the boat slowly but surely, up, up, up, until Laura felt herself sliding downward across the deck.

Pawpa meowed—and jumped onto her lap.

Then, with a sharp quickening lurch, the sailboat toppled forward and slammed down onto the water with a powerful splash. Laura let out a small yelp. Which was echoed by Pawpa. Who was snuggled securely in her arms. After a few more rises and falls of the waves—much smaller than the first—the boat began to steady itself. Thirty seconds later, it was smooth sailing again. As if the whole thing never happened.

Laura and Jake were still catching their breaths—and gripping the rails—when Jilly popped out of the cabin with an armload of swim fins and masks.

"Okay, guys! Who's ready to snorkel?"

The coral barrier reef of the Florida Keys attracts millions of people each year.

And for good reason.

It is the only coral barrier reef in North America and the third-largest coral barrier reef system in the world—with nearly fourteen hundred species of marine plants and animals, five hundred species of fish, and forty varieties of stony corals. The corals are made up of thousands of tiny organisms, or polyps, which maintain a symbiotic relationship with the microscopic algae that live in their tissue and provide them with oxygen. When the corals die, their calcified skeletons provide a foundation for additional layers of corals and algae— a process that has repeated over time to create a dazzling underwater terrain of reefs, channels, and other striking formations.

This process began more than six thousand years ago.

Laura Lange showed up six thousand years later.

"Just remember to not touch anything down there," Jilly warned her. "The corals are very delicate, and a single touch can kill them."

"Yikes."

Laura glanced at Mack, who was treading water alongside her and Jilly. He widened his eyes in mock horror inside his snorkel mask. Laura tried not to laugh. Then she looked across the water at *The Jolly Crabb*, bobbing gently up and down about fifty feet away. Jolene was at the wheel, smiling at them. Pawpa was sitting on the bow, watching them. Jake was nowhere to be seen.

"It's a shame Jake got seasick," said Laura. "I feel so bad. He warned me."

Mack snorted through his snorkel tube.

"He'll be okay," said Jilly. "Those motion sickness pills I gave him should be kicking in soon."

Laura was impressed by how calmly Jilly handled the situation. When Jilly saw that Jake was sick, she rushed over and put her arm around him, patted his back, and told him to focus on the horizon line. Then, once his stomach had settled, she led him to the cabin below and tucked him in a sleeping berth. Now here she was—as calm and cheerful as ever—giving Laura and Mack a quick tutorial on the fine art of snorkeling.

"Okay, so you know how to breathe through the tube, right? You know how to blow air into your mask, right? And you know not to touch any of the marine life if you dive below the surface, right?" Jilly waited for Mack and Laura to nod in the affirmative, which they did. "Are you sure you don't want to wear life jackets? There's no shame in wearing them."

Mack said no.

Laura said, "I'll be fine. I'm a pretty good swimmer. And these fins are incredible! I feel like the Little Mermaid wearing these." She kicked her feet and swam off, splashing around the other two in a swift-moving circle.

"Great," said Jilly. "Any questions?"

Laura looked around at the wide-open sea. "Yeah. Where are the other boats? I thought it would be crowded out here."

"Oh, we sailed out a little farther than they usually do," Jilly explained. "Besides that, they might have been scared to come out this far because of those clouds."

Laura turned and stared at the stormy dark puffs on the horizon. They looked a lot closer than they did a few minutes ago. And a lot more ominous.

"They are kind of scary looking, aren't they?" said Laura. "Are we going to be all right?"

"According to the weather reports, we should be in the clear." Jilly shielded her eyes and looked at the clouds again. She frowned. "But just to be safe, we should probably cut this short. Let's say twenty minutes of snorkeling, then we can start heading back. Just in case."

Laura didn't like the look in Jilly's eyes. But she figured that if anyone knew about sailing these waters, it would be the Crabb sisters.

Laura looked at Mack. "Ready?" she asked.

"Ready as I'll ever be," he answered.

The coral reef was one of the most beautiful things Laura had ever seen.

Full of rich, vibrant colors and strange amorphous shapes, teeming with an abundance of marine life, the seafloor below her looked like some magical land on a distant planet. The sharply angled rays of light from the slowly setting sun made everything glimmer and glow, as if bathed in liquid gold. Bright yellow fish swarmed around her feet in swift-moving clusters, tickling her legs. She gazed downward through her mask, in awe of the endless variety of corals: a miniature green mountain with small rounded peaks, a purple claw-like mass with long, thickened fingers, a multi-colored conglomeration of flat pinkish plates, small blueish spikes, and yellow feathery extensions. To Laura, they looked like a lost race of aliens, hiding from the world.

Mack swam up next to her. "Do you want to dive down deeper and get a closer look?"

Laura nodded enthusiastically.

They both took a deep breath and dived downward, kicking their fins to propel themselves toward the colorful seascape below. Ten, fifteen, twenty feet down, they found themselves surrounded by the magnificent flora and fauna. Mack tugged on Laura's arm and pointed at something resting on the sandy floor: a beautifully shaped, brilliantly orange starfish.

Laura pantomimed her delight and gave Mack a thumbs-up. Then she put one hand on her neck and pointed upward. Together, they swam rapidly to the surface.

Laura pulled down her mask and panted to catch her breath. "That. Is. So. *Amazing!*"

"Isn't it?" said Mack, grinning. "I never get tired of this reef. I could spend every day out here, just exploring."

Laura smiled and nodded. "Let's do it again. Ready?" she asked.

Mack was about to say yes when a voice rang out behind them.

"Hey! You guys!"

They turned to see Jilly treading water about forty feet away. She pointed to *The Jolly Crabb* behind her.

"Jolene just signaled me to come back! I'm going to see what she wants!"

"Should we come, too?" Mack shouted back.

"No! That's okay! Just don't swim too far! Stay in sight of the boat!"

"Got it!"

Mack turned back to Laura. "Okay then. Let's do this."

On their second dive, they spotted a strange red fish with long blue fins that resembled feathers. Upon surfacing, Laura called it "very stylish" and "very Royal Wedding."

On their third dive, they followed behind a slow-moving turtle—and noticed a small shifting change in the light. Upon surfacing, Mack called the turtle "very cool" and the clouds covering the sun "very uncool."

On their fourth dive, they explored a large, jagged formation of mossy green coral that looked like a crumbling gothic castle in an old horror movie . . .

And that's when the sea turned black.

The storm took the Crabb sisters by surprise.

One minute, the ominous dark clouds were safely in the distance. At least an hour away, by Jolene's estimation.

The next minute, those "safely in the distance" clouds were racing toward the boat at an alarming speed, blurring the horizon line between air and water, expanding outward and upward into the sky like a giant ink stain, blotting out the sun.

In between those minutes, Jake's moaning and groaning had gotten worse. Jolene was less concerned about a storm that still seemed far away than a sick passenger who was right there in her cabin. That's why she signaled Jolene back to the boat, to look after Jake so she could stay on deck and try to get a weather update.

And that's when the storm hit.

It started with a massive gust of wind that sent the sails rippling, boat tipping, and Pawpa zipping across the deck to join Jake down below. Next came the rain, spitting and spattering at first, then lashing down in waves from above. Jolene and Jilly jumped into action. Quickly, expertly—and yes, calmly—they lowered the sails, eased the sheets, and reduced the heel, stabilizing *The Jolly Crabb* from a possible broach.

Now came the hard part.

"Mack and Laura! Can you see them?" Jolene yelled, gripping the wheel.

"No!" Jilly yelled back. "They were right there a minute ago! About a hundred feet away!"

The sisters started shouting, "Mack!" and "Laura!" as the rain grew heavier.

Jake came running up from belowdeck. "They're still out

there?" he asked. "Where?" He grabbed the rail and looked around frantically.

"I don't know!" Jilly screamed. "We lost them!"

When the sea turned dark, Laura and Mack immediately knew something was terribly wrong.

Mack reached out and grabbed Laura by the arm. Together, they started kicking their fins as fast they could and swimming to the surface—having no idea what to expect when they got there. As their heads emerged from the water, lungs gasping for air, they discovered a very different world from the sun-soaked seascape they left only a minute ago. The sky was like a giant charcoal smudge, with heavy, restless clouds rolling overhead. The rain whipped around them in wild, throbbing torrents, and the waves lifted them up and lowered them down as if they were nothing at all.

Laura had never felt so small and helpless—or afraid—in her life.

"Where's the boat?" she asked nervously. "I don't see it!"

Mack tried to get his bearings. "We were right in between the boat and the sun."

"Where's the sun?"

Mack looked upward—but saw nothing but clouds. It was as if they'd swallowed it whole. "Wait! Look! There's the sun! See that patch of light behind that cloud? That's it. So that means the boat should be over there." He pointed in the opposite direction.

He looked Laura in the eye—and saw her fear.

"We're going to be okay, all right? Here, take my hand. Let's swim this way."

As they started swimming, the rain started coming down harder. The waves got choppier, too, making it hard for them to be sure they were swimming in a straight line. Then the storm got even wilder, windier, worse than before. They could barely see anything.

That's when Mack started getting scared, too.

Like, really scared.

After a large wave crashed over them and they managed to steady themselves again, he stopped and pulled Laura closer. They looked at each other for a moment, their lips trembling, water streaming down their faces, eyes wide and wet with emotion.

"Look, Laura. I know you're scared. So am I. This is not looking good, is it? Well, if this is it . . . if these are our last moments on earth, well, I just want to . . ."

He kissed her.

Slowly, deeply, passionately, he kissed her. As if it were the last kiss he'd ever give. The last kiss he'd ever know.

He pulled her in closer and held her body tighter as another rolling wave lifted them higher, and more water splashed over them, and more rain showered down upon them—

Then, as suddenly as it started, the kiss ended.

Mack pulled away. But he didn't let go. He kept holding on to Laura's arm as another large wave lifted them up and dropped them down. Then he looked at her and said, "I'm sorry. I shouldn't have done that. I should have asked you first before . . ."

"Shut up." Laura grabbed Mack's face with both hands . . .

And kissed him hard.

PART 2

WEATHERING THE STORM

A cat has absolute emotional honesty:
human beings, for one reason or another,
may hide their feelings, but a cat
does not.
—Ernest Hemingway

Chapter 9
Diary of a Mad Housecat

After everything that happened, Laura decided she should keep a journal.

Not a gushy "Dear Diary, do you think Brad will ask me to prom?" kind of thing that a heartsick teenager would write. And definitely not a *Sex and the City*–style "I couldn't help but wonder" collection of laptop musings on the lifestyles of the rich and single.

No. Laura wanted to keep it simple.

Her journal was going to be a no-nonsense, no-frills record of people, places, and events. *Just the facts, ma'am.* Like something from the notepad of a newspaper reporter. Or like Ernest Hemingway, who honed his straightforward writing style as a foreign correspondent.

Hemingway once said, *"In order to write about life, first you must live it."*

Well, Laura's life had taken a wild turn in the past few weeks. Key West was full of fascinating people, places, history, and happenings that made her life back in Syracuse seem dull by comparison. She wanted to get it all down on paper—or cell phone or laptop— for future reference. Just in case she decided to start writing again. Maybe, if she stuck to the facts and stopped worrying about "style" and "craft," she could stifle the voice of that high school English teacher who lived inside her head.

What does he know anyway?

So—on the night of her tense ordeal at sea—Laura Lange wrote her very first journal entry. She returned to the bungalow with the Crabb sisters, took a long, rejuvenating shower, then shut the door of her bedroom and created a new document on her cell phone. She titled it "Just the Facts." And from that moment on, she managed to log a few entries in it every day.

Even when the hurricane struck.

August 27th.

Went snorkeling. Almost died.

Jolene and Jilly invited Jake, Mack, and me on a snorkeling trip aboard *The Jolly Crabb*. We had two surprise guests: Pawpa Hemingway and Tropical Storm Sally. Pawpa loved sailing. Jake got sick. Mack and I got caught in a brief storm: a ripple effect of Sally in the Florida Panhandle. For several minutes, Mack and I lost sight of the boat. Very scary. Luckily, the rain stopped and the sky cleared almost immediately. We returned safely. No one was harmed.

Also, Mack kissed me and I kissed him back.

Not sure what that means. Trying not to think about it.

August 28th.

Went to work. Got wet. Again.

The day started off sunny. Saw Rooster feeding gypsy chickens on my way to Hemingway House. He asked if I was all right after my sea storm adventure. Said Mack told him all about it. I know they're close, but somehow I doubt if Mack told him *all* about it.

Footnote: Rooster looks *hot* with his new haircut. Didn't recognize him at first.

Ran into Rick and Ricardo walking their Chihuahuas, Lucy and Desi. They were arguing about money. I heard Rick say, "Do you have any idea how much dog trainers cost?" Ricardo apparently had no idea how much dog trainers cost.

Or how to make Lucy and Desi stop barking at me.

Arrived earlier than usual at Hemingway House. Caught Margarita doing the cha-cha on the front porch with Nessie. I joined them. *One-two cha-cha-cha!* Saw Millie heading to the ticket booth, still sporting the fancy hairdo she wore on Dance Night. *A farewell to ponytails!* Had coffee with Jake in the lounge. He's still embarrassed about getting sick on our boat trip, still shaken up over me and Mack getting "lost at sea," and still interested in taking me to see Tennessee Williams's house. We agreed on tomorrow after work. *Is it a date, though?*

Started raining during my second tour group. Mayhem ensued.

Dozens of cats came running inside the house to escape the rain. Larry, Curly, and Moe chased each other in between the tourists' legs. Spinderella did her slip-and-slide routine in the hall, tripping people up with every spin. Lady Bratt Ashley threw a hissy fit when Jackie Chan tried to join her on Hemingway's bed. I had no choice but to stop the tour and wait for the chaos to end.

Who can compete with a houseful of cats?

Not me. I lost my tour group when an impromptu "cage match" broke out between Boxer and Bullfighter beneath the dining room table. Everyone crowded into the room, jostling for "ringside seats" to watch the big-pawed brothers go at it. People cheered when Boxer landed a successful left hook and gasped when Bullfighter bounced back with a matador twirl followed by a full body slam.

I think I saw two older men placing bets.

Fortunately, the rain didn't last long. The afternoon was sunny. Unfortunately, it started raining again on my walk home. I didn't have an umbrella. But guess who did? Mama Marley! She pulled up next to me in her pink taxicab, rolled down her window, and handed me a collapsible umbrella.

"I always keep extras," she said. "For extra tips."

August 29th.

My date with Jake. Sort of.

Woke up with a cat on my chest. At first, I thought it was Nessie because of the fluffy tail tickling my arm. It was Tallulah. She finally came in to say hello. Lovely cat. Hungry, too, I suspected. Got out of bed and fed her some Cat Chow from the Crabbs' kitchen pantry. The sisters have it stocked with more animal food than people food. After Tallulah and I finished our breakfasts, she let me pet and stroke her—but not for long. She obviously had other things to do. Me, too. So we went our separate ways. Me, to work. She, to places unknown.

Today was . . . challenging.

My first scheduled tour was a group of small children from a day care center. Since most of them weren't old enough to read—let alone read Hemingway—I had to alter my script to keep them interested. At various times, I pretended to be a fisherman, a bullfighter, and a big-game hunter on an African safari. The kids loved it. But one of the day care workers gave me a dirty look when I pretended to be holding a gun, so I told the children it was a camera and I was taking the animals' pictures. It didn't matter. The kids were really only interested in one thing:

Hemingway's cats!

Throughout the tour, they couldn't keep their eyes off the random cats roaming around. So I cut the house tour short and led them outside to the cat-sized replica of the Hemingway House. They loved it, of course. Jake even came out to teach the kids about polydactyl cats. He let them pet some of them, too. Afterward, I rushed the children past the cat cemetery—no need to freak them out—but I did show them the cats' drinking fountain. It's made out of an old ceramic urinal that Hemingway brought home from Sloppy Joe's Bar. His wife was tempted to throw it out but instead decided to tile it, top it with a Spanish urn, and turn it into a fountain for the cats.

"Urinal?" asked one little boy. "Like where you pee?"

I said yes—and the children went wild, laughing and screaming, "Ewww!"

It was a successful tour.

Met up with Jake again after work. Thanked him for helping me with the kids. He said he loved kids. "They're so open and honest," he said. "They don't hide their feelings." I did my best not to read anything into that. We started walking down Whitehead Street, turned onto Truman Avenue, and came across a lovely yellow bungalow with a sign that said: *Tennessee Williams Key West Exhibit.* Jake explained that it wasn't the actual house Williams lived in—it was a museum and art gallery dedicated to the playwright and his work. If I was up for it, we could walk to Williams's real home on Duncan Street.

I was up for it.

Along the way, Jake told me about some of Key West's other famous residents including: children's book writer Shel Silverstein, young adult author Judy Blume, poet Wallace Stevens, and President Harry S. Truman—whose winter home came to be known as the "Little White House." He pointed out picturesque spots like Duffy's Steak & Lobster House and the Basilica of St. Mary Star of the Sea.

When we reached the house where Tennessee Williams lived, I told Jake about my schoolgirl dream of being a writer—and my parents' insistence on being practical. Jake told me about how he couldn't go to veterinary school because his father's medical bills ate up all of their savings. He died when Jake was seventeen. Jake had no money and no plans. Thankfully, Margarita offered him a job at the Hemingway House—she already knew him through Mack and Rooster—and Jake was able to help support his mom *and* work with animals all day. He said the job was a godsend, like finding a new home away from home. And a new family that he loved.

I'm starting to feel that way, too.

Afterward, we walked around aimlessly. Talked about our favorite books and movies and stuff like that. Ended up at the Schooner Wharf Bar where we had Oysters on the Half Shell, Coconut Dipped Shrimp, Key West Conch Fritters, and Key Lime Coladas. After paying the tab—I insisted we split it—we watched the sun set on Sunset Pier.

Then I did something stupid. And dangerous, too, since Jake is my coworker.

I kissed him good night.

★ ★ ★

August 30th.

FaceTime with Mom. Somebody shoot me.

Mom insisted we try FaceTime, so I could show her where I'm living. For the first few minutes, I was staring at her ear. Had to explain how to hold the phone so I could see her. Gave her a quick tour of the Crabbs' bungalow. Introduced her to Polly Parton, Romeo and Juliet, Iggy Popstar, and the other animals. She was horrified. Especially by Antony and Cleopatra (the tarantulas) and Sammy and Delilah (the boa constrictors). She did, however, like my bedroom in the converted sun-room. "It's small but very bright," she said. "Very tropical."

Then Mom dropped a bombshell:

"There's a teaching assistant position open in the S.U. English ed department. Your old advisor recommended you. So I submitted your résumé."

I was speechless. But not for long.

After recovering from the initial shock, I tried to explain—calmly—that I'm where I want to be and doing what I want to do. Also, that she shouldn't have submitted my résumé without asking me first.

She apologized up and down but then added, "Well, it's too late now. I already sent it in. Let's just wait and see what happens."

Tried to stay cool. Didn't want to get into an argument. Said good-bye and hung up.

My day only got worse.

Received a text message from Devin ten minutes later:

Your mom said you might be coming back to Syracuse. True? Call me PLEASE.

Ugh. Devin.

My ex-boyfriend doesn't seem to understand what "ex" means. Probably because I never officially broke up with him. I simply announced, out of the blue, that I'd accepted a job in Key West and was leaving in six days. I know. It was a crappy thing for me to do.

We'd been dating since our freshman year of college. But I had my reasons:

1. I hate drama.
2. I had no idea what I wanted to do with my life.
3. I was slowly going mad—like Devin's poor housecat.

Devin used to have a cat named Veronica, a frisky little Manx who liked to scratch up the furniture, the drapes, anything she could get her claws on. One day Devin's mom decided to redecorate. She bought an expensive new leather sofa, new armchairs, new drapes, the works. Henceforth, Veronica was banned from the living room. Devin had to keep her locked up in his bedroom. The poor cat. At first, she was depressed and sluggish. Then, she started acting weird, chasing things that weren't there, refusing to eat, swiping at Devin when he tried to pick her up.

Finally, one night, Veronica made her escape.

She scratched a hole through the window screen and took off. She never returned. I saw her once, a year later, in the park near Devin's house. She was chasing a pigeon—and looked healthier and happier than I'd ever seen her.

Little Veronica . . . free at last!

Oh, how I envied her.

August 31st.

More Mack. More problems.

The day started innocently enough. Woken up by Polly Parton. Recruited by Crabb sisters for a search-and-rescue mission to find Iggy Popstar, who somehow managed to get out of his iguana tank. Found him under my bed. Showered, dressed, went to work. Remembered to bring an umbrella. Didn't need it. But the clouds looked ominous all day.

Led two tour groups in the morning and three in the afternoon. Got stumped by a woman's question: "Do you know the name of the paint color on those shutters?" she asked. "It's too bright to be olive green and too muted to be lime green." I didn't know. Had to ask Lucky Leo. He said it was a custom blend mixed just for the Hemingway House.

Interesting footnote: Leo wasn't wearing one of his usual golf shirts today. Instead, he had on a lovely new button-down with a subtle print. Very tasteful.

Is he getting fashion advice from Mama Marley now?

Margarita asked if I'd stay a couple hours after work to help her and Millie fix the centerpieces for tomorrow's big wedding at the Hemingway House. The couple wanted Caribbean-themed decorations, but the bride hates the little plastic bananas the florist used. The wedding planner—who's apparently on the verge of a nervous breakdown—begged Margarita to help out and remove the bananas from the centerpieces. Margarita agreed, thinking it would be an easy job. It wasn't. The bananas were attached with wires, and the centerpieces needed to be rearranged to fill the gaps.

Margarita also asked if I wanted to make some extra money working the wedding tomorrow. "Just as a backup," she explained. "The caterers will be serving the food and drinks, but you can help me coordinate things. Jake and Mack's band is playing! You don't want to miss that."

No, I did not want to miss that. Of course I agreed.

Jake asked if I wanted to grab a drink after work. Had to say no. Joined Margarita and Millie in the lounge at five. The tables were covered with centerpieces bursting with gorgeous tropical flowers— and tacky plastic bananas. We went to work. So did the cats, who seemed weirdly fascinated by it all. A few of them started fighting over the discarded bananas, batting them around the lounge with their paws like soccer players. It got so bad, we had to send Bette Davis and Joan Clawford to the "penalty box," which, in this case, meant out in the yard with the other cats.

Finished up in time to catch an amazing sunset.

The ominous clouds in the sky looked like they were on fire. I couldn't stop looking up at them. Ran into Mack McCloud—almost literally because I was looking up—on Whitehead Street outside the lighthouse. He was standing next to a tiny elderly woman wearing wire-framed granny glasses, bright floral pants, and a Greenpeace T-shirt. Mack introduced her to me as "Shelly the weather goddess on WKEY Radio."

Shelly laughed. "I told him to stop calling me 'weather girl.' I prefer 'analyst' but have to admit 'weather goddess' has a nice ring to it. Nice to meet you, Laura." She shook my hand and pointed up. "That's one awesome-looking sky, isn't it? You can thank Tropical Storm Sally for that."

Mack told her about the flash storm on our snorkeling trip.

"You're lucky. Sally is one fickle lady. She's been bouncing around the gulf all week, changing direction every day. She reminds me of those girls who won't commit to one guy and won't settle down—she's just playing the field. Of course, I'm one to talk. I was the same way in my younger days. It's probably why I'm still single." Shelly snorted. "But anyway, back to Sally . . . I think she'll tire herself out in a few days. I'm more concerned about Harry."

"Who's Harry?" asked Mack.

"Hurricane Harry," she explained. "He's a sneaky one. Just a few days ago, he was Tropical Storm Harry. Practically a baby, born from a wave in the Atlantic. By the time he reached Puerto Rico yesterday, he was a full-blown hurricane. Category Three. Luckily, he passed north of the island and didn't do much damage. According to the big-city meteorologists, Harry was losing steam already. But he can't fool me! Just today, Harry turned into a Category Four— and he's still a growing boy, if you ask me. Haiti, Dominican Republic, Turks and Caicos—they're all under severe hurricane watch right now." Shelly stopped, noticing the shocked look on my face. "Don't you listen to my weather show?" she asked me.

"No," I said. "But I definitely will from now on! You make the weather sound so . . . exciting."

"Weather *is* exciting."

"Scary, too," I added.

"Yes, that, too," she said. "We'll see what happens over the next few days. If Scary Harry intensifies when he gets to Cuba, it'd be a real disaster for us here in the Keys. Why, a Category Five hurricane would be more devastating than anything we've ever seen! We'd have to evacuate. Immediately."

After scaring the bejesus out of me, Shelly told us to have a lovely evening and moseyed off down the street. Mack and I stood there on the sidewalk, looking at each other awkwardly. I wasn't sure what unnerved me more—the news of a killer hurricane heading our way or the fact that Mack and I shared a secret make-out session when we thought we were going to die.

Finally, Mack broke the silence. "Do you want to check out the sunset from the top of the lighthouse?"

I did.

By the time we reached the top, the sky was even more dramatic than before. The clouds were darker and deeper. The sun was riper and richer. And—maybe it was the light or the dizzying height or the wildly romantic setting of the old Key West Lighthouse, but I swear Mack looked sweeter, scruffier, and sexier than ever. . . .

Dear Diary, do you think Mack will try to kiss me again?

No! Stop it! Now!

I promised myself I wouldn't turn this journal into a lovesick teenager's boy-crush diary. And here I am, breaking that promise already. Get a grip, Laura.

Just the facts.

Here's what we talked about: Mack's love of music and his dream of becoming a record producer. Mack's uncle Rooster and how he took him in after his mother abandoned him. Mack's friendship with Jake and how they'd been competing with each other since grade school. I told him my life story. (Well, some of it, not all. Nothing about Devin.) Then I brought up what happened on the snorkeling trip.

Mack got real quiet. He looked down over the railing of the lighthouse for a long moment before saying anything. Then he looked up at me again, his eyes dark and glistening.

"It was . . . intense," he said in a soft, low, hesitating voice. "It was . . . crazy, I know. I shouldn't have kissed you. Jake really likes you, and he's my best friend. But it was something I wanted to do . . . from the first moment I met you. It was something I *had* to do . . . if it was our last moment on earth."

I didn't know what to say. The emotion in his eyes, the tenderness in his voice . . . I wanted to grab him and hug him. Or kiss him. Or both.

"Do you want to grab a drink at Sloppy Joe's?" he asked. "First round's on me!"

"Um . . . okay."

I wasn't sure if he wanted to change the conversation or simply wanted a change of scenery. Either way, I was on board. I've been dying to check out Hemingway's favorite bar ever since I got here.

Sloppy Joe's Bar!

Established on December 5, 1933—the day Prohibition was repealed—the famous Key West saloon managed to retain the atmosphere of a neighborhood dive bar even after several name changes and locations on Duval Street. Ernest Hemingway himself suggested the name Sloppy Joe's to the owner, Joe Russell, who kept the drinks flowing to Papa and his "mob" of cohorts including author John Dos Passos and artist Waldo Peirce. Hemingway met his third wife, Martha Gellhorn, at Sloppy Joe's—as well as the sea captain who gave him his first polydactyl cat. Literary scholars believe Sloppy Joe's served as the inspiration for the bar in Hemingway's novel *To Have and Have Not.*

Me? I was trying to decide whether to have or have not a frozen margarita with Mack.

"Come on, just one," he coaxed, pulling up a stool for me at the long curved bar.

"I probably shouldn't," I said. "I feel like I've been drinking a lot since I got here."

Mack laughed and held up his hands. "Welcome to Margaritaville."

I shrugged. "Okay. Why not. Hemingway once said, *'If you want to know about a culture, spend a night in its bars.'* Who am I to argue with a Nobel Prize winner?"

As Mack ordered our drinks, I gazed around the bar. The aged wood paneling and blue tiled floors looked like they hadn't changed in decades. The walls were covered with old memorabilia, fishing trophies, and framed photographs—many of Papa himself—and the ceiling had a couple wobbly fans hanging from it. One thing Hemingway wouldn't have recognized: a gift shop in the corner selling Sloppy Joe's T-shirts and Key West souvenirs.

"Here you go," said Mack, handing me a frozen margarita. "What should we drink to? A long and happy life? Our dream careers? A farewell to snorkeling?"

"Let's drink to . . . Hemingway's cats!" I said.

"To Hemingway's cats it is!"

We clinked our glasses together and started sipping. As the icy cocktail tickled and numbed my tongue, I saw someone out of the corner of my eye—someone standing on the street outside, gazing through the window of the bar, then shaking his head and moving on.

I'm pretty sure it was Jake.

And I'm pretty sure he saw us.

September 1st.

Red skies in morning. Sailor's warning.

Woke up to scary news. Listened to Shelly's weather report on WKEY Radio. Turns out Tropical Storm Sally is on the move again. Heading straight toward the Keys.

"Sally's got her eye on us," is how Shelly put it. "But I think she's just flirting. There's a handsome young pressure system developing that could sweep her off her feet and carry her out to sea. Right now, though, it looks like Sally's keeping her options open. We might see some heavy winds and rain over the next couple days, so be prepared. On top of that, we've got Hurricane Harry coming our way. He seems to be losing steam over Cuba, thank goodness, and got downgraded to Category Three. I'm hoping he's plumb tuckered out by the time he reaches the Keys. Even so, if Sally is still here when Harry shows up . . . look out. Things could get awfully stormy awfully fast. Stay tuned for updates."

I turned off the radio. Made a mental note to bring an umbrella to the big Caribbean-themed wedding at the Hemingway House this afternoon.

Footnote: If I'd known just how stormy this day was going to be, I would have stayed in bed.

Since I didn't have to go in to work until the afternoon, I cooked up a big breakfast for Jilly, Jolene, and myself. Pancakes, eggs, bacon, the works. Told the sisters about Mack and Jake and our kind-of, sort-of dates. Our kisses, too. They listened intently but said very little. I guess they don't want to get involved. Or they know something that I don't. Jilly, in particular, looked like the proverbial cat who swallowed the canary.

Speaking of birds, I spent the morning trying to teach Polly Parton a new song. Lynyrd Skynyrd's "Freebird." No luck. Guess she's not a Skynyrd fan.

Hung out with Tallulah in the backyard. She chased a lizard around the Crabbs' nautical knickknacks and lawn ornaments. The lizard managed to get away, hiding under a mermaid statue. Tallulah gave up, came and sat on my lap. Didn't expect that. Also didn't expect her to be so heavy. "You're getting fat, Tallulah," I said. "Are you getting meals from the neighbors, too? Maybe you should try cutting out the carbs."

I stroked her the same way Nessie likes to be stroked. Slowly from the top of her head to the tip of her tail. She purred the same way Nessie purrs, too.

It was weird: Meeting two cats who were so much alike and yet so different.

Also weird: Kissing two guys who happened to be best friends. Who played in a band together. Who I was going to see today. At a wedding. At the Hemingway House.

For whom the wedding bell tolls . . . ?

Not for me, not anytime soon. It's hard to imagine making that kind of commitment when I can barely decide what to wear to this wedding—or what to do about Jake and Mack.

"Help me out, Tallulah," I said, lifting the cat from my lap.

Got up, went to my room. Tallulah followed. Opened my wardrobe, pulled out a few outfits, held them up for her approval. No reaction. Reached for my Little Black Dress, held it in front of me, did a little twirl. Tallulah swished her tail. Done.

If only all of life's decisions were that easy.

Later, at the Hemingway House . . .

Margarita, Millie, and I finished placing the centerpieces—minus plastic bananas—on the tables around the dance floor. We stood back to admire our work. The decorations looked great. And surprisingly tasteful. Considering the bride's Caribbean theme, it could have gone wrong in so many ways. The wedding planner created a lovely arch of tropical flowers for the ceremony, and the caterers brought in a bar and serving stations made of bamboo and palm fronds that somehow managed not to look like a tacky hotel tiki bar. The tablecloths—in muted shades of classic Caribbean colors—set off the flowered centerpieces beautifully. Even the frazzled, and fussy, wedding planner was thrilled how nicely everything came out.

The cats also loved it. Maybe a little too much.

Larry, Curly, and Moe kept nibbling the palm fronds on the side of the bar. Chew-Chew and Whiskey were already staking out the food service area. Kilimanjaro tried to climb the flower-covered arch and had to be chased away several times. At one point, she knocked off one of the flowers, which Bette Davis and Joan Clawford started fighting over. Meanwhile, Boxer and Bullfighter waged war on the snake's nest of audio cables for the wedding band.

Ah, the wedding band.

The whole time I was helping Margarita, I kept checking out Jake and Mack, who were setting up equipment with their bandmates. They looked very handsome in their suits, though they hadn't buttoned up their shirts yet or tied their ties. They caught me looking. Both of them gave me a big smile and a little wave. I asked Margarita if it was okay if I said hello to the band.

"Of course," she said. "I think we have this under control now. The decorations are done, the wedding planner is happy, even the bride has finally calmed down. Just keep your eye on the cats. Make sure they don't do too much damage—or, worse, upstage the bride."

I glanced at the dance floor, where Spinderella was sliding around playfully. "I'll try," I said. Then I turned and walked over to the band area.

"So this is the band I've heard so much about," I said, smiling at Jake and Mack.

Jake played me a short riff on his guitar. "Everything you heard is true," he said. "The Off Keys are rock and roll legends . . . in their own minds."

Mack flipped one of his drumsticks in the air, caught it, and played a Caribbean-sounding melody on a steel drum. "Just wait until you hear our calypso covers of AC/DC. It'll blow your mind."

I laughed. They introduced me to their bandmates, Lilly and Kane, who seemed very nice and very cool and very busy—making last-minute changes to the music playlist. Mack excused himself to get yet another drum from the van, leaving me alone with Jake.

"This isn't the kind of music we normally play," he told me. "The bride wanted a Caribbean sound, but with the usual wedding songs like 'Just the Way You Are' and 'Unchained Melody.' And lounge music, too, like 'The Girl from Ipanema.' Mack says he hates 'The Girl from Ipanema,' but I think he secretly loves it. He's just not a fan of playing weddings."

"But it's a Hemingway House wedding," I said. "That's got to count for something."

"I heard the bride's father is a dead ringer for Ernest Hemingway. He could have entered the Hemingway Look-Alike Contest we have every year. It's in July."

"I heard about that. Isn't it part of a week-long festival, with fishing contests and a 'Running of the Bulls' through the streets and stuff like that? I'm sorry I missed it."

"Maybe next year. If you're still here." A strange, sad look flashed across Jake's face. Then he smiled again. "They judge the Look-Alike Contest at Sloppy Joe's, Hemingway's old hangout. Have you been there yet?"

Uh-oh. I wasn't sure how to answer that. My mind started racing. *I couldn't help but wonder—*

Ugh, no! I'm doing the *Sex and the City* thing! Another journal rule broken!

But seriously, I couldn't help but wonder if Jake was testing me. That he saw Mack and me at Sloppy Joe's last night and wanted to see if I'd lie about it. If maybe there's something going on between us.

"I was there last night," I said. "With Mack. I ran into him outside after helping Margarita with the centerpieces. We went to Sloppy Joe's for a drink. Cool place. Still divey after all these years. And so much history! I loved all the pictures and stuff on the walls. I was even tempted to buy a T-shirt but . . ."

I was rambling. Luckily, Mack returned with another steel drum, giving me an excuse to change the subject. Then Margarita waved to me from the side of the house as if she needed me for something. Good timing.

"Looks like I'm being summoned," I said. "Good luck today, guys. I mean, break a leg."

Oops.

Pre-wedding cocktails.

The band sounded great. They played soft Caribbean-flavored lounge music—Jimmy Buffett's "Margaritaville," Bob Marley's "Stir It Up"—while the wedding guests sipped tropical cocktails from hollowed-out pineapples with long pink straws. I was especially impressed by Mack's masterful performance of "The Girl from Ipanema" on the steel drums. It was smooth and sexy and very cool. You'd never guess he hated the song. And Jake? He looked like a handsome young crooner from another era, strumming his guitar seductively, swaying gently to the beat. Very suave, even swoon-worthy.

Something brushed across my leg.

Nessie! My wedding date had arrived!

The ceremony.

Held Nessie in my arms as the bride and groom said their vows. Got choked up watching them exchange rings and kiss, even though I'd never met these people before. At least I wasn't the only one getting emotional. Margarita had tears in her eyes, too. Millie was practically sobbing.

"So beautiful," she whispered.

I tried to avoid looking at Jake and Mack. But I couldn't help myself. They were standing with their instruments on the bandstand—both of them glancing at me every few seconds. I started to wonder if they were really that serious about me. As in "Could she be the one?" serious. But then I realized, no.

They were watching Millie sob uncontrollably.

Ha.

The reception.

Bride and groom said, "I do." Guests cheered. Newlyweds danced their first dance. A calypso version of Elvis Presley's "Can't Help Falling in Love." Jake sang the lead, sounded great. Looked dreamy. Then some speeches were made, servers brought out the food, and everyone sat down to eat—under the watchful eyes of Chew-Chew and Whiskey, who circled the wedding party like a pair of hungry sharks.

Throughout the dinner, guests clinked their glasses with spoons and the newlyweds kissed. More champagne bottles were uncorked, more toasts were made, and more food was consumed. Empty plates were quickly cleared away by servers.

That's when the real party started.

Jake, Mack, Lilly, and Kane—the artists presently known as The Off Keys—kicked off the evening with a crowd-pleasing set of dance hits. Everyone leapt onto the dance floor. Lilly was amazing. Not only did she look like a young Whitney Houston; she sang like her, too. Kane, who reminded me of Prince, was a curly-topped musical genius who played at least five different instruments including keyboards, guitar, and saxophone. Jake and Mack were no slouches either. They played incredibly well together. Great harmonies and stage presence.

Who knew?

The biggest surprise, though, was how well the band managed to make each song sound Caribbean—just as the bride ordered. You haven't lived until you've heard a calypso version of "Uptown Funk," a Caribbean riff on "Love Shack," and a reggae-style rendering of "The Electric Slide."

Hemingway's cats didn't know how to react.

Some of them ran away and hid (Larry, Curly, and Moe), some of them found a safe spot to watch (Nessie, Pawpa, and Kilimanjaro), and a few tried to get in on the action (Spinderella, Boxer, Bullfighter, and, of course, Chew-Chew and Whiskey). At least the troublemakers gave me a good excuse when a drunken wedding guest asked me to dance. "Sorry, I'm working now," I told him. "Gotta wrangle these cats!"

In the middle of all this, the caterers started putting up canopy tents over the bar and service tables. At first, I didn't understand why. Then I looked up at the sky.

Yikes.

Huge gray storm clouds rolled overhead like a stampeding herd of cattle. I hadn't noticed them before, probably because the sky was darkening as the sun set and the party lights were on. As I continued gazing upward, I noticed that the palm trees were starting to sway, their green fronds rippling in the steadily growing wind. It was incredibly ominous.

What did Shelly the weather goddess say about Tropical Storm Sally?

We might see some heavy winds and rain over the next couple days, so be prepared.

"Don't do it, Sally," I whispered to the sky. "Please don't ruin this wedding."

Suddenly the music stopped. I turned and looked toward the bandstand to see Jake grab the microphone. "And now I'd like to introduce a special guest singer to the stage," he said. "The one . . . the only . . . Margarita Bouffet!"

Everyone burst into applause. Especially me. I had no idea Margarita could sing!

I watched my boss step onto the stage and take the mic. Her eyes sparkled as she gazed at the crowd. "Thank you," she said. "On behalf of the Ernest Hemingway House, I would like to dedicate this song to our wonderful newlyweds, and to anyone who's ever searched for a dream and was lucky enough to find it . . . 'At Last.'"

She glanced down at the ground as the band played the opening strains of the immortal Etta James classic, "At Last." The bride and groom jumped to their feet and walked to the middle of the dance floor. Margarita waited for her cue, looked up slowly, and began to sing.

She was magnificent.

Her voice was so deep and rich and filled with emotion, it took my breath away. Soon other couples joined the newlyweds, dancing closely and romantically, as the music swelled and soared. Others, like me, were too mesmerized to do anything but stand there and listen, swept away by the song, the words, and the woman who brought them to life. As the melody continued, I began to notice something: Margarita's eyes were fixed on a point in the distance, somewhere over my shoulder. I turned and looked.

It was Rooster McCloud.

Leaning against the side of the house, the ruggedly handsome lighthouse keeper watched Margarita from afar—his eyes so blue and soulful, it made my heart hurt a little.

Then I felt something else: Pawpa Hemingway rubbing against my leg!

You could have knocked me over with a feather, as Rooster likes to say. Pawpa had stopped stalking me since our sailboat adventure together, but he'd never been actively friendly with me before. This was a major turning point in our relationship.

I reached down to stroke him.

And he let me!

This had to be my favorite moment of the wedding: petting Pawpa Hemingway while listening to Margarita Bouffet sing Etta James to Rooster McCloud.

What was my *least* favorite moment?

Everything that happened afterward.

It started with a loud clap of thunder. Then a strong gust of wind came blasting through the garden, blowing flowers and tablecloths and even some chairs across the yard. Then a massive downpour of rain started pummeling us from above—sending everyone screaming and scrambling toward the Hemingway House for shelter.

Things only got worse after that.

After that . . .

Everyone was wet and miserable. The wedding guests were wet and miserable. The caterers were wet and miserable. The cats were wet and miserable.

As the rainstorm howled outside, the bride howled even louder in the main hallway. Lifting and dragging her soaking-wet mess of a dress across the floor, she pushed her way through the chattering crowd of wet and miserable guests until she reached the staircase. She plopped herself down on the steps and started crying and cursing and wailing. "Why?!!! Why me?!!! Why now?!!!" The groom tried his best to console her.

No luck.

Meanwhile, the cats who came in from the storm began drying themselves off in the roped-off areas of the house. They scampered and frolicked and rolled around playfully—to the delight of the dripping-wet guests. Once again, Boxer and Bullfighter staged a fighting match beneath the dining room table. Once again, the crowd cheered them on.

"That one's got a mean left hook," said the father of the groom.

I went to check the other rooms. Saw Margarita and Millie talking to the wedding planner. Saw Rooster, too, a few feet away, watching. Didn't see Jake or Mack or the rest of the band. Made my way through the crowd to one of the windows. Looked out, saw a pair of figures across the yard in the bandstand. It was Jake and Mack. They were frantically trying to tie down a large plastic tarp over the band equipment, but the wind kept blowing it off.

It looked like they were yelling at each other.

Margarita came up behind me. "Laura, sweetheart, do you think you could grab a couple mops from the utility room?" she asked. "With all this water getting tracked around in here, I'm afraid the floors might get damaged. Or worse, someone might slip and fall."

I said sure, no problem. Then I looked out the window again. The rain seemed to be easing up a bit. I could see the bandstand much more clearly now. The plastic tarp appeared to be fastened down securely.

But Jake and Mack were nowhere to be seen.

I made my way to the back of the house, past the sobbing bride, dripping guests, and cavorting cats. Managed to reach the back door when I felt something brush against my leg.

"Nessie! There you are! I knew you were smart enough to get out of the rain." I gave her warm, furry, but still damp head a quick rub. "Unfortunately, I have to go back out there. Wish me luck!"

Taking a deep breath—and wishing I had Mama Marley's umbrella on me—I ducked my head and dashed outside. As I made my way toward the building out back, I saw Jake and Mack standing next to the pool.

They were arguing. In the pouring rain. About me.

"You kissed her?" Jake shouted. "You kissed her!"

"You kissed her, too!" Mack shouted back.

"We had an agreement!"

"And you broke it!"

"You broke it, too!"

I couldn't believe what I was hearing. *They had an agreement?* I barely had time to process that when the two best friends started shoving each other. Jake shoved Mack first. Mack shoved Jake back. After a few more forceful shoves, they were locked in arm-to-arm combat. Like Boxer and Bullfighter, but not nearly as cute. It was an awful thing to see.

"Stop it!" I screamed out. "What's wrong with you two?!"

They ignored me and kept fighting, pushing and slamming each other harder and harder.

Until they plunged into the pool.

That was it. I'd seen enough. Shocked—and a little disgusted—I left the boys to sort out their stupid macho rivalry on their own. I went to get the mops for Margarita.

Jake and Mack could clean up their own mess.

Chapter 10
When Hurricane Harry Met Tropical Storm Sally

Every year, at the peak of hurricane season, a funny thing happens to the people who live in the southernmost regions of Florida State.

Weather experts call it Hurricane Amnesia.

Now the funny thing about Hurricane Amnesia is how common it is among those who should know better—namely, the longtime local residents who've already lived through some terrible storms but seemed to have forgotten how terrible they are.

Possible side effects may include: an overconfident sense of security, an overwhelming denial of the danger, and an overly optimistic feeling that everything is going to be just fine.

In other words: They don't take hurricanes seriously.

This is especially true in the Florida Keys.

Many residents of Key West, for instance, had grown so accustomed to the endless barrage of tropical storm warnings, hurricane watches, and coastal flood advisories that it had become routine. These proud Key Westerners liked to think they were prepared for anything. They'd seen it all before. And more often than not, it amounted to nothing.

Much of the blame could be placed on the "action news" teams looking to boost ratings with their over-the-top, up-to-the-minute panic attacks. Reporting live on a beach wearing designer-label slickers during mild-looking rainstorms, these local TV "personalities" could teach the proverbial Boy Who Cried Wolf a thing or two.

After a while, people stopped listening.

This year was especially bad. Depending on which news station a person listened to, the chances of a storm making landfall were either rapidly increasing, slowly diminishing, or constantly fluctuating from hour to hour. *Stay tuned for updates!* Even the National Weather Service—a reliable source of information—kept changing their warnings, watches, and advisories throughout the day. There were so many conflicting reports, people didn't know whom to believe or what to think.

The problem was Harry and Sally.

They were—to quote Shelly of WKEY Radio—"awfully skittish."

Just yesterday, the U.S. National Hurricane Center (NHC) downgraded Hurricane Harry to a Category 2 as he blew past the Turks and Caicos Islands and headed northeast into the Atlantic—only to change directions a day later. At the same time, the NHC demoted Tropical Storm Sally to a tropical depression as she drifted westward into the Gulf of Mexico. She, too, changed her mind—and got upgraded again—as she headed back to Florida for another visit.

The weather experts did their best to keep up. They upgraded the storms, issued more warnings, and eventually urged the Florida governor to order an evacuation. But for some of the residents of Key West—especially the famous Hemingway cats—leaving the island was not an option.

When Hurricane Harry met Tropical Storm Sally, they had no choice but to hunker down and ride it out.

Come hell or high water.

When Mama Marley met Lucky Leo Trout at the Green Parrot Bar—five days before Harry met Sally—they thought the worst was over.

"You can stop worrying about Harry and Sally," said Leo, pulling up a chair for Mama. "They won't touch us here. Believe me, I know a lot about storms. I've lived through two Category Five hurricanes and so many tornadoes I've lost count. When I was in Kansas, a twister actually picked up my house, spun it around a few times, and dropped it like a hot potato. Every window in the place was busted out."

Mama smiled. "You're lucky to be alive, Leo."

"That's right." He smiled back. "I'm one lucky man. Lucky to be here, alive, with you."

Mama continued smiling as she ordered the Happy Hour Special—a spiced rum and pineapple concoction called the Parrot Punch—and tried not to think too hard about Leo's wildly exaggerated stories. Yes, they were amusing. No, she didn't believe them. Why he felt the need to tell such tall tales . . . well, that was something Mama wasn't ready to dive into. Not just yet. Not on the third date.

"I love that new shirt on you," she said, changing the subject. "It really brings out the green in your eyes. You look very handsome."

Leo blushed. "I never would have bought it if you hadn't pointed it out," he said. "You have excellent taste."

"In shirts or men?"

Leo blushed even harder.

Mama thought it was adorable that Leo actually took her advice. Walking home after their second date—it was Ukulele Night here at the Green Parrot—they passed by a men's clothing store. Mama used the opportunity to rave about some of the shirts in the window, hoping Leo would take the hint. The very next day, she saw him outside the Hemingway House wearing one of the shirts she liked. This impressed Mama. A lot. Most of the men she'd dated were set in their ways. They always wore the same clothes, went to the same restaurants, even ordered the same thing every time—and always resisted trying anything new.

Leo was different.

"Uh . . . Mama? Can I . . . ask you something?"

"Of course you can, Leo. Shoot."

Leo looked nervous. "It's, um . . . well, your name. I feel a little . . . weird . . . calling you Mama. That's what I used to call my
mother."

"Oh, dear."

"Yeah. Well, I was wondering if, maybe . . . Do you have another name I could call you?"

"You mean, like my real name?" Mama smiled slyly. "My real
name's a secret. I never tell anyone my real name. But for you? I'll
make an exception. My real name is . . . Marla."

"Marla?" he said, breaking into a smile. "Marla. What a beautiful name! I love it. Marla."

"That's my name; don't wear it out."

At that moment, the live music started to play. It was a local band
called The Kool Kats. Their music could be described as Southern-
Fried Honky-Tonk with a Key Lime Twist. They were very loud,
very rowdy—and very danceable.

"You wanna shake a leg, Marla?" Leo held out his hand.

Mama didn't answer at first. She tilted her head to the side and
listened to the opening bars of the band's ramped-up version of
Little Feat's "Dixie Chicken." She looked at Leo and smiled. "Okay.
Let's do this."

Five songs later . . .

Mama and Leo were still dancing up a storm. The band's raucous mix of musical styles inspired them to come up with ever-
more-creative dance moves. Mama did the spinning while Leo did
the dipping, each totally in sync with the other's next step as if they'd
been dancing together for years. Some people in the crowd started
cheering them on, giving them space on the dance floor to really go
wild. It was a hell of a lot of fun.

Until it wasn't.

When Leo stepped away to reach for his beer, a broad-
shouldered brute in a cowboy hat started pressing up against Mama

Marley, grinding his hips against hers. She pushed him away with a hard shove—and things turned ugly real fast. The cowboy grabbed Mama by the arm. She kicked him in the groin. And then Leo came out swinging.

It all happened quickly.

It ended quickly, too.

Leo managed to land one solid punch on the cowboy's jaw when a huge bouncer appeared out of nowhere, grabbing Leo by the shoulders, dragging him to the door, and tossing him outside—into the rain. Mama Marley came running out after him. She helped Leo up from the wet sidewalk and opened an umbrella, shielding him from the downpour.

"I always carry extra umbrellas," she explained. "Come on, Leo. My cab is parked around the corner."

Once they were safely inside Mama Marley's cab—and ten blocks away from the bar, the bouncer, and the brute—the two of them burst out laughing.

"Man, oh, man, oh, *man*! That was *beautiful*, Leo!"

Mama hooted and whistled and pounded her palms on the steering wheel. Leo had to hold back his laughter as he attempted to apologize for causing a scene—and getting them eighty-sixed from the bar—but Mama wasn't having it.

"Are you kidding me? That was *awesome*, Leo. You are the man! Defending my honor like that? I mean, wow. That guy was *huge*! You're lucky he didn't kill you!"

Leo snorted. "I *told* you I was lucky!"

"Oh, no, you're more than lucky. You're my hero! You actually threw a punch! *For me!* I'm gonna start calling you 'Left Hook' Leo!"

They were still laughing when Mama pulled her cab up the famous red pier on the southernmost point of the island. Thanks to the rain, they were the only ones there. No tourists. No picture takers. No souvenir peddlers. Just Marla and Leo and the rain falling down on the deep blue sea.

"Yes, sir, you are really something else, Leo," she said, turning off the ignition. "I'll bet you never expected to get into a bar fight tonight. You ever been in a bar fight before?"

"Oh, yeah, sure," said Leo, leaning back. "Dozens of them. I've been in so many bar brawls, I've lost count. I used to train with professional boxers, you know."

Oh, no, Mama thought. *Not this again.*

"Really, Leo? That's interesting." She fiddled with the radio until she found a slow, soft reggae song. "But to tell you the truth, I don't follow boxing. Let's talk about something else."

"Like what?"

"Like, how can you work around all those cats all day?"

"You don't like cats?"

"They scare me. Those gypsy chickens scare me, too. All animals do, actually. I try to avoid them if I can. Been that way since I was little."

"Where did you grow up?"

Mama looked out at the sea and didn't say anything. Then she looked back at Leo. "You go first. Tell me something about your past. How about your ex-wife? Tell me about her."

Leo scoffed. "Oh, I don't know if that's a good idea. Every dating show I've seen on TV says you should never, *ever* talk about your past relationships on a date."

"That only applies to the first date. This is our third date." Mama leaned in closer, pressing against his arm. "Anything can happen after the third date, Leo. Anything and everything. The rules no longer apply."

Leo chuckled softly. "Oh? Is that right?" He put his arm around her.

"That's right." She laid her head on his shoulder and nuzzled his neck.

"In that case," said Leo, "would you consider coming to my place for a nightcap?"

"I would. Any other questions?"

"Yeah. Why did your parents name you Marla Marley?"

"Oh, that's not my real last name."

★ ★ ★

When Foster Lee Jackson met Millie Graham at the Hot Tin Roof Restaurant—four days before Harry met Sally—the island was under a tropical storm watch.

Millie wondered if they should cancel their plans and make a rain date for the following week. But Foster wouldn't hear of it.

"I'm not about to let a little bad weather keep me from enjoying the company of a beautiful woman," he said over the phone. "Especially one with such a sunny disposition."

"Aw, that's sweet," she said with a girlish giggle. "But are you sure? They say Tropical Storm Sally is heading our way again."

"Well, Miss Sally will just have to wait until I've wined and dined Miss Millie," he said. "And besides, I've already made a reservation."

When they arrived at the restaurant, the hostess told them that the outdoor veranda was closed due to possible wind and rain. Foster insisted on being seated there anyway.

"What is the point of bringing a lady to this fine establishment if we can't gaze out at the Key West Harbor, sipping rosé as we take in the sunset?" he said. "If you could possibly arrange that, I would be forever grateful. And also, could I see your wine list, please?"

The hostess begrudgingly obliged.

As Foster studied the wine selection, Millie watched the restaurant staff scramble to set up a table on the veranda. The main dining room seemed to have a lot of empty seats tonight—probably because of the storm warnings—but it was incredibly chic and elegant. Millie would have been happy to eat inside. But once she saw the waterfront view from the veranda, she was glad Foster convinced the hostess to let them sit there. It was just so beautiful and romantic looking—even with the clouds blotting out the sun.

"This place is awful fancy," she whispered to Foster after the waiter seated them. "I've always wanted to come here. I've heard the food is yummy."

Foster nodded. "It is indeed. The Hot Tin Roof is my favorite dining spot on the island. Just look at that view!"

Millie gazed across the harbor at the massive blue and purple clouds rolling across the horizon. "It's stunning," she said. "But . . ."

"But what?"

"Those clouds are pretty scary looking. And see those choppy waves out there? Looks like a pot of stew on the stove ready to bubble over. Must be a strong wind coming in."

Foster tried to reassure her. "It's nothing. Just a little squall, perhaps. Tropical Storm Sally is at least a hundred miles away right now. There's nothing to worry about."

"What about Hurricane Harry?"

"Harry? He's somewhere in the middle of the ocean by now."

"That's not what Shelly said this morning."

"Shelly? Rooster McCloud's weather lady? She's not a meteorologist."

"No, but she sure knows her stuff. She said that Hurricane Harry changed his itinerary last night and booked a flight to the Bahamas. He got upgraded again, too. He's Category Three now and moving west. Shelly's afraid he might try to pick up some Cuban cigars next. She said if he does that, we could all get smoked!"

Foster broke out laughing. "Oh, that Shelly. She has quite an imagination, I must say. Me? I have quite an appetite." He opened his menu. "Do you mind if I order for both of us?"

"Um, I guess not. You know what's good here, right? I can trust you?"

"Of course you can trust me. I used to order all the time for my ex-wife."

Foster called the waiter over and started rattling off items from the menu—Wild Mushroom Bruschetta, Octopus Salad, Seared Scallop & KW Pink Shrimp, Filet Mignon and Florida Lobster—while Millie sat there thinking about Foster's ex-wife.

"What was she like?" Millie asked when the waiter left. Foster looked confused. "Your ex-wife," she said. "I only met her once, years ago. What was she like?"

"Oh! She was very high society. One of those genteel Southern belles from a prominent family in Savannah. She was very quiet, very demure, and very accommodating. She took care of my every need. Until she took off and ran away. Along with the cat."

"She took your cat?"

"No," Foster sighed. "The cat ran away after my wife ran away. It seemed the cat didn't like me either. To this very day, I have no idea where either one of them are."

Millie was about to ask another question when it started raining—and raining hard. Luckily, the veranda had a roof. Then the wind started blowing, too. Millie glanced across the water at a nearby pier set up with dining tables, yellow lawn umbrellas, and party lights. A small crew of service workers were trying to close the umbrellas as quickly as they could, but then another blast of wind started knocking the umbrellas over.

"Oh, my," she said, scooting her chair away from the railing. "I don't want to get my hair wet. My neighbor Connie—she's a stylist—did it up real special for me tonight."

"It looks lovely," said Foster. He reached out to shield the candle on their table so it wouldn't blow out.

"Connie lent me this dress, too," Millie went on. "She has a lot of designer stuff that don't fit her anymore since she put on some weight."

"Very stylish."

"Thank you, Foster . . . oh, look!" Millie pointed across the water.

The party lights on the pier were flickering on and off as the wind and rain intensified. Yellow lawn umbrellas rolled across the pier, plunging over the side and into the water below. The rain-soaked crew of service workers gave up trying to save them. The workers dashed for shelter as the wind sent tablecloths and dinnerware flying. Next to the veranda, a large tropical tree swayed wildly back and forth. A few of its leaves ended up in Millie's new hairdo.

Then the restaurant lights went out.

Before the diners could react, a massive *whoosh* of wind blasted across the veranda. It blew the napkin off Millie's lap, the silverware off the table . . .

And the toupee off Foster's head.

It happened so fast, Foster didn't even realize he'd been exposed. Not until Millie pointed up at his bald head. "Foster, your hair! It's gone! With the wind!"

It took them five minutes to locate the flyaway hairpiece—it was stuck in a branch of the tropical tree—and another five minutes until the rain tapered off enough for them to make a run for Foster's BMW. Dinner was out of the question since the lights of the restaurant never came back on. The power seemed to be out in the whole neighborhood. It wasn't until Foster drove a few blocks south that they saw lights in the houses.

"Well, at least I got you home safely," he said, pulling up in front of Millie's house. "Other than that, I'm afraid this evening has been a total washout. I do apologize."

"What are you talking about?" said Millie. She unbuckled her seat belt and turned to face him. "We just had ourselves a little adventure, that's all. It's actually pretty funny if you think about it. Those umbrellas rolling off the pier. Your hairpiece getting stuck in the tree . . ."

Foster groaned. "Don't remind me. I was completely and utterly humiliated. I don't think I've ever been so embarrassed . . ."

"Why? Because of the hairpiece? That's silly. You have no reason to feel embarrassed. It's a very good toupee, Foster. Very high quality."

"Millie, please, you don't have to . . ."

"No, I mean it. I really do. I didn't know you even wore a toupee," she said. "And I know everything about everyone in this town. But I swear, I did *not* know that Foster Lee Jackson wore a toupee. Didn't even suspect it. I mean, it looks so natural. And you're such a handsome man. With or without the toupee."

Foster didn't say anything, just stared at the windshield wipers going back and forth.

"Want to come inside?" she asked, leaning closer. "I have a box of Chardonnay in the fridge. And a chili bean casserole I can heat up. We could Netflix and chili."

Foster looked at her, smiled, and started to laugh.

"Sounds delightful," he said.

When Rooster met Margarita at the lighthouse museum—three days before Harry met Sally—the weather advisories had become much more serious.

Category 4 serious.

Early that morning, the National Weather Service upgraded Hurricane Harry as he veered southwest toward Cuba. Wind speeds were as high as 150 miles per hour, with waves peaking at thirty-five feet. That, plus twelve inches of rain, caused massive flooding along Cuba's north coast. The destruction was immeasurable—and still ongoing.

This did not bode well for the Florida Keys.

In response to Harry's resurgence, the governor of Florida declared a state of emergency. Residents in southern Florida and the Keys were advised to evacuate immediately, if possible. All road tolls were suspended, all schools were closed, and five hundred troops of the Florida National Guard were deployed to assist with preparations.

How did Key West respond to the governor's response?

With mixed responses of their own.

Some people panicked. They started packing their bags as soon as Harry started slamming Cuba. Others weren't quite sure whether to stay or go. They made phone calls to friends and relatives to get their opinion on the matter—and, they hoped, an invitation to stay with them until the storm passed. Then, of course, there were the longtime locals with Hurricane Amnesia. They were convinced that *this* storm couldn't be worse than the *last* storm. They weren't going anywhere. As long as they were stocked with candles, batteries, toilet paper, and extra cans of SpaghettiOs, they'd be fine.

And then there was Rooster McCloud.

Rooster was no hurricane denier. He knew all too well the dangers of a major storm. But as Key West lighthouse keeper, he felt it was his duty to stay and keep the lights burning. Literally, if not figuratively.

Also, he got a text from Margarita:

I need your help! Are you at the museum now?

He texted back with a thumbs-up emoji. She replied:

On my way!

Rooster turned off his phone and gazed at the lonely-looking displays around him. The Key West lighthouse and museum were officially open today—but the only visitors so far were a young family from Virginia. They zipped through the museum and climbed to the top of the lighthouse in five minutes flat. "We want to get out of Key West before the storm hits," the mother explained.

"That's smart," said Rooster. "Drive carefully. These roads are slippery when wet."

Watching the family's car speed away in the rain made him a little nervous.

Getting a text from Margarita—asking for help—made him a lot nervous.

What's going on? he wondered.

He walked to the entrance of the museum and looked outside. Through the downpour, he could make out a bright red umbrella coming down Whitehead Street.

Margarita.

"What's new, pussycat!" she called out as she ran up the sidewalk.

Rooster held open the door and ushered her inside. "Are you okay? Is everything all right? How can I help?"

Margarita closed her umbrella and brushed the water off her arms. "I'm fine, Rooster," she said. "Just a little out of breath."

"What is it? What's wrong?"

"Oh, dear. I'm getting water all over your floor." She pointed to the bottom of her flowered dress. It was soaked and dripping. "All over my cha-cha shoes, too," she sighed.

"Margarita, you're freaking me out. You said you needed my help."

Margarita took a deep breath. "Okay. Here's what happened. I sent the staff home this morning as soon as we heard about Hurricane Harry. The problem is, I forgot about the windows."

"The windows?"

"We board up the windows of the Hemingway House whenever there's a Category Two or higher. I should have taken care of it yesterday, but Tropical Storm Sally didn't seem too severe and Hurricane Harry was moving east. Thank goodness Jake stuck around today to feed the cats. He's bringing the plywood up from the basement now. Is Mack around? Jake could use his help."

Rooster nodded. "Mack's in the lighthouse. I'll get him." He turned on his phone and sent his nephew a text message. Then he looked up at Margarita. "You know, those boys aren't talking to each other right now. Seems they got into a fight."

"A fight? Over what?"

"The new girl."

"Laura?"

"Laura. They both like her and they both kissed her."

"Oh, dear."

"They've been avoiding each other all week. It's a sad thing to see."

"That's ridiculous," said Margarita. "Those two have been best friends since grade school. I remember when they'd come to the house to play with the cats. They were inseparable."

"Well, now they're separable." Rooster sighed and shook his head.

Neither of them spoke for a moment. They stood there listening to the sound of the rain outside. Finally, Margarita broke the silence.

"You know, Rooster. I've had this strange feeling that you've been avoiding me, too. Ever since the dance party."

Rooster shifted uncomfortably. "I've been busy is all. Between the radio station and the museum and feeding those chickens . . ."

Margarita rolled her eyes. "You mean, your normal routine? I'm talking about the way you act around me now. It's not normal. You seem, I don't know, distant. Even a little shy. Which is weird, considering how bold you were on the dance floor with me. I mean . . . *dios mío*." She fanned herself with her hand, as if she were having a hot flash. "You really surprised me, Rooster. You swept me off my feet!"

Rooster blushed. "Really?"

"Really! I haven't had so much fun on the dance floor in ages. How did you learn to dance the paso doble like that?"

"I lived in Spain for a year after high school. Had the hots for a girl in Pamplona who loved to dance. She taught me."

"She certainly did," said Margarita, smiling and nodding. "How is it that I've known you all these years and this is the first I'm hearing about this?"

Rooster looked her in the eye and took a long, slow breath. "There's a lot you don't know about me, Margarita."

The soft, low tone of his voice took Margarita by surprise. He sounded so . . . what? Serious? That wasn't it. There was something else in his voice, something sweet and sad and unexpected. . . .

There was tenderness.

Margarita let out a little sigh. "Well, you'll have to tell me more of your stories, Rooster. I'd love to hear them. We should spend more time together. In fact, I was hoping you might consider joining our dance club."

Rooster laughed. "Me? The paso doble is the only dance I know!"

"I can teach you! It'll be fun! Just a few short lessons with Señorita Margarita, and you'll be dancing like a pro. We'll do the cha-cha . . . the rumba . . . the fox-trot . . . the waltz. . . ."

She performed each of the dances as she spoke, shaking her hips and twirling and gliding through the museum, her arms wrapped around an imaginary partner.

Rooster shook his head and laughed. "You're crazy, Margarita," he said. "I can't move my hips like that."

"Oh, just wait until I get ahold of those hips of yours." She winked and broke into a samba. "I have ways of making them do things that'll drive the ladies wild. The ghost of Elvis Presley is going to be jealous of your hips."

Rooster laughed again, even harder. Margarita grabbed him by the hand and spun herself into his arms, swaying her body against him as he swayed along.

They stopped when the door swung open.

It was Mack—grinning ear to ear.

"I hate to break up the party," he said, "but . . . you wanted to see me?"

"Mack! Darling!" said Margarita, slipping out of Rooster's arms. "I need to ask a favor."

Mack looked confused. "Sure. Anything. What's up?"

"Grab your raincoat and gloves," said Rooster. "We have work to do."

"We do?" Mack glanced around the empty museum. "What?"

"Not here. At the Hemingway House. Jake needs help boarding up the windows."

Mack's face fell. "Oh. That could be a problem. Jake and I aren't in a good place right now."

Rooster scoffed. "Well, you'd better get yourselves out of that place—fast—because Harry and Sally are coming. And frankly, my dear, they don't give a damn."

When Nessie met Laura on the front porch of the Hemingway House—two days before Harry met Sally—the rest of the fifty-four cats were nowhere in sight.

They knew something bad was coming.

It wasn't unusual for felines to sense an approaching storm before humans did. For centuries, people thought that cats possessed supernatural powers. Some believed they actually conjured thunderstorms through the magic stored in their tails. This was not true, of course. According to modern zoologists, cats have always been finely tuned to their environments and sensitive to barometric pressure changes.

They responded to weather shifts swiftly and instinctively—often gathering their young, seeking an enclosed shelter, and sometimes pawing their faces to relieve the pressure. This ability to "predict" a coming storm was one of the reasons eighteenth-century sailors and fishermen brought cats along as shipmates.

They would have loved Nessie.

Nessie sensed the danger long before the other cats. She felt it in her bones weeks ago. When the wind knocked that branch onto the roof of the gift shop—and Laura showed up at the house with her bags—Nessie knew it was coming. And it was going to be bad.

Not all of it, though.

Nessie had a feeling something good was going to come out of all this, too—and that Laura was going to bring it to her. She'd had that feeling since the day she met the girl many, many years ago. That's why Nessie waited for her on the front porch of the Hemingway House, instead of running for cover like the other cats.

"Nessie! What are you doing outside?"

The cat looked up to see a person in long pants, black boots, and a shiny jacket with a big hood walk through the front gate. From the voice, Nessie knew it was Laura. Normally she identified people using her sense of smell. But today, with all this rain and wind, Nessie could barely recognize her old friend.

The funny-looking clothes didn't help.

"Hey, Nessie. How's it going, girl?" Laura stepped onto the porch and out of the rain. "I'd pet you, Ness, but I might get water all over you. I know how much you hate water."

Nessie looked up and waved her tail.

"I'm surprised to see you out here," Laura went on. "Were you waiting for me? Well, the Hemingway House is closed, you know. The governor said we should evacuate. It's not mandatory, but I'm leaving with the Crabb sisters tomorrow morning. They have cousins up north who'll take us in. Mack is going to drive us there in his van."

Nessie didn't understand what she was saying but listened intently anyway.

"The Crabbs don't want to leave their animals behind, so we're bringing them along. That got me thinking about you and the Hemingway cats. I'm worried about you, Nessie!"

Laura stopped and looked around.

The place was deserted. There was nobody in the garden—human, feline, or otherwise—just the rain-soaked plants with low drooping leaves and the tall swaying palm trees rustling in the wind. The house looked as if it had been abandoned. All of its windows were boarded up with large sheets of plywood.

"Hello?" Laura shouted out. "Is anybody here?"

Laura tried the front door. It was open. She stepped inside. Nessie followed behind her, tiptoeing around the tracks left by Laura's wet boots.

"Hello? Margarita? Jake?"

Nessie recognized the names. She knew that "Margarita" was the First Lady and "Jake" was the Food Man. They were very important humans as far as Nessie was concerned. Laura seemed to think so, too. Nessie would watch her eat food with the Food Man in the room with the hot brown liquid maker. They used to eat food together almost every day.

Until recently.

It started last week. That's when Nessie noticed something different. Laura seemed to be avoiding the Food Man. She ate her food alone on a bench in the garden with Nessie. Which was fine with Nessie. She liked getting all of Laura's attention. But she also liked seeing Laura and Jake together. They laughed a lot when they were together. Not so much now.

"Hello! Anybody here?"

Laura stepped into the main hallway and looked around. At first glance, the place seemed empty. Then, as she walked from room to room, she began to notice furry clusters of cats nestled throughout the house.

Bullfighter and Boxer were curled up together beneath the dining room table. It seemed the big-pawed rivals had finally called a truce.

Chew-Chew and Whiskey were huddled under a glass display case of Hemingway's fishing mementos. They must have thought it was a food bar. Or a liquor cabinet.

Larry, Curly, and Moe were snoozing in one of the armchairs. The little knuckleheads were tangled in a ball of kitten arms, kitten legs, and kitten tails, making it hard to know what belonged to whom. They didn't seem to know either. They kept pawing each other's faces to scratch an itch.

Spindcrella was hiding in the kitchen sink. Actually, she was sliding more than hiding. The tiny kitten with the oversized paws seemed to be having a ball slipping around on the ceramic. She only ducked down to hide when Laura entered the room. "Ha-ha, I see you there, kitty."

Upstairs, Lady Bratt Ashley was lounging in her usual coveted spot on Hemingway's bed. But this time, she had Jackie Chan, Bette Davis, and Joan Clawford surrounding her. Maybe she thought a barricade of cats would protect her from the storm.

Meanwhile, Kilimanjaro gazed down from her perch next to the Picasso sculpture. With her snowy white fur and impenetrable green eyes, she looked even more enigmatic than Picasso's abstract art. Laura couldn't begin to guess what she was thinking.

"Is somebody up there?"

It was Margarita, shouting up the stairs from the main hallway.

"Yes! It's me: Laura! I'll be right there!"

Laura picked up Nessie and ran down the staircase. She stopped on the bottom step when she saw that Margarita wasn't alone. Behind her stood Lucky Leo, Millie, Rooster, and Jake. All of them were wearing raincoats—and very grim expressions on their faces.

"What's going on?" Laura asked. "Is something wrong?"

Margarita took a breath. "It's Hurricane Harry. He's been upgraded to a Category Five. They predict he'll make landfall—here—in two days."

"That's not all," said Millie. "Tropical Storm Sally is coming at us from the other side."

Lucky Leo held up his phone. "The governor just ordered a mandatory evacuation. They want everyone to leave the island by tomorrow."

Laura felt like she'd been punched in the stomach. She hugged Nessie tighter. "What about the cats? Can we evacuate them, too?"

Jake shook his head. "There's no way we can evacuate fifty-four cats. It's just not possible."

"So what are we going to do?"

Jake looked Laura in the eye. "I'm staying here with them."

"Me, too," said Rooster.

"We're all staying," said Margarita. "Leo and Millie, too."

Millie nodded vigorously. "These cats are like family to us. We can't just leave them behind. Right, Leo?" Leo nodded, too.

Laura looked at her coworkers. She saw the passion and determination in their eyes—and the worried look on Jake's face. He knew what she was thinking.

"You should go with Mack and the Crabb sisters, Laura," he said. "I'll feel better knowing you're safe with them up north."

"But . . ."

"It's for the best," said Rooster. "Things could get pretty bad here."

"Yes, dear, it's dangerous," said Margarita. "And the governor ordered the evacuation. It's mandatory."

Laura felt Nessie breathing against her chest. She caught a glimpse of Pawpa Hemingway at the end of the hall, watching her from a doorway. The old gray white-bearded cat looked different to her somehow. Not grumpy or annoyed or suspicious, like he usually did. No.

Pawpa looked scared.

That was enough to convince Laura. "I'm staying, too," she said. "I don't care what the governor said. I don't care if it's dangerous. I'm staying here with the rest of you . . ."

She paused, glancing at Pawpa.

". . . and Hemingway's cats."

★ ★ ★

When Hurricane Harry met Tropical Storm Sally—forty-eight hours later—the famous six-toed cats of the Hemingway House would be surrounded by the people who loved them.

And that's when the kitty litter really hit the fan.

Chapter 11
The Purrfect Storm

By twelve o'clock the next day, the news about Hemingway's cats had gone national.

And people were worried.

It started when a local TV reporter got wind of Margarita's decision to defy evacuation orders. An "action news" camera crew showed up at the Hemingway House to interview the manager and her staff—and also get some adorable cat footage. Margarita told the reporter, "We love these cats too much to leave them behind. We're going to ride this out together." Jake explained why they couldn't evacuate them all: "You've heard the expression 'herding cats,' right? Well, imagine trying to round up fifty-four free-range cats in a place this big. It can't be done." Lucky Leo pointed out the unique weather-resistant features of the house: "These walls are made of eighteen-inch blocks of solid limestone. They've withstood dozens of hurricanes over the years, even the big one in 1919. This baby was built to last. It sits on the highest point of the island, so flooding shouldn't be a problem. We're going to be just fine."

The rest of the world wasn't so sure.

The story was picked up by the newswire services and, in a matter of hours, was splashed across the pages of *USA Today*, *The Washington Post*, and *The New York Times*. Magazines like *People* and

Southern Living started digging up photos of the Hemingway House and its famous six-toed occupants to run "feline interest stories" on the developing situation.

Soon the whole country was concerned for the cats' welfare.

Some people thought it was a mistake not to evacuate them. Mariel Hemingway—the Academy Award–nominated actress and granddaughter of Ernest Hemingway—told TMZ that the house manager should "get all the cats in the car and take off." Others thought it was incredibly brave of the staff to shelter in place for "the Storm of the Century."

Either way, everybody in America was rooting for Hemingway's cats.

If they lived in Key West, they were also trying to get out. . . .

Shelly woke up early that morning to gather her things and meet Rick and Ricardo at the Lighthouse Hotel. She didn't need an evacuation order from the governor to convince her to leave Key West. She'd been tracking the courses of Harry and Sally all week. The only thing crazier than the paths of those storms was the number of people who vowed to stay here when they collided. Shelly wasn't crazy. She called up Rick and Ricardo and talked them into driving her to a motel upstate. She booked rooms for all of them. "Bring Lucy and Desi," she told them. "They allow dogs, as long as they're well behaved."

Shelly liked to be prepared. Her bags were packed. She was ready to go.

Unfortunately, Rick and Ricardo were not.

"We still have one guest left in the hotel," Rick explained. "He refuses to leave."

"We told him the evacuation is mandatory," added Ricardo. "But he says he wants to make sure he gets his money's worth."

Shelly rolled her eyes. "So give him a refund. He's got to go."

"We tried that," said Rick, stroking his mustache. "He finally agreed to leave, but not until checkout time. Three o'clock."

Shelly looked at her watch. "That's cutting it close." She glanced at the sky. The rain had subsided for the moment, and the clouds seemed to have lightened up. "Too bad we can't leave now. This is the perfect time to go."

Ricardo picked up Lucy, who was sniffing Desi's butt, and gazed up at the lighthouse. "It doesn't look so bad right now," he said. "Are you sure the hurricane won't pass us by? He's been zigzagging all over the place."

"Oh, he's coming," said Shelly. "Harry's got a hot date planned with Tropical Storm Sally. He wouldn't miss it for the world."

"I think Sally's just a tease," said Rick. "I mean, look how nice it is now."

"Trust me," said Shelly. "This is the calm before the storm."

Mama Marley spent most of the week driving tourists to the airport.

Nobody wanted to be stuck in Key West right now, no matter how pretty their Airbnb's hand towels were. It was time to go, and they didn't need the governor or Mariel Hemingway or anyone else to tell them. Over the past few days, Sally had served up a hot steaming gumbo of crappy tropical weather. No one was anxious to see what Harry brought to the table.

This was all fine with Mama Marley. *More trips, more tips!*

But once the last flight departed from Key West International Airport—which was then closed until further notice—she didn't know what to do next.

So she switched off the reggae, drove herself home, and called Leo Trout.

"Hey, Lucky Man," she crooned. "Have you changed your mind yet?"

Nope. Leo hadn't changed his mind. He was staying at the Hemingway House with Margarita and the others. *And those scary cats.* Hearing Leo's calm and reassuring voice, she briefly considered joining him. *But those scary cats.* Nope. No way. She couldn't do it.

She asked Leo about the latest forecast. After chatting a few minutes, they told each other to be careful, be safe, and be free next Friday for Dance Night. *It's a date.*

Then she called her sister in Atlanta.

"Hey, Lana Banana in Atlanta. Does your offer still stand?" It did. Lana told Marla she could stay with her as long as she needed. "Thanks, Sis. Traffic's gonna suck, so don't wait up for me. I know you need your beauty sleep." Lana's comeback was swift, harsh, and hilarious.

It was a sister thing.

As Mama packed her suitcase, she started thinking about Leo. *Why does he have to lie so much? What's the deal with that?* Then she started to worry about him. He was taking a huge risk staying here. A Category 5 was major. As in devastating. And deadly. *What if he gets hurt? What if the house collapses? What if . . . ?*

Mama stopped herself. She looked up and caught a glimpse of herself in the mirror on the closet door. She saw the worry lines on her face. And the watery pools in her eyes.

What if . . . I'm actually falling in love with Lucky Leo Trout?

"No way," she told herself. "Get out of town."

Foster Lee Jackson knew he'd never convince Millie into leaving Key West with him.

But he thought he'd try. Just one more time.

"Won't you please reconsider, Miss Millie?" he asked over the phone. "The evacuation is not only mandatory; it's the sensible thing to do. It's crazy to risk your life for . . . for . . ."

"Cats?" she said. "It's crazy to risk my life for cats? Well, Foster. If risking my life for cats is crazy then, yes, I'm crazy. Crazy for cats."

"I'm sorry, Millie. I didn't mean to offend. I know you love those cats. Who doesn't love cats? Anyone with a modicum of taste loves cats. Cats are the most civil and refined of domesticated beasts."

"They're not beasts, Foster," she said. "They're little furry people with souls. Just because they don't use big fancy words, and have a few extra toes, doesn't mean they're beasts. They're my friends. I can't leave them here to face a hurricane all by themselves."

Foster knew he'd screwed up. "Forgive me, Millie. Please. It was not my intention to disparage the divine nature of the feline soul. You are truly a kind and giving person. It's one of the many things I admire about you. That . . . and your magnificent chili cheese soufflé."

"You mean, my casserole? It's good, right?"

"Good? It was absolutely *yummy*. I had such a lovely time the other night and . . . I look forward to seeing you again and . . . honestly? I feel really awful about leaving without you."

"Aw. That's sweet, Foster. But the governor gave an order, and you've got to follow his order because you work for the historical society. That's part of the government, isn't it?"

"Um, not exactly. . . ."

"Whatever. You're a very important man in this community. I'm just Millie. I'm just the ticket booth lady at a tourist attraction. You might think I'm crazy, but I'm just doing my job . . . and what I think is right. For the cats. That's just who I am."

Foster didn't know what to say. He had to let her words sink in for a moment.

"Well, just Millie," he said. "I think you're just wonderful."

Their phone call ended a few minutes later. Foster finished packing, put on his Burberry raincoat, and carried his bags out to his car. It was a red 1983 classic BMW. His most prized possession. An hour ago, he was worried about driving it through the rain and mud and sand.

Now he was worried about Millie. Just Millie.

And maybe the cats, too.

Mack McCloud's van was a total piece of junk, but it got him where he needed to go.

Most of the time.

He bought the van five years ago from an old fisherman who

used it to transport whatever he caught from the nets of his trawler to the local seafood stores. It took Mack more than a year to get rid of the fish smell. In addition to deodorizing, Mack had the van custom-painted by the artist who did his tattoos. It looked really cool—a phantasmagoria of deep-sea creatures, sunken shipwrecks, and coral reef castles—but it was still a piece of junk. The engine was in constant need of repair, and the muffler barely muffled anything.

The best feature of the van? It was big. Big enough to hold the band's instruments, speakers, and sound equipment. Big enough to squeeze in some extra steel drums for a calypso-themed wedding. And big enough for the occasional odd job.

Like evacuating snakes.

And spiders, and turtles, and birds.

And one very mellow iguana.

"Iggy Popstar is going to love the change of scenery," said Jolene, sliding the tank across the floor of the van. "You wouldn't think it by looking at him, but he's quite the explorer."

"Put his tank near the front," said Jilly. "So he can see out the window."

Mack rubbed his scruffy beard and sighed. "I'll have to move Rocky and Rambo," he said, pointing to the turtle tank behind the driver's seat.

"That's okay," said Jolene. "They'll probably spend most of the trip inside their shells."

"Yeah," said Jilly. "Rocky and Rambo aren't as tough as they look. They're hard on the outside but soft as a pussycat on the inside."

"Pussycat! That reminds me," said her sister. "Have you seen Tallulah around? I fed her last night but haven't seen her since."

"I'll go look."

As Jilly searched the bungalow for the missing cat, Mack and Jolene finished loading up the van. They wedged Antony and Cleopatra's tarantula tank in between the iguana tank and the boa constrictor tank. Even though they each had eight eyes, the furry spiders didn't seem to notice Sammy and Delilah. The two coiled snakes were pressed against the glass watching them—trying to decide if the spiders were edible or not. Next in the van were Romeo and Juliet. Surprisingly, the star-crossed lovebirds weren't quarrelling today. Probably because they had a lot of things to look at besides each other. Last up was Polly Parton. As her Victorian birdcage was being loaded in the van, the Dolly-loving parrot kept repeating the first two lines of "Nine to Five" over and over. Thankfully, she stopped when Jolene covered the cage with a blanket.

"Done," said Jolene, smiling at Mack. "Now we can start loading up the supplies."

"Supplies?"

"Pet food, cat litter, nesting material, crickets—"

"Crickets?"

"For Antony and Cleopatra. They love them."

When they returned to the bungalow to get the supplies, Jilly was still looking for Tallulah. "I can't find her anywhere. I've checked all her usual spots. I don't know what to do. What if she—?" Jilly's phone buzzed. It was a text from Laura:

Don't forget Tallulah!

Jilly texted back:

I can't find her!

Laura responded:

Did you look in my wardrobe? She built a nest in there with my socks.

Jilly checked the wardrobe in Laura's room. "Tallulah! There you are!"

Mack and Jolene let out a sigh of relief. Then they went back to work, loading various supplies into the van. Jilly held Tallulah in one arm while she dropped time-released fish food into the aquariums. "I wish we could take the fish with us," she said to the others.

Mack looked at her. "I think we have enough animals, Jilly. My van is not an ark."

"Relax, Noah, the fish are staying," said Jolene. "Hurry up, Jilly. We should set sail before Noah here chickens out."

"The chickens!" Jilly gasped. "What's going to happen to the gypsy chickens? They live on the streets!"

"They'll be fine," said Mack. "Uncle Rooster told me a bunch of his fellow chicken feeders are driving around town, rounding them up, and putting them in the backs of their cars for shelter. They even wrap the chickens in newspaper to keep them calm."

"Really?" said Jilly with a skeptical look on her face. "Is that true?"

Mack answered in his deepest voice.

"Never doubt the Rooster."

Twenty minutes later, they were on U.S. Route 1 heading out of Key West.

But they weren't moving.

The traffic was backed up all the way to the IHOP on North Roosevelt Boulevard. The northbound lanes were packed with cars, but the southbound lanes were empty. Occasionally a large green supply truck from the Florida National Guard would pass by. That was about it.

"Look at the sky over there," said Jolene, pointing to the left.

A massive wall of black churning clouds loomed above the sea on the other side of the highway. It was Tropical Storm Sally moving in from the northwest.

"Look at the sky over *there*," said Jilly, pointing to the right.

An even bigger wall of black churning clouds loomed above the palm trees and blue angled roof of the IHOP. It was Hurricane Harry moving in from the southeast.

"I know this sounds weird, but I'm really hungry for pancakes right now," said Jilly.

"You're weird. They're closed," said Jolene. "Most people packed up and left yesterday. Except the stragglers. Like us."

"Sorry about that," said Mack, knowing he was the reason they'd waited. "Boarding up the Hemingway House took longer than Jake and I thought it would."

"So you two are speaking again?" asked Jilly.

Mack sighed. He was thinking about how to answer when a state trooper car pulled up beside them. Mack rolled down his window. The trooper explained that there'd been an accident on Stock Island. "We should be moving again shortly," he said.

Two hours later, they were still sitting there.

And the weather was getting worse by the minute. The light drizzle had turned into a heavy downpour. The wind was blowing like crazy, making the palm trees next to the IHOP thrash wildly back and forth. Leaves and branches and other debris swirled in the air and spilled across the highway, smacking the side of the van and sticking to the windshield.

"It's like we're under attack," said Jolene, hugging Tallulah.

Mack leaned forward and looked up at the massive walls of clouds on either side of them. They seemed to be rushing toward each other, as if they were getting ready to embrace.

The walls were closing in.

"This doesn't look good," said Mack.

He tried the radio again. After a few turns of the dial, he managed to pick up an emergency broadcast station. A man's voice crackled through the speakers: "It's just been confirmed that US 1 has been flooded in at least five locations in the Florida Keys. Evacuation is not possible at this time. Residents are urged to seek out the nearest emergency shelters. I repeat, US 1 has been flooded—"

Mack turned off the radio and turned on the windshield wipers. Up ahead, barely visible through the teeming rain, he could see several of the cars pulling off the road and turning around. They must have gotten the message. *Evacuation is not possible at this time. . . .*

"What are we going to do?" asked Jilly, sitting on the floor next to Iggy's tank.

"I don't know, but we can't stay here." He started up the engine and waited for a few cars to pass. Then he pulled off the highway and into the parking lot of IHOP.

"Where are we going?" asked Jolene. "Back to the bungalow? I'm not sure that's a good idea. That old shack is pretty shaky, even on a good day."

"We're going to the Hemingway House," said Mack, turning the van around. "It's on higher ground. We'll be safe there."

He started to pull out onto the highway when the muffler let out a few loud bangs. Smoke started spewing out of the sides of the hood. The engine sputtered and coughed.

Then it died.

Mama Marley didn't hear the emergency broadcast on the radio—she was listening to reggae—but it didn't take long for her to figure out that the only road out of Key West was flooded.

She could see it with her own eyes.

After being stuck on the northbound US 1 for two hours, she considered turning around and joining Lucky Leo at the Hemingway House. She tried calling him but no luck. So she sat there in her taxicab gazing across the highway at the incoming waves from the Salt Pond Keys. As the weather grew worse, the waves got higher. Soon they were smashing against the low concrete seawall and splashing onto the southbound lanes.

"You got to be kidding me," she muttered.

She watched in disbelief as another giant wave swelled up and crashed down on the road. The foaming water spilled across the highway—and splashed against the tires of Mama's cab.

"Oh, hell, no!" she exclaimed.

Grabbing the steering wheel, she hit the gas and pulled onto the shoulder of the road. Making a hard U-turn, she started driving south against the traffic. She glanced in her rearview as she looked for a turnoff and noticed that some of the cars behind her were doing the same thing.

She saw an IHOP coming up on the left. "Great. I can turn off there."

That's when she spotted the stalled van in the parking lot. She recognized it from the customized paint job—all those icky sea monsters—even before she saw Mack McCloud standing over the open hood. Smoke was billowing from the engine.

Mama pulled up next to him, rolled down her window, and said, "Need help?"

"Mama!" Mack shouted happily, wiping the rain from his eyes. "Thank God you're here! Do you think you could give us a lift to the Hemingway House?"

"That's where I'm headed," she said. "Who's *us*?"

Jilly and Jolene Crabb jumped out of the van and ran toward the cab.

"Mama Marley!" Jilly cried out. "Hallelujah!"

"We're in trouble!" Jolene shouted over the sound of the wind. "We need to get these animals to safety!"

"Animals? What animals?" Mama looked nervously at the van.

The twins turned and opened the back doors, showing her the tanks and cages inside.

"You got to be kidding me."

The van was filled with birds and turtles, spiders and snakes, a long green lizard—and one big-pawed cat in the passenger seat.

"Oh, hell, no."

Foster Lee Jackson was stuck on the highway—three cars behind Mama Marley—when the first waves started crashing onto the southbound lanes of US 1. Sixty seconds later, a voice on the radio confirmed that the highway was flooded. Evacuation was out of the question.

Foster tried to look on the bright side. *I can join Millie at the Hemingway House now.*

He wasn't sure, though, how he was going to do that. The cars were lined up on the northbound side, and no one was moving. He hoped the state troopers or National Guards were redirecting traffic up ahead. In the meantime, Foster thought he'd try calling Millie. His phone still had a connection. But when he called her number, he was sent to voicemail.

"My dear Miss Millie," he said. "It appears that the roads are closed and I will not be able to evacuate. If you don't mind, it would be an honor and a pleasure to take refuge with you and your cherished cats before the hurricane hits. Actually, it looks like it's already here—"

His connection was cut off.

Foster sighed. He glanced to his right to see Mama Marley's pink taxicab zoom past him. On the shoulder of the road. Going the wrong direction.

Well, that's one way to get off this highway, he thought. *But if every driver did that, it would be chaos.*

He decided it was more prudent to wait until the cars started moving in an orderly fashion. So he turned on some classical music and settled back. He started to close his eyes when another big wave crashed onto the highway—and splashed onto the side of his BMW.

Screw this. I'm getting out of here.

Pulling onto the shoulder of the highway, he made a sharp U-turn and started heading south. Back to town—and back to Millie. In a way, Foster was glad it turned out like this. When Millie insisted on staying, he should have insisted on staying with her. It was the gentlemanly thing to do. He gripped the steering wheel tighter and tried to focus through the rain-streaked windshield. The storm was getting worse by the minute. It looked like Hurricane Harry was trying to knock over some palm trees next to the IHOP.

That's when Foster saw Mama Marley's cab and Mack McCloud's van. The Crabb sisters were helping Mack move things from the back of the van to the trunk of Mama's cab. They seemed to be having a rough time of it, leaning into the wind to keep from being blown over. Foster wondered if he should pull over and help them.

Of course I should, he thought. *It's the gentlemanly thing to do.*

He steered his BMW into the IHOP parking lot, drove up next to Mack's van, and called out from his window, "Greetings, fellow travelers! May I be of assistance?"

Ten minutes later, Foster's trunk was packed with pet supplies and the back seat was covered with a blanket for the snake tank and iguana tank. Mack sat next to him in the passenger seat, holding a tank of tarantulas on his lap.

Meanwhile, Mama Marley was trying not to freak out.

"Can't you shut those birds up?" she asked Jilly in the back seat of her cab. "Between those damn lovebirds and that damn parrot and that damn Dolly Parton song, my nerves are shot. How am I supposed to concentrate on driving?"

"Sorry, Mama," said Jilly, putting covers over the birdcages. "I just wanted to give them some air."

"At least they're not spiders and snakes," said Jolene, sitting in the front passenger seat with Tallulah on her lap.

"That's where I draw the line," said Mama. "No spiders and snakes in the cab. Cats and birds are bad enough. Just make sure that furry-tailed devil stays on your lap."

Jolene laughed. "Don't worry. Tallulah's a sweetheart. She likes everybody."

"As long as you're not a mouse," said Jilly.

"I knew it!" Mama hooted. "She's a killer. I can see it in her eyes. Just look! She's staring at me! Probably wants to claw up my face. She's got those extra claws, too, just like the Hemingway cats. I don't like it."

The Crabb sisters laughed again and tried to reassure her, but Mama was focused on the road. The rain was pounding down hard now, and the wind was intense. Leaves and debris blew across the street, some of the bigger pieces forcing Mama to swerve around them. As she turned onto Whitehead Street, a small uprooted tree came flying out of nowhere. It crashed down in the middle of the street—right in the path of the cab. The sisters screamed, the birds screeched, and the cat jumped.

Mama slammed on the brakes.

They sat there for a few moments, catching their breath. No one said a word. Finally, Mama broke the silence, speaking calmly and quietly.

"Okay. We're fine. Now somebody get this damn cat off my lap."

Laura helped Jake carry the last of the litter boxes down to the basement of the Hemingway House, being careful not to trip over the cats who ran up and down the stairs. For the past twenty-four hours, the cats had been following their every move, fascinated by all the preparations they were making—and sticking their noses into absolutely everything.

Laura wiped her hands on her dripping raincoat and looked up at Jake. "Is that it? Can we finally take a break now? And I mean a real break, not one where I have to test batteries while I'm eating lunch."

Jake smiled and nodded. "We're done. Good job, Laura. I really appreciate the help."

Laura let out a sigh of relief, sat on one of the basement steps, and closed her eyes.

She was exhausted from lugging supplies through the teeming rain, unloading crates of flashlights, lanterns, and candles, unpacking bags of food and jugs of water—for cats *and* humans—and cranking up the hand-cranked radios until her arm ached.

At least the cats enjoyed it.

Larry, Curly, and Moe—that troublemaking trio—kept pawing at her hand while she turned the crank of the radio. They thought it was a game. If it was, Laura was losing. She had to distract the kittens with an empty plastic bag so she could finish cranking in peace. Chew-Chew and Whiskey were—unsurprisingly—interested in the food and beverages. They kept running off with small bags of chips, and Laura had to hunt the cats down before they hid the chips away somewhere, never to be found again. Boxer and Bullfighter were attracted to the batteries. They kept knocking them off the tabletops and rolling them across the floor for sport. Spinderella, the poor little thing, kept getting stuck inside every box or bag she could crawl into. Then she'd cry until someone pulled her out. Even the aloof Kilimanjaro came down from her perch to get a closer look at what was going on. The cats were everywhere, getting into everything.

Jake said they should have their own reality TV show: *Cats Gone Wild* or *Cats Behaving Badly*.

And then there was Nessie.

Laura's golden-furred friend climbed onto her lap as soon as

Laura sat down on the basement stairs. She seemed agitated. "It's going to be okay, Ness." She scratched the cat's ears, then looked up at Jake. "She keeps clinging to me as if she's afraid I'll abandon her. Or something will happen to me. It's weird. She's usually so mellow."

"Maybe she understands the danger we're in," said Jake. "I've always thought Nessie is the smartest cat in the house. The most sensitive, too. It's like she's tuned into things that the rest of us can't . . ."

Nessie sat up suddenly, glared at the ceiling, and arched her back. Seconds later, there was a loud *boom, boom, boom* upstairs.

Someone was pounding on the front door.

Laura looked at Jake. "Who do you think that is?"

"I have no idea."

They heard some footsteps and the door opening, followed by the sound of howling wind and rain and people talking. They ran upstairs to see what was going on.

"Of course you can stay here," Margarita was saying. "It's safer than the hotel."

Standing in the doorway were Rick and Ricardo—holding Lucy and Desi in their arms—along with Key West's favorite weather goddess, Shelly. The Chihuahuas were quieter than Laura had ever seen them. Probably because they couldn't take their eyes off Larry, Curly, and Moe, who came running to check out the strange new houseguests. The Chihuahuas seemed as curious about the kittens as the kittens were about them.

"Come on in, get dried off," Margarita said, ushering everyone into the hallway. "And Shelly, dear, could you please close the door behind you before we all blow away? Thank you, dear. Rooster! Leo! Millie! We have guests!"

Suddenly the hall was crowded with people. And cats. And dogs now, too. Rick and Ricardo set the Chihuahuas on the floor while they removed their wet jackets. Laura expected the little dogs to start barking any second now, but they didn't. Probably because they were surrounded by a small gang of curious cats.

They were in enemy territory.

Shelly started giving everyone a weather update as Margarita led them to the next room. "Hurricane Harry arrived ahead of schedule. I guess he couldn't wait to meet Tropical Storm Sally. She might surprise him, though. Might even knock some of the wind out of him. That's what I'm hoping for. A good woman can have a calming effect on a man, you know. I dated a guy once who . . ."

Speaking of a calming effect, Laura was amazed at how quiet the Chihuahuas were in the presence of so many cats—even when Boxer and Bullfighter started circling them like a pair of tag team wrestlers sizing up their opponents. Lucy and Desi, to their credit, didn't bark or move. They stood frozen in place as the two cats—who were bigger than they were—crept closer to investigate. Boxer touched noses with Lucy. Then Bullfighter raised one of his giant paws and poked Desi's shoulder. Desi licked it. For some reason, that seemed to relieve the tension. Boxer and Bullfighter strolled back to their spot under the dining room table. To Laura's surprise, Lucy and Desi followed them! And lay down next to them! And started cuddling!

"Will you look at that?" Jake whispered in Laura's ear. "Isn't it incredible how two different species can get along so well?"

"Certainly better than two best friends can." Laura turned to see Jake's reaction when she noticed someone tall, dark, and dripping at the end of the hall.

It was Rooster McCloud in a mud-spattered raincoat. He looked like an old-timey lighthouse keeper straight out of central casting. Or a *Scooby-Doo* cartoon.

"Jake, could you help me and Mack? We need to reinforce the plywood out back. The wind blew some of the boards loose."

"Sure, Rooster." Jake gave Laura a wounded look, then followed Rooster down the hall.

Which left Laura alone with the cats. She still had her rain-coat on. She could feel her phone vibrating in one of the pockets—probably the five-hundredth text message from her panic-stricken mom. But instead of taking off her coat or checking her phone, she listened to the wind howling in the trees outside and the rain pounding against the boarded-up windows. She looked at the cats around her—Bette Davis and Joan Clawford fighting over a piece of duct tape, Jackie Chan trying to dislodge a bag of potato chips from under a cabinet where Chew-Chew secretly stashed it, Lady Bratt Ashley stretching her legs after a long nap on Hemingway's bed—all of them seemed perfectly fine, blissfully sheltered from the storm. Then she noticed something else. Something missing.

Where are the kittens?

Larry, Curly, and Moe were nowhere to be seen. Laura started looking from room to room, calling their names. She knew she'd seen them just a few minutes ago. In the entry hall. By the front door. When the others arrived.

And the door was open.

Laura's heart started racing. She ran back to the front door. Sitting there on the floor—sniffing and pawing the door—was an old gray bearded cat.

Pawpa Hemingway.

"Pawpa? What are you doing there?"

Pawpa looked at her with his big blue eyes. He blinked, turned, and pawed at the door again, then looked back at Laura.

"What's out there, Pawpa? The kittens? Did you see the kittens go outside?"

Pawpa turned to the door and meowed.

Laura knew it was crazy, but she had a hunch that the old cat was actually trying to tell her where they were. She stepped forward and grabbed the doorknob, positioning her leg in the doorframe to keep Pawpa from running out. Slowly, carefully, she inched the door open and peeked outside.

The storm was raging now. The sky was almost black and filled with clouds. The rain pelted down in waves. The wind was like some sort of invisible, undefined monster, ripping through the palm trees and plants, scattering leaves and broken branches all across the garden.

Laura took a deep breath and stepped outside. "Larry! Curly! Moe!"

She started to close the door behind her when Pawpa jumped out onto the porch.

"Pawpa! No!"

It was too late. Before she could grab him, Pawpa scampered across the porch and ducked under a bush. Laura didn't know what to do—except start looking for the missing kittens. And Pawpa, too. "Larry! Curly! Moe!" She looked from side to side, trying to see a place where they might hide for shelter. Pulling her hood over her head, she ran out into the rain and searched under the steps, the flowerpots, the benches—everywhere she could think of. She considered asking Jake and the others to help her look when she spotted Pawpa.

The old gray cat stepped out from under a thick, low shrub—holding Larry by the scruff of his neck.

"Pawpa! You found Larry!" She rushed forward and bent down. "Are the other ones here?" She lifted some leafy branches—and saw Curly huddled next to the shrub's woody trunk. She reached in and gently pulled her out. "I've got you, Curly! Now where's Moe?"

Pawpa carried Larry to the front door. Laura ran after them, holding Curly to her chest. She opened the door, let Pawpa take Larry inside, and placed Curly down next to them. Then she shut the door and went back to the shrub to look for Moe. Frantically she searched under every plant in the immediate area—but couldn't find him anywhere. Then she gazed down the garden path toward the entrance.

"Moe! Don't move!"

The furry little kitten was huddled against the door of the ticket booth, shivering in the rain. Laura lowered her head and started running toward him. But before she was halfway there, a deafening boom of thunder filled the air—frightening Moe so badly that he bolted out of the gate, across the sidewalk, and into the road. "Moe! No!" Laura watched the kitten run for cover underneath Rooster's old Buick in front of the Lighthouse Hotel. "Stay right there, Moe! I'm coming!"

She charged into the street so quickly, she didn't see the car coming.

Screeeeech!

The driver of the car slammed on the brakes, managing to stop just inches away from hitting her. The shock of it made Laura freeze like a statue. Her heart pounding, she slowly turned her head toward the blinding beams of the car's headlights. At first, she thought she was seeing double, because there were two pairs of lights.

Then she realized she was looking at two different cars.

A pink taxicab and a red BMW.

After a frenzied scramble to unload the cars—just minutes before the hurricane made landfall—everyone was safe inside the Hemingway House. This included twelve people, two Chihuahuas, two boa constrictors, two box turtles, two tarantulas, two lovebirds, one parrot, one iguana, and, by last count, fifty-four cats.

It felt like a slumber party. In a zoo.

Rooster and Margarita rolled out a bunch of sleeping bags in the living room while Jake and Mack brought out snacks and bottles of water.

Shelly played with the dials of the hand-cranked radio to see if she could get an update on the storms. No luck. She finally gave up and left it tuned to the only broadcast she could find: one of Mack's mixed music tapes on auto-play at the WKEY Radio station in Rooster's garage. A selection of Motown's greatest hits.

Laura sat on the floor, drying off the kittens with towels until their fur was extra fluffy. Larry, Curly, and Moe loved it. Even Pawpa Hemingway didn't seem to mind when she wrapped him in a towel and dried him off from beard to tail. As if on cue, the radio started playing "Papa Was a Rollin' Stone."

Millie Graham and Foster Lee Jackson settled into a cozy corner next to Hemingway's fishing mementos. Millie couldn't hide the fact that she was delighted to see Foster. She kept smiling from ear to ear and fidgeting with her blond bouffant, hoping and praying her hairdo would hold up under the weather. She brought a can of hairspray with her in case it didn't. Foster had his own must-have items: a couple bottles of his favorite wine. He uncorked one of them, poured the wine into red plastic cups, and made a toast. "To the brave, beautiful, and bighearted Millie Graham," he said, gazing into her eyes. Then he noticed Whiskey and Chew-Chew sniffing the open bottle. "And to Hemingway's cats!" he added.

Lucky Leo Trout shared a bag of chips with Mama Marley on the other side of the room. He couldn't stop laughing when she started describing her harrowing drive to the Hemingway House with the Crabb twins. "There I was, trying to navigate my little pink taxi through the biggest storm since Noah, and my windshield looks like a tidal wave hit it. Zero visibility. I'm squinting my eyes to see and squeezing the wheel so hard my knuckles hurt. Meanwhile, I got a parrot singing Dolly Parton in the back seat, along with two screeching lovebirds who obviously hate each other. I've seen happier couples in divorce court. What's worse, there's this huge monster cat in the front seat. She's got the biggest paws I've ever seen, with too many claws to count. Must be polydactyl or pterodactyl or whatever it is. Anyway, she's looking at me like I'm a big can of Fancy Feast. Then—get this—a giant palm tree slams down in the middle of the road, I slam on the brakes, and that cat jumps on top of me! She's climbing up me, pawing my face—I'm lucky I'm alive. Well, maybe not so lucky. It was a black cat."

Laura stopped petting Nessie and looked up at Mama. "Where *is* Tallulah?" she asked. "I didn't see anyone bring her in."

She turned to ask the Crabb sisters, then remembered that they were upstairs, setting up the tanks and cages in Hemingway's bathroom so the cats wouldn't mess with them.

"Let me think," said Mama Marley. "We grabbed the cages first and unloaded the supplies from the trunk and . . . oh, jeez. We must have left the cat in the cab."

"The poor thing!" said Laura, climbing to her feet. "I'll go get her. Can I have the keys, Mama?"

"It's unlocked."

"I'm not sure it's safe to go out there now," said Leo. "Do you hear that wind? Sounds like the storm is peaking."

Laura reached for her raincoat. "I'll be fine. The cab's parked right outside. It'll take two seconds. I can't leave poor Tallulah out there. She must be terrified."

Leo nodded. "Okay, but I'll wait by the door and watch. Just in case."

They walked into the hall. Nessie followed them to the front door. She looked up at Laura with her big green eyes. "Don't worry, Ness," said Laura, leaning down to scratch her ears. "I'll be coming right back. With a brand-new friend for you! I think you'll like her."

She stood up as Leo slowly opened the door. A strong blast of wind and rain blew into the house, along with some leaves and twigs. Laura braced herself, nodded to Leo—and then dashed through the open door. Leo closed it behind her, leaving a small crack to peer through.

It was worse outside than Laura imagined.

In fact, it looked like the end of the world.

The sky didn't resemble a sky at all. It was just a swirling mass of blue and gray and brown. The rain wasn't falling down like normal rain either. It slashed through the air sideways, whipping through the garden in all directions. Even worse was the wind. It blustered and bellowed in wild erratic gusts that reminded Laura of the powerful choppy waves that almost swept her and Mack out to sea. She could feel it trying to knock her over as she headed down the path to the front entrance.

She spotted Mama's taxi right away. Its cheerful pink exterior stood out against the grayness of the storm. Reaching for the cab's door handle—and finding it unlocked—Laura breathed a sigh of relief, then jumped inside and shut the door. "Tallulah? Are you in here? Where are you?" For a moment, she was afraid the cat might have gotten out unnoticed when they were unloading. But then she heard a soft *meow* beneath the driver's seat. "Tallulah!"

The large black cat crawled out from under the seat and hopped onto Laura's lap. "Poor kitty," she said, stroking her fur. "You must have thought we abandoned you. Don't worry, girl. I'm going to get you inside where it's nice and dry. I have a friend I want you to meet."

Unzipping her raincoat, Laura placed Tallulah on her chest. Then, holding the cat carefully, she zipped it up again. "Fasten your seat belt, kitty," she whispered. "It's going to be a bumpy night." She opened the car door, took a deep breath, and climbed out.

The trip back to the house was worse than the trip to the cab. The wind was blowing even harder now, making Laura stumble and swerve as she struggled to keep her balance. She could feel Tallulah freaking out under the raincoat, digging her claws into her skin. Laura ignored the pain and forged ahead, trying to stay focused on the slim crack of light at the front door. When she reached the porch, Leo flung the door open. She dashed inside and heard it slam behind her.

"Laura! Are you crazy?"

She looked up to see Jake and Mack and a few of the others standing in the hall. Everyone looked mortified.

"Why did you go out there?" said Jake. "You should have asked one of us to go."

"Yeah, what were you thinking?" said Mack. "We could have handled it for you. We're less likely to get blown away. We weigh more than you."

"Well, I do, at least," said Jake.

"I'm taller," said Mack.

Laura sighed. "Okay, I know this is Hemingway's house, but you guys need to cool it with the macho crap. I'm fine. It's done. Mission accomplished." She unzipped her raincoat and looked down at Nessie sitting quietly by the door. "Nessie, I would like you to meet my sometime roommate Tallulah. Tallulah, this is my long-time friend Nessie."

She placed the black-furred cat down next to the gold-furred cat.

At first, they just stared at each other, neither of them blinking. Then, they slowly raised their heads and leaned forward at the same time. They looked like that old mirror routine with Lucille Ball and Harpo Marx mimicking each other's movements. Nessie touched her nose to Tallulah's. Tallulah did the same. They took a few sniffs.

Then a few more. Then they reared up on their back legs, raised their front paws, and rushed toward each other They collided and tumbled onto the floor. It took Laura a second to realize they weren't fighting—they were embracing. And cuddling. And playfully rolling around as if they were high on catnip.

"Aw, look at them," said Millie. "They're kissing!"

Actually, they were licking each other, but no one corrected her.

"Tallulah! Thank God you're all right," said Jolene, rushing down the stairs with her sister. "I was just saying to Jilly, 'Where's Tallulah?' And she said, 'I don't know, didn't you bring her in?'"

"She was still in the cab," said Laura. "I went out and got her."

"Thank you, thank you, thank you," said Jilly, rushing down the hall and leaning over the cats. "Can you ever forgive us, Tallulah? We didn't mean to . . . oh, wow. You were right, Laura. These cats really do look alike."

"Yeah," said Jolene, joining her sister. "Same tails, same paws, same white streaks. Just different-colored fur."

They started stroking the look-alike felines when they heard someone behind them, clearing his throat.

"Excuse me, ladies," said Foster Lee Jackson. "But I do believe that's my cat."

Everyone turned and looked at him.

Then the lights went out.

Chapter 12
Cat's Out of the Bag

Everyone stood there—in total darkness—for a surprisingly long time before anyone did or said anything. Maybe it was because they were startled by the suddenness of the power outage. Maybe it was because they were stunned by Foster's shocking claim of cat ownership. Or maybe it was because they were a bit thrown off by the Motown music still playing on the hand-cranked radio.

The song was "Standing in the Shadows of Love."

Finally, Mack spoke up. "Hold on. I set a flashlight down right over . . . here? No, wait . . . it's around here somewhere."

While Mack fumbled around in the next room, Foster started chuckling in the dark.

"What's so funny?" Millie asked.

"I'm sorry, but I really owe everyone an apology," said Foster, still chuckling. "I didn't mean my last statement to be so dramatic. If this were a murder mystery, the lights would come back on and I would be dead. The rest of you would have to solve my murder."

"That's not funny," said Millie. "Nobody wants to murder you, Foster."

"You should talk to my ex-wife."

"Should I?"

"No, you should not."

A voice rang out from the other room. "Hallelujah! Let there be light!"

Mack returned with two flashlights beaming. He illuminated the way for the others as they shuffled back to the main room. Rooster, Leo, and Jake turned on the battery-powered lanterns they'd placed around the house while Margarita brought out a large pitcher of frozen margaritas she'd prepared.

"The power's off, so we might as well drink this now before it melts!"

A few minutes later, everyone was settled in with their drinks of choice. They sat on the floor on sleeping bags, arranged in a circle around a small glowing campfire—actually a "flickering flame effect" lantern that Millie bought online. While the hurricane raged outside, they felt calm, safe, and secure huddled together inside. Some of them were paired off, like Mama and Leo, Foster and Millie, Rooster and Margarita, Rick and Ricardo—yet the others fit comfortably in the circle. Even the cats were drawn to this warm little gathering. Before long, there were at least two dozen felines prowling the perimeters, staking out spots to lounge and nap, some even cuddling up next to one of the humans.

"Isn't this cozy?" said Margarita. "Now that we're all settled in, maybe Foster will tell us more about the cat he claims is his."

"Yeah," said Jilly. "You said Tallulah's your cat. But she's been with us for years."

Foster sighed. "It's a long and shameful story."

"We've got time," said Jolene.

Foster glanced at Millie, then at the black cat curled up with Nessie. He took a deep breath. "Okay. I might as well confess to my crime. It's been weighing on my soul for years. The truth is, your cat Tallulah—I used to call her Queenie—is one of the Hemingway cats."

Everyone gasped.

"I knew it," Laura muttered.

Margarita glared at Foster. "If she's one of the Hemingway cats, how did she end up with you? Don't tell me you stole her from here. . . ."

"Please, let me explain," said Foster, pulling a handkerchief from his pocket and patting his brow. "My wife, my *ex*-wife, was a delicate yet demanding young woman. I did everything I could to keep her happy. Bought her the finest clothes, took her to the finest restaurants, escorted her to the finest social events. All to no avail. She was bored and disappointed by everything—me, the clothes, the food, the events. But mostly me. One day she decided that a child was what she needed to fill the hole in her heart. But I, alas, was physically unable to fill it."

Millie flinched. "You mean, you can't . . . ?"

"Oh, I can," Foster quickly interjected. "Of course I can. I simply have a low sperm count." He paused and blushed. "Anyway, we tried a number of medical treatments but eventually had to give up. My wife was distraught, and more depressed than ever. I didn't know what to do. Then one night, I attended an event here at the Hemingway House. An awards dinner for the local historical societies. Before dinner, a cat keeper showed me the newest litter of kittens. They were very cute. When dinner was over, I lingered at the bar, dreading to return home to my miserable wife. After my sixth or seventh drink, I began to crave a cigarette, so I snuck around back for a smoke . . ."

"You smoke?" asked Millie.

"Not anymore," said Foster. "Anyway, when I got there, I saw two of the little kittens from the litter playing by the pool. A black kitten and a yellow kitten."

"Tallulah and Nessie," said Laura.

Foster nodded and went on. "As I stood there enjoying my cigarette, I watched the kittens tumble and roll around. I started getting nervous as they got closer and closer to the edge of the pool. Finally, I rushed over to grab them before they fell in. But I was too late. In they went."

Everybody gasped.

"I'll never forget it. The sight of those tiny little kittens, struggling in the water . . . it haunts me to this day."

"What did you do?" asked Millie.

"I tried to save them, of course. And I did. But it wasn't easy. I was able to pull out the black one pretty quickly. But my arm couldn't quite reach the yellow one. She kept kicking and splashing and sinking below the surface, I was sure she was going to drown."

"Poor Nessie," Laura whispered, glancing at her feline friend. "No wonder you hate the pool so much."

"Just when I thought I'd lost her," Foster continued, "she raised her paw out of the water and I was able to grab it. I pulled her out and laid her next to her sister. She coughed up a bit of water but seemed okay. Then, as I was drying them off, I started thinking. Maybe, just maybe, my wife would be happier if she had a little kitten to take care of. A sweet little baby kitten . . ."

Margarita sighed. "So you decided to steal one of Hemingway's cats."

"You have to understand, I was drunk. And desperate. And if it makes you feel any better, the cat never liked me anyway."

"Probably because you stole her away from her home," said Margarita. "And her sister."

"I know, I know!" said Foster. "I've been wracked with guilt about it ever since I took her. And to make things worse, the cat ran away after my wife left me. First I stole the cat and then I lost her. I'm a terrible person who did a terrible thing, and I am deeply, deeply ashamed."

He lowered his head and let out a long, quavering sigh.

Against her better judgment, Margarita began to feel sorry for him. "Okay, Foster. I can forgive you. But I want to know, just out of curiosity, why did you take the black cat and not the yellow cat?'

Foster's face turned red. "I know this sounds awful," he said, hesitating. "But I took the black cat because . . . she matched our home décor."

His answer was met with sneers and snickers from the rest of the room.

"That's okay, Foster. I understand," said Millie, patting his back. "I think it was very brave of you to confess your secret to everybody. In fact, I have a secret to confess, too."

Everyone stopped and looked at her.

Millie took a breath. "This is not my natural hair color."

Margarita raised an eyebrow. "Really? You're not a natural platinum blonde? I'm stunned."

The others tried to stifle their laughs as another Motown song started playing on the radio: "I Heard It Through the Grapevine."

Jilly jumped up off the floor. "This song!" she said. "It just gave me an idea for a game we can play. Just to pass the time."

Jolene looked up at her sister. "What game?"

"It's kind of like Truth or Dare. But without the Dare part."

"Does this game have a name?"

"Yeah. It's, um . . . I Heard It Through the Grapevine!"

"Did you just make this game up?"

"Yes, and it's really cool. Do you remember when we took Laura out for drinks on her first night in Key West? Remember when we told her all the crazy rumors we've heard about everyone in town? Well, wouldn't you like to know if there's any truth behind those rumors?"

Margarita looked up from her cocktail. "I don't know if I like the sound of this game. I have some board games in the back we could play instead."

"Aw, come on, Margarita. We're all friends here. Would you prefer to let people think that those weird, awful rumors just might be true?"

Margarita glanced nervously at Rooster but didn't say anything.

"Look what Foster did tonight," Jilly went on. "He confessed his deepest, darkest secret to all of us."

"I did, too," said Millie.

"Yes! And Millie, too. It's out in the open now, and everything's fine. Let's just try it, okay? I'll start." Jilly walked around the circle from person to person—and stopped in front of Rick and Ricardo.

The mustachioed hotel owners stopped petting Lucy and Desi and looked up at Jilly timidly. "Us?" they said.

"Yes, you. Here goes," she said, taking a breath. "I heard it through the grapevine that you guys won the Lighthouse Hotel in a poker game with Las Vegas gangsters."

Their jaws dropped at the same time.

"That's ridiculous," said Rick. "We won it in Reno. And they weren't gangsters."

Ricardo rolled his eyes and scoffed. "They were gangsters."

"No, they weren't. They worked in the sanitation industry."

"They were gangsters. Their 'assistants' had guns. I saw them."

"But they had their wives with them."

"Mistresses."

"They didn't kill us when we won everything."

"So? They're nice gangsters."

Rick sighed. "Okay, fine. The rumors are true."

"See?" said Jilly. "That wasn't so bad, was it?"

"No," said Ricardo. "I'm just surprised anyone knew about it."

"It's a small town. People talk," said Jilly. "Anyway, you're next."

"Great," said Ricardo, rubbing his hands together and scanning the room. His eyes stopped on a certain dreadlocked cabdriver. "Mama Marley. I heard it through the grapevine that you were a big reggae star in Jamaica, but your career crashed and burned when your fans found out you were lip-syncing to someone else's voice. True?"

Mama Marley glared at Ricardo for an agonizingly long time, with a stone-cold expression that made everyone in the room nervous—even the cats.

Then a tiny smile crept over her face, and she burst out laughing.

"Jeez Louise, that is *hilarious*! I mean, *really*? That's what people are saying? That is *so* messed up. I mean, *lip-syncing*? *Me*? Never in all my days . . ." She shook her head, chuckling. "It's like the Telephone Game. You know, that game you played as kids? Where one kid whispers something to another kid who whispers it to another, and by the time it reaches the end, it's been twisted and turned into something else? It's like that. Sure, there's a teeny-weeny grain of truth in the rumor. But it's not the real story. Not even close."

"So what's the real story?" Ricardo asked.

Mama closed her eyes and sighed. "Okay. I might as well fess up. My real name isn't Mama Marley. It's Marla Jones. I changed it because I got tired of people saying, 'Marla Jones? One of the Jamaica Joneses? Whatever happened to them?' You see, me and my sister became local celebrities when we were really young. I was ten, she was eleven, and we lived in Chicago with our parents, our Jamaican grandmother, and our uncle Bob. Uncle Bob was a music freak who had all this equipment in his room for recording and sound mixing. He wrote some reggae songs and laid down the tracks for me and my sister, Lana, to sing along with. Lana and I thought it'd be fun to sing them with Jamaican accents, like our grandma's."

"You mean, the accent you still use to get better tips?" asked Lucky Leo, nudging her with his elbow.

"Sure, why not? A girl's gotta eat," she said. "Well, anyway, the songs came out really good. Uncle Bob started booking us gigs at street fairs, block parties, even some churches and weddings. We called ourselves the Jamaica Joneses. The next thing you know, we get a call from the *Chicago Sun-Times*. A reporter heard about us and wants to do a feature story with color photos and everything. Lana and I were thrilled. We dressed up in our Sunday best and used our Jamaican accents through the whole interview. Even worse, we told all these wild made-up stories about growing up homeless on the streets of Jamaica and coming to America as stowaways on a fishing boat. We even said we were twins, which we aren't. Yeah, we dished up some real whoppers. But we were just kids. The whole thing was a game to us, you know? We thought it was hilarious. Lying was fun."

She shot a quick glance at Lucky Leo and continued.

"Well, the paper printed the story—and our parents hit the roof. They couldn't believe we told all those fibs and were ready to ground us for life. But then the offers started pouring in. The concert hall bookings. The local TV appearances. The Jamaica Joneses were an overnight sensation. The hottest ticket in town. Soon we were getting approached by the big record labels, and there was a bidding war. We ended up signing a million-dollar contract! We were gonna be living on Easy Street! But then—before we recorded a single song—it all went up in smoke."

She paused for dramatic effect. Everyone in the room leaned forward. Even Nessie and Tallulah stopped playing to look at Mama Marley.

"Well?" said Laura. "What happened?"

Mama sighed. "The record company found out we were lying. They said our stories about Jamaica were part of 'the package' and we had misled them. They called it a breach of contract or something, I don't know. All I know is, they canceled the contract and I ended up driving a cab in Key West, Florida." She shrugged. "At least I still get to use my grandma's accent. The tourists sure like it. So that's that. Is it my turn now?"

Leo looked at her and smiled. "You certainly earned it," he said. "That was quite a story, Marla. I guess this means I can use your real name from now on. In front of everybody."

She smiled back at him. Then she took his hand in hers and gazed into his eyes.

"Lucky Leo Trout," she said in a soft, gentle voice. "I heard it through the grapevine that you like to exaggerate the truth and that all of those life-or-death disasters you were lucky to survive never really happened. What's up with that?"

Leo looked surprised—and deeply embarrassed.

"Well, um, I don't know. You know how it is." He let out a little sigh. "I guess it all started when I joined the army. I grew up in a boring little town in Ohio. Everything about it was average. The people were average, the houses were average, my folks were average. I was average, too. Average looks, average grades, average intelligence. You couldn't find a more average guy than me. Then, in my final weeks of high school, I signed up for the army and *boom*—suddenly I'm different than the other guys. The girls start talking to me, asking me where I'll be stationed and stuff like that. I liked the attention. I felt noticed. Then I went through basic training, got stationed in Europe. I started telling people back home about my adventures there. I quickly discovered that if I tweaked the story a bit, added a little more drama and excitement, they liked the story more. They liked *me* more. As the years went by, my life got more interesting—and my stories got more exaggerated. I've found that people enjoy them more if, say, it's a plane crash instead of a bumpy landing. Or a tornado instead of a whirlwind. Even if people don't believe my stories, I don't care. I get a kick out of telling them—the crazier, the better—and then watching people's reactions. It's like you said, Marla. Lying is fun."

Mama Marley chuckled. "Yeah, I guess I'm not one to talk, am I? I've been lying my whole life. It's my business model! And yes, I'll admit, it's fun. But I gotta say, Leo, some of your stories are so outrageous, so out-there over-the-top, it's just ridiculous." She paused and smiled. "Those are my favorites."

"You see? That's why I think we make a good match. We appreciate the outrageous things in life, even if they aren't true. But I want you to know something, Marla, and this is no lie." Leo placed his hand over hers and squeezed. "When it comes to the important stuff—the things that really matter—I'll always keep it real with you."

Mama was clearly touched. She looked at him tenderly, her eyes glistening. "Wow. Thank you, Leo. I appreciate that. I really do. That's no lie! And neither is this: I promise to keep it real with you, too." She leaned over and kissed him.

Everyone in the room let out a collective sigh.

A few of them said, "*Awwww.*"

This was turning out to be a very interesting evening for the fifty-four cats of the Hemingway House. (Fifty-five including Tallulah.)

On the one paw, there was a big, scary storm raging outside.

On the other paw, there was a warm, friendly gathering inside.

As far as the cats could tell, the inside beat the outside paws down. The calming sounds of familiar human voices and soft, bouncy music made it easy to ignore the muffled roar of wind and rain outside. The cozy circle of humans also provided them with bodies to snuggle up to, laps to lie down on, and hands to get stroked by. Even the more standoffish cats couldn't resist the comforting lure of the pack—or the "flickering flame effect" of Millie's lantern.

Pawpa Hemingway, for example, curled up next to Laura, his "fellow shipmate." She casually stroked his back as he gazed, sleepy eyed, at the light in the middle of the room. Chew-Chew and Whiskey set up camp with Foster and Millie, sprawling lazily among the fancy cheese wrappers and bottle corks. Foster had to admit the tuxedo cats looked pretty classy lounging next to his premium wine. Larry, Curly, and Moe cuddled up next to Mack's feet—they seemed to think his shoelaces were cat toys. Then there were Boxer and Bullfighter, who'd apparently retired from both boxing and bullfighting—at least for the evening. They wrapped their big paws around their new little friends, Lucy and Desi, settling in for a long group snooze.

Other interesting matchups included: Bette Davis and Joan Clawford, who fought over the comfiest spot on Rooster's lap; Lady Bratt Ashley, who flirted shamelessly with Jake; and the usually aloof Kilimanjaro, who kept trying to climb to the top of poor Shelly. Probably because of her white hair.

But of all the cats in the house, no one was more blissfully content than Ernestine Hemingway—better known as Nessie.

Lying there on the floor next to Tallulah, her long-lost sister, Nessie felt a profound sense of peace and calm that she hadn't felt since she was a kitten. Of course, being a cat, she didn't have a clear memory of being a kitten or having a sister. It was more of an impression or instinct, something she felt in her bones.

The moment she saw Tallulah, she just knew that she knew her.

Nessie felt the same way about Laura. When she arrived with her suitcases on that storm-struck morning, Nessie knew right away.

They shared a connection.

And now they shared Tallulah.

This made Nessie very, very happy. She rubbed her nose against Tallulah's neck and gazed up at Laura, sitting a few feet away. Nessie felt safe here in this circle of humans. Safe and happy. She turned her head and looked around, studying each of the humans' faces. She stopped when she got to Margarita, the "First Lady of the House." Her old friend looked nervous. She was worried about something. Nessie wondered what it was.

She stretched and yawned. After such a long day, she could use a little cat nap.

But tonight, with so much going on, Nessie wanted to stay awake.

She didn't want to miss a thing.

It was Leo's turn to play the game now.

He peered across the circle at his boss, Margarita Bouffet. She noticed him looking at her and reached for the pitcher of frozen margaritas. Leo thought she seemed jumpy. He wondered if he should pick someone else instead. But then he figured, what the hell. It would be good to finally clear the air about all the nasty rumors people were spreading around.

"Margarita," he said, clearing his throat. "I really hate to do this to you. But I think you should know what people are saying about you."

Margarita looked at him and poured herself a drink.

"I, personally, don't believe a word of it," he went on. "I've known you for many years now, and I think you're a wonderful person, a terrific boss, and an all-around great lady. I know the rumors can't be true. If you want me to shut up and keep it to myself, just tell me and I will."

Margarita sighed. "It's okay, Leo. Everyone here has probably heard it already." She took a long, slow sip of her frozen margarita, then looked back at Leo with frosty cold eyes. "Let's do this."

Leo took a deep breath. "Okay then," he said. "Margarita. I heard it through the grapevine that you fled here from Cuba on an inflatable pool toy shaped like a flamingo to escape your abusive first husband. You headed to the finest resorts of Miami, where you seduced, married, and murdered three very old, very rich men in rapid succession. You killed them with poison, inherited their fortunes, and changed your name multiple times. The only reason you're here in Key West, working in a house full of cats, is because you're on the FBI's 'Most Wanted' list. You can't travel anywhere or spend anything without getting caught. I don't believe any of this, of course, but that's what I heard."

Leo finished and sat down. Everyone looked at Margarita to see how she'd react. But her eyes were dark and distant, her face unreadable. Finally, she spoke.

"This is incredibly hard for me. I think of you all as my family— every one of you—and I really don't know what to say right now." She paused. "Because it's all true."

Everyone gasped.

"Except the part about the inflatable flamingo. And the murders. *Are you kidding me?*"

Everyone burst out laughing.

"I knew it!" Leo hooted. "I knew it wasn't true!"

"Of *course* it's not true! *Me? A murderess?* The only thing I've ever killed was a spider plant back in the eighties and I still feel guilty about it." Margarita laughed and took a sip of her drink. "The reason I'm so secretive about my late husbands is because our marriages weren't legal. I'm still married to my first husband back in Cuba."

Everyone stopped laughing.

"Wait," said Millie. "So you're a bigamist?"

Margarita nodded. "Bigamist, trigamist, something like that. But definitely not a murderess. Let's get that part out of the way. I never married for money, always for love. Contrary to rumor, my dear departed husbands were not 'very old' and 'very rich.' They were mature and comfortable. I did not marry them in 'rapid succession.' They were spread out over several decades. And they didn't die from poisoning, either, or anything else suspicious. I did change my name 'multiple times,' but that's because I was married multiple times and took the last names of my husbands."

"But you said you weren't legally married to them," said Millie. "Why didn't you divorce your first husband?"

"Because he was a monster. He said he would kill me if I ever tried to leave him. And I knew he meant it. So I plotted my escape. I snuck out while he slept and came to America on the Mariel Boatlift—not a blow-up flamingo. That was in 1980. A few months later, I met my second husband in a dance hall in Miami. We fell madly in love and he asked me to marry him. I said yes—but didn't tell him I was still married. We had a lovely beach wedding and lived in a beautiful condo and thought we'd live happily ever after. Then he was killed in a car wreck. Well, his money-grubbing family decided they wanted his condo and hired a lawyer to do some digging. The lawyer found out that I never divorced my first husband and threatened to have me arrested on bigamy charges unless I signed over the lease and all of his investments. I was so scared, I agreed. I never told anyone about it, not even my third or fourth husbands. When they died, I let their families take everything because I was terrified of being found out."

Rooster—who'd been strangely quiet all evening—looked at Margarita and said, "There must be some legal way to annul your first marriage."

"Maybe there is. I don't know. It would be nice to know I could get married again without ending up behind bars." She smiled at Rooster, then turned to the others. "If it's all right with everyone, I'd like to take my turn now. I want to know what's going on with Jake and Mack. I heard it through the grapevine that you boys got into a fight and aren't speaking to each other. What's this all about?"

Laura stopped stroking Pawpa and looked up. She glanced back and forth between Jake and Mack, who sat on opposite sides of the circle looking very uncomfortable.

Jake sighed. "Go ahead, Mack," he said. "Tell them."

Mack frowned. "I think you should tell them, Jake. It was your idea."

Jake glanced at Laura, then looked at Margarita. "I'm not sure how to explain this, but I'll try. You see, Mack and I are best friends, and one of the rules of the Guy Code is that if one friend likes a girl, the other friend backs off. Well, when Laura started working here, we both liked her right away. So Mack and I sort of made a deal with each other."

"A deal?" said Laura. "Why didn't you just flip a coin to decide which one of you Neanderthals gets to club me on the head and drag me back to your cave."

"It wasn't like that, Laura," said Jake. "We wanted you to be the one who decides who you like. Maybe it would be one of us; maybe it would be neither of us. Maybe it would be Lucky Leo Trout."

"Hands off, girl," said Mama Marley. "He's mine."

Jake continued: "Anyway, Mack and I agreed to let you settle into your new home, new job, new life, and get to know the island, the people—and us, too—before anyone made any moves. We agreed to play it cool and leave it up to you." Jake stopped and turned to Margarita. "Then Mack kissed Laura on our sailing trip."

"And Jake kissed Laura on a date," said Mack.

Jake shot back at Mack: "You took her out for drinks at Sloppy Joe's!"

Mack countered: "You've been flirting with her at lunch every day!"

Margarita slapped her knee like a judge pounding a gavel. "Boys! Boys! Settle down! If you ask me, it sounds like you both broke the rules of the Guy Code. I think each of you owes the other an apology. You both screwed up. Just admit it. And apologize to Laura, too, while you're at it. She's not some stuffed animal you win playing ring toss at the fair."

Foster raised his hand. "Excuse me, but what is this 'Guy Code' everyone keeps talking about? Is it a book? Where can I get a copy?"

Millie told him to hush.

After an awkward silence, Mack looked at Jake and said, "She's right. We screwed up. I'm sorry, Jake. And I'm sorry, Laura. Really, I am."

Jake sighed. "I'm sorry, too, Mack. I just want to be friends again. We've been at it too long to stop now. Besides, The Off Keys have a gig next week. How can we harmonize if we aren't speaking?" He turned to Laura. "I owe you an apology, too, Laura. Margarita's right. You're not some carnival prize to compete over; you're a person with a mind of your own. I'm sorry you had to see Mack and me fighting at the pool like knuckle-dragging idiots. There's no excuse for that. Again, I'm sorry."

Laura looked at Jake and then Mack. She took a breath. "All right. I accept your apologies. I just want you two to be friends again. And if it's okay with Jilly, I want to take my turn at this game now."

Jilly tilted her head, thinking. "I don't know. That's not following the rules."

"Rules? You made up this game twenty minutes ago," said Jolene. "Go ahead, Laura."

"Thank you. This is for you, Jolene. And Jilly, too. I heard it through the grapevine that you dated Jake and Mack back in high school. But whenever I ask anyone for details—like who dated who and what went down—I never get a straight answer. Why? What happened?"

By the looks on their faces, the twins were more than a little embarrassed by the question. Laura glanced over at Mack and Jake—they looked embarrassed, too.

Jolene took a deep breath. "It started in junior high, actually. We were really young and really stupid—which is our only excuse. I passed a note in class to Mack saying Jilly liked Jake. Mack showed it to Jake, who told Mack that he liked me better. Mack passed a note back saying 'Jake likes you'—meaning me, Jolene—but he passed it to Jilly accidentally because he couldn't tell us apart. Jilly was crushed. But two years later, in high school, Jake asked Jilly on a date. She was thrilled. Meanwhile, I was dating Mack, and Mack told me that Jake still liked me, but he was dating Jilly because she's the next best thing. I told Jilly, and she got real upset. So we decided to play a trick on Jake and Mack and switch places on our dates to see if they noticed. Jake couldn't tell it was me, but Mack knew it was Jilly—and it turned out he liked Jilly better! But Jilly thought Mack still liked me, and I thought Jake liked Jilly. Well, this went on for a whole summer. We kept trading dates and changing our minds until we all finally gave up and decided to be just friends. Does that answer your question?"

"My head is spinning," Millie whispered to Foster. "Do you think it's the wine?"

"It's not the wine," said Foster.

"Okay, Laura," said Jolene. "Now I have one for you. I heard it through the grapevine that you have a boyfriend back in Syracuse. Do you?"

Laura's jaw dropped. "Where did you hear that?"

"Okay, I didn't hear it through the grapevine. I saw it in the texts on your phone. They started popping up after you left it on the kitchen table. Who's Devin?"

Laura sighed. "Devin Ferrari. My next-door neighbor. And high school boyfriend. And college boyfriend. He's a great guy, really smart, but I felt like I'd outgrown him. After graduation, I really wanted to get out of Syracuse and meet new people, experience new things. But I didn't have the heart to tell Devin. We'd spent half our lives together, and he was dropping hints about getting married. I just wanted out. When I got the job here in Key West, I waited until the last minute. I was, like, 'hello, Devin, I'm breaking up with you and moving to Florida, good-bye.' I know, it was awful of me. But I knew he'd try to talk me out of it. So I made a clean break and took off."

"Judging from his texts, he's having trouble letting go," said Jolene.

"Yeah, I know." Laura sighed and looked over at Mack and Jake. "But here's the thing. I came here to start over. I need to figure out who I am and what I want out of life. I may not know what's right for me in the long run, but I'm right here, right now, and I'm working on it. Just one day at a time. I'm having a blast, too. Everyone's been so great. Mack, Jake, I love you guys. But—as you just heard through the grapevine—I'm fresh out of a *very* long-term relationship. I need to breathe for a while, just be on my own. I'm not ready to jump into another relationship, so it's good you guys decided to 'play it cool' and not make any moves. I've only been here a few weeks. I'm still getting to know you both, and everyone here. I'm looking forward to spending more time with all of you and can't wait to see what happens next. That's it. That's all I wanted to say. I'll shut up now."

She went back to stroking Pawpa Hemingway, and a hush fell over the room. Most of the cats were asleep now. The pitcher of frozen margaritas was almost empty. And the last song on Mack's mixed tape played through to the end: "You Can't Hurry Love."

But the game wasn't over quite yet.

Millie raised her hand. "Would anyone mind if I took a turn? There's a rumor I heard years ago and it's been bugging me ever since. I'm dying to know if it's true."

Everyone shrugged and nodded. Millie turned to Rooster and smiled.

"Mr. Rooster McCloud, my favorite deejay," she said. "I heard it through the grapevine that you're the man who invented the iPad and you sold the idea to Apple for millions and millions of dollars. Is this true, and if it is, could you get me a discount on one?"

Rooster leaned back, stroked his mustache a few times, and burst out laughing.

"Millions and millions of dollars?" he roared, eyes twinkling. "Oh, Millie. If I had millions and millions of dollars, I'd buy you a hundred iPads! And a new van for Mack's band, and veterinary school for Jake, and a weather station set-up for Shelly. Oh, man, I would love that! But sorry, no, I did not invent the iPad. I did, however, create an internet domain name that I sold to a big tech company—whose name I cannot disclose—that paid for my radio equipment. So the rumor, sadly, is false."

Millie looked disappointed.

"But I have something else I'd like to share with everyone," he said. "And trust me, it's a whole lot juicier than any rumor."

The whole house went silent.

Rooster stood up and walked to the center of the circle. All eyes in the room were on him. There was something about the expression on his ruggedly handsome face that made everyone sit up and take notice. Even the cats seemed to know he was going to say something important.

"I have a secret," he said in a soft, low voice. "A secret that I've been keeping for many, many years. Now here's the strange thing about this secret. I didn't just hide it from everyone I know. I hid this secret from myself. But deep down, in my heart of hearts, I always knew it was true."

He turned around slowly and faced his longtime friend.

"Margarita Bouffet . . ."

She looked up at him.

"I'm in love with you."

He waited for a reaction. Something, anything, in her eyes to let him know he wasn't making a huge mistake. But even if he was, he couldn't stop now.

"I was scared, Margarita. I was scared that if I told you, it would ruin everything. Our friendship means so much to me. I actually tried to talk myself out of it, tried to convince myself that I don't really love you. But I just couldn't do it. Because I do, Margarita. I do love you. I've been in love with you for years. I was just too afraid to admit it—to myself, and to you."

Margarita held her breath as he spoke. When he was finally done, she slowly exhaled, gazed into his eyes, and raised her right hand. "Help me up," she said. "I'm too old to sit on the floor this long."

Rooster laughed and helped her to her feet. Once he got her up, he was relieved to see a smile on her ruby-red lips. She straightened her blouse and patted her hair, then looked him straight in the eye.

"Rooster, are you sure?"

"That I'm in love with you? Yes, I'm pretty sure I am."

"Pretty sure?"

"Very sure. I'm very sure I'm in love with you."

"How sure? Ballpark figure."

"If I had millions and millions of dollars, I'd buy you a big fat diamond ring."

Margarita laughed. "Let's not jump the gun. Maybe we should start with dinner and a movie first, or a walk along the pier, or . . . oh, I know! You can join my dance club! *One-two cha-cha-cha* . . ."

She grabbed Rooster's hands and started dancing to her own beat.

"Too bad we don't have any music," said Mack. "My mixed tape at the radio station must have reached the end."

"I think I have some Justin Bieber on my phone," said Jilly.

"Oh, we don't need that," said Margarita. "I have a better idea. We can sing! And dance! Come on, get up, everybody. I'm going to teach you to waltz. Get off the floor, Foster. You, too, boys."

Soon she had everyone paired off: Foster and Millie, Leo and Marla, Jake and Jolene, Mack and Jilly, Rooster and herself. Which left Laura and Shelly. Laura said she'd dance the man's part. After a quick review of the basic waltz steps, Margarita said they were ready to go.

"You said we were going to sing," said Jilly. "What's a good waltz song?"

"I was thinking 'The Rainbow Connection.'"

"The *Muppet Movie* song? The one Kermit the Frog sings?"

"Yes, do you know it?"

"Of course. Everyone knows 'The Rainbow Connection.'"

"Great," said Margarita. "Places, everyone! I'll set the beat and we can start. And *one two three, one two three, one two three* . . ."

All the cats of the Hemingway House gathered round to watch as Margarita Bouffet and her beloved family of friends, both old and new, began to sing and dance their way around the room. The couples twirled and swirled, stumbled and laughed, as they belted out the bittersweet lyrics of "The Rainbow Connection" (or hummed along if they didn't know the words). Meanwhile outside, Hurricane Harry and Tropical Storm Sally engaged in a spellbinding dance of their own. He blustered and bellowed. She swiveled and swerved. He swept her off of her feet. Crosswinds clashed and clouds collided as the two storms merged in a single savage embrace. They kicked over trees, flooded the streets, and raised up the roofs of the houses below.

When Hurricane Harry met Tropical Storm Sally, it was truly a night to remember.

Rooster would never forget it, that's for sure.

As he danced with Margarita, he felt like he was dreaming. He couldn't believe that he actually did it, that he actually told her how he felt. And she didn't freak out! Or so she said when he asked her, "Are you freaking out?"

Margarita assured him that she was not freaking out, adding, "I had a big crush on you years ago, Rooster. I thought you knew. But I wasn't sure you thought about *me* that way, so I stopped thinking about *you* that way. Then you showed up at the dance party with that suit and tie and movie star face of yours and, *wham*, the crush was back."

Rooster laughed and hugged her. Then he kissed her. And . . . wow.

Margarita pressed her lips to his ear. "Maybe later tonight we should sneak upstairs to Hemingway's bedroom."

"Oh, you're bad. I'm telling the manager."

The next morning, there was a loud pounding on the front door that boomed through the house and startled the sleepers right out of their sleeping bags. Laura rubbed her eyes and crawled to her feet, along with the other drowsy humans and cats. When she got to the hall, she saw Margarita and Rooster talking to a couple guys from the Florida National Guard. "We just wanted to check in on you and see if everything's okay. The whole world is watching, you know. Everyone's worried about Hemingway's cats!"

After they left, Laura picked up Nessie and leaned out the door to check things out. It was still a bit stormy outside, but the wind and rain were a lot lighter and there was a big bright patch in the sky. Leaves, branches, and random debris were scattered everywhere. A tree had fallen and broken a window at the Lighthouse Hotel across the street. "What do you think, Nessie?" she asked the cat. "Looks pretty bad, huh? At least the lighthouse is still standing. As is the Hemingway House. We survived!"

Mack, Jake, and the Crabb sisters came up behind her to look. Jake was holding Tallulah like a baby and tickling her tummy.

"Whoa, what a mess," said Mack. "Millie's poor ticket booth never stood a chance."

"I wonder if our bungalow is still standing," said Jolene.

"I wonder if our fish are all right," said Jilly.

"Hey, guys," said Jake. "Did you know Tallulah is pregnant?"

"What? Awesome!" Jilly cried.

"Way to go, Tallulah!" said Jolene. "Getting some action on the side. No wonder she sneaks out so much."

Laura stepped next to Jake and held Nessie up to Tallulah. "Congratulate your sister, Nessie. She's going to be a mommy! And you're going to be an aunt!"

Margarita, Rooster, and the others stepped out onto the porch to see what the fuss was about. Everyone was thrilled to hear the news.

"Hey, guys! Look! Someone must have heard us singing last night," said Jilly. She pointed up at the sky. "It's a little one and hard to see, but it's right over there, above the lighthouse."

"Oh, wow. How cool is that?" said Jolene.

"Beautiful," said Margarita.

"Yes, it certainly is," said Rooster.

Laura kept looking but couldn't find it. All she could see was a bunch of big gray clouds. But after shifting her focus away from the clouds, she was finally able to see the rainbow.

Chapter 13
"What Has Six Toes and Nine Lives?"

In the days and weeks that followed, a lot of things happened on the southernmost island of the Florida Keys. First of all, Hemingway's famous six-toed cats became even more famous.

This was not surprising.

After the big buildup to "the Storm of the Century"—and the irresistible drama of furry fearless felines defying evacuation orders to stay in their home—the story was like catnip to a large cross section of weather watchers, animal lovers, and general interest readers. By the time the storm was finally over, the whole world was dying to know: *Are the cats okay?*

Luckily, they got through it without a scratch.

The story had a happy ending, and the media had a field day. *The New York Times*, *The Washington Post*, and *USA Today* cut to the chase with headlines as simple as "Hemingway's Cats Survive," efficiently telling readers what they wanted to know: *Are the cats okay?*

Other media outlets did variations on "Cats Rode Out Storm" or "House and Cats Spared." But the best line came from the writers at *Southern Living* magazine:

"What has six toes and nine lives?"

Meanwhile, back at the Hemingway House, the most famous and celebrated cats in the world had absolutely no idea any of this was going on. Even when the reporters, photographers, and camera crews arrived, the cats weren't fazed at all. Living inside a tourist attraction, they were used to large groups of people looking at them, taking pictures of them, and reaching down to pet them. It was business as usual.

But not for the humans who worked at the Hemingway House.

Margarita Bouffet—being the manager who made the decision to stay with the cats—received the most attention from the media. She loved every minute of it. Especially the TV interviews. "I think we humans can learn a lot from cats," she'd say. "Hemingway said that cats have 'absolute emotional honesty' while human beings hide their feelings. Well, I'll tell you this. When we barricaded ourselves in here with these cats, it was just . . . magical. We began to open up and share our secrets, let down our defenses and reveal our true feelings. Some of us fell in love on that night. I know I did."

Then she'd wink at the camera.

Lucky Leo Trout loved the attention almost as much as Margarita did. He would lead the cameramen and reporters through his usual tour of the house's storm-resilient features—but add in some personal asides that were so outrageous and over the top, the directors had to yell, "*Cut!*" Like this one: "The bricks of this house are carved from solid limestone. Now limestone is incredibly dense, hard, and heavy. I should know because my daddy owned a limestone quarry and he made baby blocks out of limestone for me to play with. Well, one day I stacked them all up and they fell right on top of me. The sheer weight of them squeezed the hair right out of my head. And that's why I'm bald today."

"*Cut!*"

Jake Jacobs received a lot of TV airtime because of his extensive knowledge of the history and nature of polydactyl felines. Also, he looked great on camera and the lady reporters thought he was hot. The segments showing him interacting with the cats were incredibly popular, receiving millions of hits on YouTube. In one of them, he introduced viewers to the oldest and the youngest members of the household: "This here is Pawpa Hemingway, spelled *P-a-w*, and he's named after Ernest 'Papa' Hemingway himself. This cat might look old and grumpy, but he's still an active sportsman who enjoys the occasional sailing voyage. He's a real hero, too. He helped save the lives of these three kittens over here. This is Larry, Curly, and Moe. They're like those old movie comedians The Three Stooges, but cuter, funnier, and more violent."

That's when the kittens jumped on top of Pawpa. Hilarity ensued.

"Curly! Moe! No! Stop it! *Ouch!*"

Millie Graham—the brassy blond ticket booth manager of the Hemingway House—didn't get asked to do as many interviews as Jake, Leo, or Margarita. But she didn't mind. She was ecstatic about her brand-new, historically authentic ticket booth—courtesy of Foster Lee Jackson, who fast-tracked the approval process for rebuilding it by pulling some strings at the historical society. She and Foster spent a lot of time together since the night of the big storm. He was teaching her about fine wines while she showed him how to whip up a yummy casserole using canned beans and processed cheese.

But the Hemingway cats and staff weren't the only superstars of the storm.

WKEY Radio's beloved ninety-four-year-old weather enthusiast, Shelly, became a celebrity in her own right. She provided the weather agencies with invaluable data on the catastrophic collision of Hurricane Harry and Tropical Storm Sally—a rare example of the Fujiwhara Effect where two storms "dance" around a central point before merging. In an interview on The Weather Channel, Shelly described the storms as "hot to trot and ready for action. Harry wanted to dance, and Sally had the moves. They were like Fred Astaire and Ginger Rogers. You might think he's the stronger dancer, but she's doing the same steps! Backward! In heels!"

The Weather Channel offered Shelly an exclusive contract.

Rooster McCloud and his nephew Mack—proud keepers of the Key West lighthouse and museum—were featured in a Sunday magazine news article on the long and rich history of the famous 1848 landmark and its ability to withstand decades of hurricanes and storms. In addition to looking rugged and handsome in the photos, Rooster made female readers swoon with his unabashedly romantic quotes: "I think of this lighthouse the same way I think of my lady. She is the true light of my life, a shining beacon in the darkest of nights. When I feel low, she raises me up. When the fog rolls in, she stays the course. And when I am lost at sea, she shows me the way home."

Rooster got a lot of fan mail from the ladies—and a big kiss from Margarita.

Mack's tattoos of shipwrecks and sea monsters caught the eyes of several tattoo fan sites and trade magazines. He received offers from editors who wanted to feature him, photographers who wanted to shoot him—and girls who wanted to see him naked. Or date him. Or both. Against his uncle's advice, he actually met up with a couple of his adoring new fans. Big mistake. The first one rambled endlessly and looked nothing like her photos. The other turned out to be a seventy-year-old man.

Never doubt the Rooster.

All of this might sound like fun. But for most of Key West's residents and businesses, it was anything but. In the aftermath of the storms, they faced the long and difficult task of repairing the damage—and rebuilding their lives. Homes were destroyed, businesses devastated, power lines down, and boat engines ruined. Surge flooding and severe winds had knocked out their water and fuel supplies, electricity and communications. It would take a lot of work, a lot of man-hours—and millions and millions of dollars—to return the island to something resembling normal. All things considered, it turned to be the costliest hurricane in Florida's history.

But in the end, the people of Key West knew it would all be worth it. For them, this was more than a tourist destination. This was their home. And the old saying applied:

There's no place like it.

Rick and Ricardo were lucky. Besides a few shattered windows and fallen trees, the Lighthouse Hotel suffered minimal damage. It still took a few weeks to get everything cleared away and cleaned up before the hotel was up and running. In the meantime, they devoted some quality time to Lucy and Desi—and taught the Chihuahuas a little self-control.

Their new friends, Boxer and Bullfighter, helped keep them in line.

Jilly and Jolene Crabb were also fortunate when it came to their sailboat, *The Jolly Crabb*. Besides a bit of flooding in the cabin, the storm-hardy craft was in tip-top shape. Their parents had trained them well in how to prepare a docked boat in the event of a hurricane. Two days before the storms hit, the sisters stripped down the sailboat, took down the mast, then lashed, sealed, and secured a long checklist of items. The bilge pump still got damaged somehow, so they had to ask some cute sailors for help.

The sailors got the job done—and the sisters got dinner dates.

And then there was Laura Lange.

In the weeks following the hurricane, she had a lot of time on her hands. The Hemingway House had survived the storm with little damage, but there weren't any tourists around for her to guide. Just a lot of reporters, photographers, and cameramen. She dropped by every day to see if she could help in some way, but mostly just to check in with her coworkers—and the cats, of course. She loved those cats and was slowly getting to know all fifty-four of them. She loved seeing Rooster at the house, too, hanging out with Margarita and practicing dance moves together with her. Margarita told her he was joining her dance club, along with two new couples: Foster and Millie and Leo and Marla (the cabdriver formerly known as Mama Marley). Laura decided to join the club, too, when she heard the news.

And speaking of news, her mother called to tell her that the Syracuse University English Department wanted to interview Laura for the teaching assistant position. Laura told her mother thanks, but no. She was happy where she's at.

Her ex-boyfriend Devin called, too. After a long and deeply uncomfortable conversation, Laura finally convinced him that it's over, she's sorry, but she's here to stay. Devin let out a sigh and said, okay, he gets it, he'd find a way to move on. And that was that. Fingers crossed.

The next morning, on her way down Whitehead Street to the Hemingway House, Laura saw Rooster tossing birdseed to the gypsy chickens and she suddenly realized something: They didn't frighten her anymore. It might have been Jake's story about Rooster's friends wrapping the chickens in newspaper to calm them and shelter them that changed Laura's mind. It made the chickens seem vulnerable. It was sweet that people looked after them, and she was glad they were okay. As she walked through the Hemingway gates, she was greeted by the always-cheerful Millie, who was cheerfully fussing over the final details of her newly built ticket booth. Foster Lee Jackson stood next to her, serving as her consultant. He tipped his hat to Laura as she passed.

Nessie was waiting for Laura on the front porch. "Nessie! What's up?" She sat down next to her fine furry friend and gazed across the garden. Slowly stroking her from head to tail, Laura watched the other cats stroll and play and tumble and snooze in the muted morning light. Laura thought the sun seemed especially lazy today. She first noticed it when Tallulah woke her up by scratching on the insides of the wardrobe—Laura suspected she was turning it into a nursery—but the sun hadn't risen yet. She turned on the pirate lamp, checked the clock, and wondered why it was still dark out. It was almost as if the sun refused to get up.

"Laura! What are you doing tonight?" It was Jake, rounding the corner of the house with a broom. "Mack heard Sloppy Joe's is open for business now, so we were wondering if you and the twins want to hang out."

"That sounds great. But I'm not sure it's a good idea to leave Tallulah alone. She looks like she's ready to pop any minute now."

"Oh, that's right," said Jake. "Well, Mack and I could drop by with some six-packs. I could check out the mother-to-be. I'm not a vet—yet—but I have some experience."

"Okay," said Laura. "It's a date."

"Is it, though?"

After Jake left, Pawpa Hemingway joined Laura and Nessie on the porch. He seemed to get chummier with Laura every day. The rest of the staff couldn't believe it. Soon they were joined by Larry, Curly, and Moe, who were chasing Spinderella across the porch—until Spinderella spun and caused a three-kitten pileup. Then Chew-Chew ran by with a cookie in her mouth. Probably stolen from the employee lounge while Whiskey kept a lookout. Bette Davis and Joan Clawford were under a tree fighting—for Jackie Chan's attention. Across the yard were even more cats. Some slept; others lounged. One cat—Kilimanjaro, of course—had managed to climb to the top of Millie's new ticket booth.

"Laura! I'm glad you're here!"

Margarita Bouffet came clicking down the path in her cha-cha heels. She had a few small chores for Laura, but they wouldn't take long and then she could go home to the expectant mother. Laura finished up quickly, then said good-bye to Margarita, Jake, and the rest of the crew, giving Nessie and Pawpa a few last strokes. She started walking home when a pink taxicab pulled up next to her and stopped. "Need a ride, miss?" She listened to Mama Marley's hilarious description of her latest date with Lucky Leo as they drove down the street toward the little pink bungalow that—miraculously—survived the storm. When Laura got inside, she found the Crabb sisters in her bedroom, crouched down in front of the wardrobe. Tallulah gave birth! To four teeny-tiny, ridiculously adorable little kittens! With big, beautiful six-toed paws! They were the cutest things Laura had ever seen in her life. Jake and Mack came over with bottles of champagne to celebrate. They popped and poured, raised their glasses, and made a toast.

"To Hemingway's cats! The next generation!"

Later that night—after everyone in the house was sound asleep, including Tallulah and her babies—Laura lay in bed, wide awake, thinking. She couldn't sleep. She couldn't stop thinking about things. All the things that happened since coming here, and all the things she loved about her new life. So many interesting people and places and cats and birds and reptiles and—it was a lot to think about. Good thing she was keeping a journal. Laura reached for her laptop and scrolled through the entries she'd written. There was a lot there. Enough for a book. It was something she'd always dreamed of doing, but she could never think of anything to write about. Her life was boring.

She thought about that Hemingway quote: *"In order to write about life, first you must live it."*

And then it dawned on her: Laura Elizabeth Lange from Syracuse, New York, was finally, fabulously, living her life. She wasn't a mad housecat anymore. She wasn't slowly losing her mind in a locked room. She was like Hemingway's cats: free roaming, independent, and, yes, a little freaky with those six-toed paws, but ready to face the storm.

She took a deep breath and started to write:

Every morning, just before dawn, a funny thing happens on the southernmost island of the Florida Keys.

The sun refuses to get up.

Keep reading for a special excerpt . . .

FOX CROSSING
Melinda Metz

**Crossing paths with a black cat is said to bring bad luck.
But crossing paths with The Fox is a whole other story. . . .**

SOME SAY THE FOX IS GOOD LUCK

In the mountain village of Fox Crossing, Maine, everyone knows the story of The Fox. According to local legend, one of the town's founders crossed paths with a curious-looking fox with a distinctive white ear and paw. The unusual fox sighting not only inspired the town's name; it sparked a fantastical piece of folklore that's been passed down for generations. Some people say that whoever sees The Fox will be rewarded with good fortune, love, and happiness. Others say it's just a silly folktale. . . .

WHAT DOES THE FOX SAY?

Annie Hatherley doesn't believe the Fox legend—even though it was her great-great-great-grandmother who spotted the critter centuries ago. But now it's part of Annie's legacy, along with her family business, Hatherley's Outfitters. For years, Annie's been selling gear to hikers on the Appalachian Trail. But she's never seen The Fox—until now. Out of nowhere, this little white-earèd vixen leads her to Nick Ferrone, a woefully unprepared hiker who needs her help. The Shoo Fly Bakery owner also spots the sly creature—who takes him to a homeless dog that needs his love. Annie can't deny that something magical is happening—because she's starting to fall for a certain foxy hiker named Nick. . . .

Look for FOX CROSSING, on sale now.

Chapter 1

One look was all it took. He's not gonna make it, Annie Hatherley thought. She watched the lanky man cross the street toward the store, the sun bringing out glints of auburn in his curly brown hair. He wasn't the worst noob hiker she'd ever seen. That would be the guy last year wearing jeans, flip-flops, and an aloha shirt, cotton of course, his pack filled with three more of the gaudy shirts, a carton of Clif Bars, and a large bottle of water. And nothing else.

This guy wasn't that guy, but his backpack probably weighed close to seventy pounds. Nope, he wasn't gonna make it.

Forget the pack and the boots, his calves showed her that he hadn't been doing the kind of training he needed to take on the 100-Mile Wilderness. They weren't scrawny. They were, in fact, nicely muscled, with just the right amount of hair, at least in Annie's opinion. She had a friend who liked her men to look half-bear. Took all kinds to make a world.

But this guy's calves, nice as they were, were the calves of a casual day-hiker. A serious hiker's calves usually expanded a half inch in circumference, thighs about two inches. Sadly, Annie couldn't see the man's thighs. His prAna Stretch Zion shorts hit him a couple inches above the knee. He'd made a smart choice there, the shorts stretchy and cool, with a wicking finish. And only two pockets. A

lot of noobs thought they needed way more pockets than they actually did. But, despite the sensible shorts, he wasn't gonna make it.
He—He was coming through the door. "Okay if I bring this in?"
he asked, holding up the paper cup he carried.

"Sure." Annie watched him take in the store, her store, since
her mother had gotten herself elected first selectman, basically CEO
of the town, about four and a half years earlier. He took his time,
looking at everything.

"These hardwood floors are amazing."

"They're juniper maple." The hardwood floors were the first
change Annie had made when she took over. Her mother hadn't
bothered much with aesthetics. Hatherley's Outfitters was the only
game in town, the only place to buy gear in Fox Crossing, and
Fox Crossing was the last town before the 100-Mile Wilderness, the
wildest, and in Annie's opinion, most beautiful stretch of the Appalachian Trail. But just because the store had no competition didn't
mean it shouldn't be inviting. Fox Crossing had changed over the
years since her great-great-great-great-great-grandmother opened
the store. An antiques store was a few doors down from Hatherley's, the Wit's Beginning Brewery was included in one of the Brew
Ha-Ha Bus tours out of Bangor, and Foxy Loxy Books had just been
selected as one of Maine's best used-book stores.

"Perfect with the slate." The man appreciatively ran his fingers
over the smooth slate counter Annie stood behind. For a crazy second, Annie flashed on those fingers running over her skin with that
same—Inappropriate thought! He was a customer. Also, a complete
stranger.

"Slate from Fox Crossing is in high demand," she said, as crisply
as a new schoolteacher being observed by the principal. "There are
several political graves in Arlington Cemetery made by the black
slate from the local quarry. Although I preferred gray for—"

"Political graves?" he repeated, raising one eyebrow. Annie had
been trying to learn to raise one eyebrow since she was about seven.
Still couldn't do it.

"Don't be pedantic." Had she actually just used the word *pedan-*

tic? People who used the word *pedantic* were pedantic. "You know I meant graves of people in politics, including Jackie and John F. Kennedy's," she continued, unable to shake the lecturing tone. At least it was keeping her brain from creating more inappropriate thoughts.

"Guilty. License to be pedantic comes with the glasses." He pushed his slightly geeky, definitely stylish tortoiseshell specs higher on his nose. "The girl—woman—who sold them to me said they gave me a 'modern intellectual look.' "

He laughed and Annie joined in. Even though he was a noob who shouldn't be within a hundred miles of the 100-Mile Wilderness, she was starting to like this guy, dammit. And not just for his perfect-amount-of-hair-and-muscles calves. And not just for his warm chestnut eyes, which she couldn't help noticing when she was looking at his glasses. He was kind of funny, and kind of smart, and had good taste in flooring and countertops.

You have to find, at the very least, a new friend-with-benefits, Annie told herself. It had been a little more than a year since Seth had decided to head west to hike the PCT, and she hadn't even started feeling lonely. Truth? Seth had been starting to get on her nerves, and she was more than kinda glad he was gone. But her zero-to-sixty attraction to this guy showed her she was getting itchy.

"So, what can I help you with?" she asked, all professional-like.

"Wait. First you have to tell me your name. I don't allow myself to be mocked by strangers."

"Annie Hatherley."

"Of Hatherley's Outfitters." She nodded. "Nick Ferrone." He held out his hand, and she shook it. His grip was also just right. Not you're-a-delicate-lady-and-I-must-not-squash-your-fingers soft, but not I-must-show-dominance-to-all hard. Also, it sent a little tingle from her fingers to low in her stomach. Dammit.

When he let go, Annie caught sight of the tattoo on his forearm, and she could feel a wide grin, the kind that gave her chipmunk cheeks, stretching across her face. The tat was of what was clearly supposed to be a fox since it had the words I'M FOXY underneath. Nick noticed the direction of her gaze and flushed. "I—"

"You had an encounter with Noah and Logan, otherwise known as Nogan," Annie finished for him. "I'm quite familiar with their hand-drawn temporary tattoos, as well as their strong-arm sales techniques. What else did you buy?"

He took a swallow of what Annie knew was Nogan's drink of the day—blackberry lemonade sweetened with local honey. She'd had one herself at lunch.

"Just a piece of the Canine Candy," he admitted.

He had a dog? Bad idea. She opened her mouth to give Nick a list of all the reasons he should absolutely not bring a dog on his hike, starting with how it would greatly lower his odds of completing the hike, and those odds were pathetic to start out with. She forced herself to take a beat. Find a way to say it nicely, she told herself. Be professional. Last hiking season she'd gotten a bunch of negative social-media reviews about her attitude. One had even called her surly. Surly! Not that it mattered. You wanted to buy gear in Fox Crossing, you bought from her.

"You're planning to hike the Wilderness?" she asked. Even though she already knew the answer.

"Yep." Those chestnut-brown eyes of his gleamed with enthusiasm.

Nick was clueless about what he was in for. Annie felt prickles of irritation run down the back of her neck. The irritation prickles were stronger than the attraction tingles. A license should be needed to hike the Wilderness, and a test—written and practical—to get one. Don't go there, she told herself. "Then I'm assuming you want to go up Katahdin when you get to the end." She managed to keep her tone pleasant. No surly to be heard.

"I couldn't say I'd hiked the whole thing if I didn't."

Couldn't *say* he'd hiked it. Was he doing it for bragging rights? Who was he trying to impress? What was he trying to prove? None of your business, she told herself. You're here to sell him stuff.

"Just so you know, dogs aren't allowed in Baxter State Park, which is where the mountain is." Yeah, that was a good approach.

Nothing personal about his hiking skills. "You'll need to board your beastie before that last stretch. There are kennels in Millinocket, but that's twenty-five miles east. It's not easy. You'll only have logging tr—"

"No dog. Just me."

"Oh. Good." She let out a breath. "Then why the Canine Candy?"

"The boys convinced me it tasted just as good to humans and that there was nothing in it that would hurt me, so . . ." Nick shrugged. "Wasn't too bad."

"Wait. You actually ate a piece!"

"Well, yeah. They were watching. It tasted like an extremely healthy, very dry, mostly flavorless cookie, if you want to know."

He's nice, too, Annie realized. Dammit. He wasn't just smart-ish and funnyish, with excellent taste, plus the calves, and the eyes. He'd humored two nine-year-old boys by buying a dog treat when he didn't have a dog. And he'd eaten it! That was exceptionally nice.

But he's also exceptionally ill prepared, she reminded herself. He wasn't gonna make it out there. The only question was, How badly was he gonna get hurt?

Not at all, if Annie could help it. She'd try to be nice herself, but if that didn't work, well, she could deal with another "she's so surly" review. Surly sometimes saved lives. "So how long have you been training?" Annie asked nicely.

"Almost three months. Every weekend, and I usually got in a few weeknights. And I carry my pack whenever I can, like now."

"Not enough." It felt like the two words hit the ground with a thud.

"What?"

"That's just not enough time to get in shape. I can tell by look-ing at you you're not up for the Wilderness." Was that surly? No, Annie decided. She hadn't raised her voice. She hadn't called Nick an idiot. She'd just given him the truth, plainly spoken, and he needed to hear it.

"Just by looking at me?" His eyes weren't warm anymore.

"Yep. I've been working here since I was a kid. I can tell when a hiker's not ready, and you, my friend, are not ready."

Nick snorted. " 'My friend,' " he muttered.

The prickles of irritation were back, but they were more like ice-pick stabs now. He was already shutting down. He didn't want to hear her. Well, too bad. "Look, you could die out there. Do you get that? This slate"—Annie slapped the counter—"it's what a lot of the rock out there is made out of. And it gets slippery as shit." She managed not to say *my friend* again, but it was truth time, and she was giving him all of it. "Which makes falling and bashing your head in a definite possibility. Also, there's snow melt. We've got snow melt this time of year, and it can turn streams into white-water death-traps. And there are swamps—"

"I read about all of this." Nick planted his hands on the counter and leaned toward her.

Annie mimicked his position, leaning in, getting right in his face, glaring at him. "Oh, you read about it. My bad. So, you know it all. Happy trails then."

"Have I interrupted something interesting?"

Annie's grandmother had come in. Of course. Why not make this situation a little worse by having her as a witness?

"Just giving a customer the rundown on what to expect out on the trail." Annie pushed herself away from her side of the counter.

Nick took a step back from his and planted a smile on his face. He turned to Annie's grandmother. "Hi. I'm Nick. The customer."

"I'm Ruth Allis. But you can call me Honey." She fluffed up her blond curls and straightened the pair of cloth fox ears attached to her hairband.

"I'm honored." The fake, being-polite smile—because, of course, he had to be polite, too—became genuine.

"Don't be too honored," Annie snapped. "Everyone calls her Honey, including me, and I'm her granddaughter. You'd think I'd call her Grandma or Grammy or Nana or the like, but, no, I'm forbidden from using any appellation that makes her sound over twenty-one." Annie knew she was taking out her frustration on the wrong person, but kept on going. "That's actually what she puts on forms, even medical ones, twenty-one-plus."

"All anybody needs to know." Honey shot Annie a reproving glance. It didn't work. Annie was way too riled to be reproved.

Nick laughed. "I agree completely. I'm going to start using that myself. Twenty-one-plus."

Honey gave Nick's arm a pat. She was such a flirt. "I hope Annie's told you how beautiful the Wilderness is."

"She was just about to tell me about the swamps," Nick answered, keeping all his attention on Honey.

"There *are* sections of trail that were blazed straight through bogs," Honey began.

Annie had to interrupt her. "Just so you know, you're not going to find much resembling an actual *trail* out there. Don't be expecting a nice dirt path."

"You'll get muddy, but you'll also see pitcher plants." Honey went on as if Annie hadn't spoken. "You're not going to get a look at those too many other places."

"I read about them!" Nick exclaimed. "Definitely going to make sure I see some of those bug eaters in the wild."

He was trail-struck. Nothing Annie was going to say would make a difference. Suddenly, she felt tired. This happened way too many times. "Was there something particular you were looking for today?" She wanted him out of there.

"I was thinking about a bug net."

"This time of year? Absolutely necessary," Annie answered. "I have several types."

"Around now, the blackflies and mosquitoes can get so thick you can't see your hand in front of your face," Honey added, finally giving Annie some backup. "The man who owns the bakery? He was found standing on a bog log shouting, 'Shoo, fly,' over and over, tears streaming down his face. And he was a marine. He got his trail name that day and has been called Shoo Fly ever since."

"Bug net it is," Nick said.

He's probably hoping for a cool trail name, like Thoreau or Seeker, Annie thought. *He's one of the ones who imagines he's going to be transformed by the journey.* She didn't bother telling him to get over it.

"Looking at your pack, I'd say you should have Annie do a shakedown for you," Honey told Nick.

"Shakedown?"

He couldn't have done that much reading about the trail if he didn't know what a shakedown was. "To let you know what's unnecessary, noob," Annie explained.

His eyes narrowed as he looked at her, and she could hear tension in his voice when he spoke. "Everything I brought is important. You're the one who said I wasn't prepared, but I have everything I'm going to need in this baby." He patted his pack.

"Take it off and open it up," Annie ordered. She wanted him out, but that didn't mean she was willing to send him into the Wilderness carrying enough weight to blow out his knees, or end up with a rolled ankle, or a stress fracture. If he managed to avoid one of the dozens of possible injuries, he could still end up so fatigued that he'd take a fall.

When Nick hesitated, Annie insisted, "Do it."

"Fine. But you'll see I have everything I need and nothing more." Nick yanked off his pack, put it on the floor, and unzipped it.

Annie crouched down and started checking out his supplies. She gave a snort of laughter when she got to a worn copy of *Walden.* Had she called it or had she called it? "Everything is necessary, huh?" She tossed it to the side.

"It's one book," Nick protested. "And it is necessary. I know a big part of the trail is mental preparation, and—"

Annie didn't bother to listen. She pulled a solar phone charger from his pack. "Don't need this. Cell service sucks out there." Annie kept on going through his stuff. She pulled out a box of Band-Aids. "Don't need this. If the injury is small enough for a Band-Aid, you don't need a Band-Aid." She pulled out a deodorant stick. "You're gonna have to stink." She pulled out three pairs of boxer briefs. "Nope."

"Come on!" Nick yelped. He probably wouldn't call it a yelp, but it definitely was.

"Bring those and you'll have to bring Boudreaux's Butt Paste for the chafing," Annie explained.

"Fine." She noticed a flush was creeping up his neck. She wasn't sure if it was caused by anger or embarrassment or both. And she didn't care. About ten minutes and fifty protests later, she had Nick's pack at a manageable weight. It took her another five to convince him to trade in the boots for trail runners.

"Is that it?" Nick asked. She noticed a little muscle in his jaw twitching. Good. Why should she be the only one who was pissed off?

"That's it." She shoved herself to her feet.

"Except that we wish you a wonderful hike," Honey said. "It's the experience of a lifetime."

"Thank you." Nick smiled at her. "Hey, we match." He held out his arm so she could see his fox tattoo.

"We're twins!" Honey smoothed down the front of her T-shirt to show off her I'm FOXY fox.

Annie took a long breath, trying to calm down. "I assume you have an extraction plan."

"I did. But the solar charger you nixed was part of the plan. I tried to tell you that."

"And I told you, you can't rely on cell service," Annie shot back. "You need a tracker."

"Yeah? And how much profit are you going to make off one of those?"

He thought this was about money? She was attempting to keep him alive, and he thought she was trying to make a profit. Not that she didn't want the store to be successful, which it was, but that didn't mean it was all she cared about. "I'll rent you one. Hell, I'll loan you one. For free. You can give it back tomorrow afternoon when you come back to town with your tail between your legs."

"Annie!" Honey exclaimed.

Nick jumped in. "I don't—"

"Shut up and take it." Annie jerked open a display case and took out one of the satellite messengers, then thrust it into Nick's hand. He stared at it, as if things were going too fast for him. "Call the number and they'll get your profile set up. If you get in real trouble, send an SOS. It will go out to a rescue coordination center. You can also send your support person a link to an app. They'll be able to watch your progress in almost real time."

Nick's forehead furrowed as he continued to look at the small device. Annie read his expression. "And you don't have a support person, do you?"

"If I needed help, I planned to call for help." He held the tracker out to her. When she folded her arms, refusing to take it, Nick set it on the counter. "I'll take the solar charger and my phone."

Annie pressed her fingers against the bridge of her nose. "Were you not listening? You might not get service and you might not always get sun for the solar. Which means"—she said the next words slowly, and deliberately—"you. Might. Not. Get. Help."

He was close to walking out. She could see that. She pressed her lips together to stop herself from saying something that would push him out the door. He needed the tracker.

"Go ahead and take it, Fox Twin," Honey told Nick. "It might come in handy." She picked up the tracker and gave it to him. He slid it into his pocket.

"I want to pay for it," he told Annie.

"Fine. How many days?"

"Ten."

"It's fifteen bucks for three days."

"Fine."

She could tell he wanted out of her place as much as she wanted him gone. She quickly rang up the bug net, the trail runners, and the rental, ran his card, and gave it back to him. "Do you need me to go over how to send the SOS?"

"I'll google it." He hefted his pack back on his shoulders. "I'll see you when I return the tracker. In ten days."

"I'll be here," Annie said to his back. He was already heading to the door. She and her grandmother watched as he crossed the street, turned the corner, and disappeared from sight.

"You can call me Grandma if you really want to," Honey said.

"I like calling you Honey."

"I know you do." Honey smiled. "That man had everything, and then some. You could have been sweeter to him. Then when he returned the tracker, he'd probably have asked you out for drinks. Or you could have asked him. Then who knows?"

Annie shook her head. "He's way too impulsive for me. He's one of those guys who thinks he's going to change his life by hitting the trail. Walking around with his copy of *Walden*. Which, fine. But you can't just *go*. You need to prep. You need to plan."

"Looked like he'd done some of both to me."

"Some. Not nearly enough. And did you see how he almost walked out of here without the tracker? Just because his pride got dinged a little? He should have thanked me for pointing out he needed the thing." Annie took her phone out of her pocket. "I have the app that will let me see how he's doing. I'm going to keep an eye on him. He clearly isn't capable of taking care of himself out there."

Chapter 2

She acted like I wasn't capable of taking care of myself out there, Nick thought as he spooned the last bite of cobbler into his mouth. He knew it was fantastic—the perfect combo of buttery crunch and sweet, tangy blueberries. But he might as well have been eating that Canine Candy. He'd made a dinner reservation at the Quarryman Inn as a treat before ten days of eating dehydrated meals, dehydrated fruit, jerky, protein bars, and instant oatmeal. Believe it or not, Annie Hatherley, he *had* researched, and he knew what he should be eating on the trail.

He'd also decided to splurge on a comfortable bed for his last night in civilization and promised himself he'd enjoy both again when he returned, scraggly bearded and stinking, since Annie Hatherley had taken away his deodorant. Probably, make that definitely, he should go upstairs and get into that comfy bed early, get a good night's sleep, but he was too wound up. He decided on a walk. He thought about getting his pack from the room, but one more night of carrying it wasn't going to make a difference on the trail. And he'd been training plenty, despite what Annie Hatherley thought she could tell by looking at him.

Annie Hatherley. Annie Hatherley. Enough with the thinking about Annie Hatherley, he told himself as he headed out of the Inn in his new, comfortable trail runners. He got that he might not make it all the way through the Wilderness. He knew people had to give up for all kinds of reasons. He wasn't an idiot, even though Annie Hatherley clearly thought he was.

He was still doing it. He had to forget about all her negative bullshit. Haters gonna hate. Crap. Annie Hatherley had reduced him to thinking in Taylor Swift lyrics. "Shake it off," he muttered.

You're in a new place. You're at the start of an adventure. Look around. Take it in, he thought. He slowed his pace, smiling as he noticed Honey in a lit store window across the street, putting a sundress with a frolicking-fox pattern on a mannequin. The sign, all flourishes and curlicues, read VIXEN's. That explained the fox T-shirt and the cloth ears. He wondered how much business it did. Was there a market for all fox stuff? At a glance, it looked like that's all the shop sold. Maybe people just went in to talk to Honey. She was a charmer. Unlike her granddaughter.

Nick gave a growl of annoyance. In another minute, he was going to have to take out the pocketknife he'd bought for the trip—an Opinel No 7—and excise the part of his brain that held the memory of those few minutes in the outfitter's. At least Annie Hatherley had let him keep the knife. She'd actually said it was one of the best backpacking blades.

Crap. He was doing it again. He shoved his hands through his hair. Maybe it was because before Annie Hatherley had turned into a shrew, he'd thought he felt some mutual attraction between them, a *click*. He knew he'd felt it on his side. That hadn't happened in a long time. Actually, not since Lisa. It's like being happily married had switched off that part of his brain. Not that he hadn't noticed attractive women, but he hadn't noticed them in the same way. He'd have a flash of speculating what they looked like naked or what it would be like to have sex with them, your basic guy stuff. But not with any . . . intent.

But he wasn't married anymore. And he hadn't been happily married for a long time. He'd *thought* he was happily married, but how could he be if his wife was thinking divorce? How could he have been happily married if his wife—ex-wife—got married the day their divorce went through? Not even one day later. The same day.

Today, in those first few moments with Annie Hatherley, it's like an old part of himself had woken up. He usually didn't like short hair on women, but her short, dark brown hair let him focus on her face, on her clear blue eyes, her perfect creamy skin, her lips, her neck, that little dip between her collarbones.

It wasn't just the physical though. He'd liked how she busted his chops, so playful, about being pedantic. Then she did almost a Jekyll and Hyde. It was like she couldn't wait to get him out of her store and out of her sight.

Enough. He needed a drink. Something to settle him down. Get him ready for that good night's sleep. He'd seen a bar with a crazy sign on his way into town. He walked up a block, then turned left. Yep, there it was. The Wit's Beginning Brewery, with a presumably dead donkey, all four legs in the air, on the sign. He'd try one of the local microbrews, then head back to the Inn. And tomorrow the adventure started!

He could have, and probably should have, asked one of his friends to be a support person, but he wanted the Wilderness to be his thing. He didn't want to be checking in every day, didn't want even that much connection to the outside world. It felt like it would . . . like it would somehow diffuse the actual experience, suck some of the meaning out of it.

As soon as Nick stepped inside, the bartender called, "Welcome, friend." He was tall, wiry, and bald, with skin the color of a pine cone. The greeting felt so genuine that Nick headed to the bar instead of settling in at one of the tables. Most were empty, although a group of about ten was settled in at a table in the back, probably town regulars. It was early in the season for hiking the Wilderness. In a few weeks, Nick bet the place would be much more crowded.

"First time here?"

"First time in Mai—"

"Banana, is it or is it not endless-nacho night? Because we are perilously close to the end over here," someone called before Nick could finish answering.

"Big Matt, you got that?" Banana—Banana?—yelled.

"Got it," a guy called back from what Nick assumed was the kitchen.

"Let's start again. As I'm sure you heard, we have endless nachos tonight, if you're interested. Big Matt sprinkles chopped radishes on top. Sounds crazy, but . . ." Banana let out a groan that sounded almost orgasmic.

"Wish I could. But I just finished a big meal."

"What'll you have? The first drink's on me."

Nick had picked the right place. A little *pleasant* conversation would help him unwind as much as a drink. "In that case, what do you suggest?"

"My specialty. The Spirited Banana. It's a wheat beer, but in the German vein, not Belgian."

"Bring it on. But I'm gonna tell you up front that I'd have an easier time telling Coke from Pepsi, than German from Belgian beer."

"Honesty is appreciated." Banana grabbed a plain brown ceramic mug and held it under one of the taps. "Belgian is more citrusy. Esters and phenols give German wheat beer banana and clove flavors." He set the mug in front of Nick.

Nick took a long swallow, trying to pick up on all the ingredients. He got the banana and clove, but also a little apple, and, weirdly, a little bubble gum. "Smooth." He took another swallow. "I wasn't sure I'd like banana in my beer, but it works. Is that why they were calling you Banana? Because of your special brew?"

"Nope." Banana grinned at him.

"Are you going to tell me why they do?"

"Nope." Banana's grin widened.

"How about a different question. What's the story with the donkey?" Nick nodded toward the display of deep blue mugs with the legs-in-the-air donkey on the front.

"It's in honor of my first donkey. I called him Bucky." Banana pressed one fist against his heart and closed his eyes for a long moment, before he opened them and continued, "He was a feisty son of a gun. But smart. I taught him all kinds of tricks. Taught him how to count to ten. Taught him to add. Even taught him to do a kind of a hula shake. Then I decided to try something harder. I decided to train him not to eat."

"Train him not to eat," Nick repeated, his shoulders relaxing with the story and the alcohol.

"Yeah. I cut his food back a little at a time, and he was really getting the hang of it, then he died. Right when he almost had it down."

Nick laughed. It might have been the stupidest joke he'd ever heard. Which is exactly why it was so funny.

Banana laughed even harder than Nick, a low, loud *haw-haw-haw*. "That's from *Philogelos*, the world's first joke book. Or at least first surviving. It was written in Greece, fourth or fifth century CE."

Now Nick understood the name of the bar. "Hence Wit's Beginning." The bartender pointed to his nose, then pointed to Nick. "So, what's the deal with the mugs. Is it a membership thing?"

"Yep, but not the usual kind. There's no membership fee. All you've got to do is walk the two thousand, and I hand one over."

The two thousand. As in miles. The whole Appalachian Trail. "Do you have one?" This was where Nick needed to be. Banana could be Nick's Yoda. He'd send Nick on his way with everything he needed to know, the stuff you couldn't read in books or blogs.

"It's my place, so I could have as many as I want. But I'm not taking one until I finish the damn thing, and I still have a hundred miles to go."

"The Wilderness?"

Banana nodded. "Made sixteen attempts, had sixteen failures."

Nick let out a low whistle. "You never wanted to just throw in the towel?"

"Of course, I did. Sixteen times, for sure. Probably a lot more. But I'm not a quitter. I only have a hundred miles left, and I'm getting them done. This time, though, I'm waiting until I see The Fox."

"What's that?" Nick asked eagerly. "Some kind of flower that blooms at the best time to start? Or when the sunrise is a certain color? Or—"

"Why don't I just tell you?"

"That might work better."

"This is a story that takes some telling."

"Why am I not surprised?" This guy was a story himself—trail hiker, teller of ancient jokes, a beer maker, a business owner. All that, and Nick felt as if he'd barely scratched the surface.

A skinny guy carrying a plate with a mountain of nachos on top headed for the back table as Banana began. "A long time ago, before you were born, hell, before I was born, before my sweet grandmama was born, back in 1803, a fox was caught in a trap around here. Now, I don't know why, because back then there weren't a lot of animal-rights types, but a woman named Annabelle rescued that fox. She'd just lost her husband, and her baby, and was desperate to keep her little boy, not more than two, healthy and safe. The whole settlement was about to go under, and the scraggly group of settlers with it. Maybe that's why she freed that fox and took her home. Maybe she was so heartbroken that she figured any company was better than none. Or maybe death had taken so much from her that she refused to let the Reaper take another, not if she could help it."

Nick bet Banana had told this story a dozen times at least, but he looked as if he was seriously considering the reasons why this woman had saved the fox. "Some say the only reason it lived was because she nursed it. And I'm not talking with a bottle."

"You're shitting me!" Nick took a long pull on his beer.

Banana held up both hands. "All I'm telling you is what people told me. And some have said the milk, the same milk Annabelle still used to feed her little boy, saved The Fox. Some say it did more than that." He turned, took a mug, one of the plain brown ones, and poured himself a drink from one of the taps.

"I don't get you. What more could it have done?" Nick had the feeling he was walking into another bad joke. But he had to ask.

"It's just rumors and supposition. Not much worth passing on."

He's messing with me, Nick thought. He tried not to sound too eager when he said, "I like a good supposition."

"What do you think, Big Matt?" Banana asked as the skinny guy headed past on his way back to the kitchen. "Should I tell our friend the secret about The Fox?"

The man rolled his eyes. "As if I could stop you," he answered without pausing.

"I do like to tell a story," Banana admitted. "I said the settlement was close to dying out. Then a gentleman, Celyn, who had immigrated from Wales, was out riding. A fox ran right between his horse's feet—a skinny, skittish gelding named Mud. Mud dumped Celyn on the ground and took off into the woods. Celyn took off after the animal, who was not nearly as smart as my donkey, Bucky. Before he reached Mud, Celyn caught sight of something sparkling along the side of a cliff. Now, Celyn had worked at a slate mine back in the old country, and he knew what he was seeing. Mica. And where there was mica, there was usually slate."

Nick jumped in. "And that was the start of the Fox Crossing Mine Company." Banana again touched his nose and pointed at him. "I saw some slate from there today. Beautiful."

"And profitable. Turned the luck of the settlement around. Annabelle's especially. She owned the land, and she teamed up with Celyn on the mine."

"This is the part where you tell me the fox was the fox that Annabelle saved, right?" Nick loved the story, even though he knew it had to be heavy on rumors and general malarkey.

Banana gave an exaggerated shrug. "She had the same markings—one white sock, one almost-white ear, black-tipped tail, same as the one Annabelle saved. Same as the one I'm waiting to see."

"Wait. You mean same as in same?" Banana nodded. "You should take this show on the road. You're a master bullshit artist. You've almost got me believing that there's a more-than-two-hundred-year-old fox running around. And that you had an exceptionally smart donkey named Bucky." Nick was glad he'd come in. He hadn't had an Annie Hatherley thought since Banana started spinning his stories. Except that one thought he'd just had, but that one didn't count, because it was about how he wasn't thinking about her.

"Well, some people think she's a descendant of the first one," Banana admitted. "I disagree. And you can see Bucky's gravestone out back." Banana crossed himself.

"And you're seriously not going to make another try at the Wilderness until you see this fox—or its great-great-great-et-cetera-granddaughter?"

"That's right. When I see The Fox and get me some of that luck, I'm heading straight to the trail. My backpack's packed. Big Matt is ready to take over." Banana's eyes flicked up and down Nick's frame. "Maybe you should wait for a sighting. It'd give you a little more time to condition."

"You, too?" All the good feeling Nick had going circled the drain. "You think you can tell just by looking at me that I'm not ready? Don't bother with the lecture. I heard it all and then some from Annie Hatherley."

Banana let out another of his deep *haw-haw-haw*s. "Our Annie, she's a pistol. She also has a good heart."

"In a jar on her bedside table," Nick muttered.

Banana laughed again. "It's why she's so hard on hikers. She doesn't want anyone to get hurt. I wasn't trying to say you're not ready, by the way. But anyone on the trail can use some extra luck." Banana pulled several baggies out of the pockets of his jeans. "I got chicken. I got ham. I got berries. I got a hard-boiled egg. I go out to likely spots in the woods every night and morning, scatter fox treats around me. The Fox is going to come to me. This is the year. This is the year I get my damn blue mug. Speaking of mugs, you need a refill." He got Nick a refill. "I like to talk, as you've probably already concluded. But now it's time for you to tell your story."

"My story."

"Everyone who hikes the Wilderness has a story."

"Ah." Nick took a swallow of the beer. "My thirtieth birthday is in a few days. Thought it would be a good way to mark the decade. A couple buddies and I used to talk about doing a thru-hike when we were in college. It ended up just being talk, but lately I started thinking about it again. . . ." He shrugged. "And here I am. Not a thru-hike, 'cause I don't have time, but a real challenge."

"Try again."

"What?"

"Try again."

"That's it. I'll have my birthday while I'm on the trail. Seems like a good way to close out my twenties and kick off my thirties doing the kind of thing I hope I'll be doing the next ten years."

"Sounds good. But, no." Banana nudged Nick's mug closer. "Try again when you finish that."

Another guy, short, stocky, starting to go gray, poked his head through the door. "Right back," Banana told Nick. Banana took a ceramic bottle from under the counter, filled it from one of the taps, and brought it to the guy. The guy handed him some cash.

"Shoo Fly, want to join—" a woman from the back table called. Before she could finish the sentence, the man had disappeared.

"You tried, Bev." Banana patted the woman on the shoulder before he headed back to Nick.

Shoo Fly. The name was familiar. For a few seconds, it wouldn't come to him, then the memory clicked into place. "The marine who cried because he got swarmed by blackflies, right?"

Banana nodded. "I'd still be crying if I was him. Those flies are little mofos. You got a bug net, right? This early in June, you gotta have a bug net."

"Yep." Nick finished his beer. "I should go. I want to get an early start in the morning."

"Before you go, let me ask you one more time. Why are you hiking the Wilderness?"

"Sorry. My reason hasn't changed. Unless my wife about to have a baby is a thing."

The good humor disappeared from Banana's face. "Your wife is about to have a baby and you're heading into the Wilderness? I'm going to have to ask you to leave my place. I misjudged you."

"Not my wife. My wife that was."

"And bingo."

"Bingo what?"

"Bingo was his name-o," Banana shot back. "Bingo, I think we've unearthed your reason for taking on the Wilderness."

Nick tilted his head from side to side. His neck felt stiff. Must have slept on it wrong. "I wouldn't say—"

Banana slapped the bar with both hands before Nick could finish. "Another drink on me if you want to share your sad story." Nick hesitated, giving a few more neck tilts. Banana refilled Nick's mug.

Fifteen minutes later, the mug was empty. "Oh, and did I mention that she got married the day the divorce got finalized?"

"You did not. And may I say, harsh."

"That same day." Nick stared into his empty mug. Banana refilled it. "Same day."

Connect with

Us

Visit us online at
KensingtonBooks.com
to read more from your favorite authors, see books
by series, view reading group guides, and more.

Join us on social media

for sneak peeks, chances to win books and prize packs,
and to share your thoughts with other readers.

facebook.com/kensingtonpublishing
twitter.com/kensingtonbooks

Tell us what you think!

To share your thoughts, submit a review,
or sign up for our eNewsletters, please visit:
KensingtonBooks.com/TellUs.